# BEYOND THE
WATER MEADOWS

# ABOUT THE AUTHOR

Maggie Allder was born and brought up in Gamlingay in Cambridgeshire, the second daughter of a village police officer. She studied at King Alfred's College, Winchester (now the University of Winchester), in Richmond, Virginia, and later at Reading University, and taught for thirty-six years in a comprehensive school. After exploring and appreciating more orthodox forms of Christianity, Maggie became a Quaker, and is happy and settled in the Quaker community in Winchester. She has previously written three novels which form a trilogy: *Courting Rendition*, *Living with the Leopard* and *A Vision Softly Creeping*. A fourth novel, *The Song of the Lost Boy*, is a stand-alone. Maggie volunteers for a not-for-profit organisation, Human Writes, which aims to provide friendship to prisoners on death row in the USA.

# BEYOND THE WATER MEADOWS

## MAGGIE ALLDER

Copyright © 2021 Maggie Allder
The moral right of the author has been asserted.

Apart from any fair dealing for the purposes of research or private study, or criticism or review, as permitted under the Copyright, Designs and Patents Act 1988, this publication may only be reproduced, stored or transmitted, in any form or by any means, with the prior permission in writing of the publishers, or in the case of reprographic reproduction in accordance with the terms of licences issued by the Copyright Licensing Agency. Enquiries concerning reproduction outside those terms should be sent to the publishers.

This is a work of fiction. Names, characters, businesses, places, events and incidents are either the products of the author's imagination or used in a fictitious manner. Any resemblance to actual persons, living or dead, or actual events is purely coincidental.

Matador
9 Priory Business Park,
Wistow Road, Kibworth Beauchamp,
Leicestershire, LE8 0RX
Tel: 0116 279 2299
Email: books@troubador.co.uk
Web: www.troubador.co.uk/matador
Twitter: @matadorbooks

ISBN 978 1800462 465

British Library Cataloguing in Publication Data.
A catalogue record for this book is available from the British Library.

Printed and bound in Great Britain by 4edge Limited
Typeset in 11pt Aldine40 BT by Troubador Publishing Ltd, Leicester, UK

Matador is an imprint of Troubador Publishing Ltd

*To Denyse Hanna and my Woodbrooke tutor Martin Layton.
Both of you have kept me on my toes and helped me to think through
so many issues that lie behind this novel.*

A nd then, suddenly, it was all over. I was fast asleep in the big attic dormitory that the girls shared. It had only been made into a room a few years earlier and the stairs up to it were steep and spiralled so that if you went down them before you were properly awake in the morning there was the danger it would make you feel slightly dizzy. Rebecca, who was the baby of the household and who slept in the little bed in the darkest corner away from the windows, once fell down them and went very white and quiet, and Ethel-nushi, who was our caregiver, looked really worried, and sat her on her lap right through breakfast, which was unusual.

Then Toby said to Rebecca, "Do you want to play pirates?"

So Rebecca slipped off Ethel-nushi's lap and ran outside, and we realised that everything was all right.

As I said, I was fast asleep, curled up under my duvet, which had my favourite cover on it – a football team's colours, in red and white, dating all the way back to the Old Days. I had it pulled right up over my head. This was partly because the curtains in the dormer window are patterned white cotton and let the light in, and it had been a clear, moonlit night, and partly because at some point in the night I must have got really cold.

It was Sophie who woke me. She was, as far as I knew, about the same age as me, although I wondered about that sometimes, and as the two oldest girls we got the best beds. Mine was three feet wide, and although it sagged a little it was really comfortable, and I had a pine cupboard next to my bed where I could keep my things. There was a rag rug on the floor which we had made the previous winter, a year ago or more from the time I am remembering now, and Sophie was standing on that rug shaking my shoulder, where I was all hunched up trying to keep warm.

"Daisy! Daisy!" Sophie was hissing as she tried to wake me. "Daisy! Wake up! I think there's a frost!"

I remember easing the duvet away and blinking in the dull light of the dormitory. There was a plug-in night light on the socket by the stairs, in case anyone wanted to go to the loo in the night, but, of course it only worked when we had electricity. Sophie's torch was on, shining into my face as I emerged.

"What?" I had been dreaming one of those confused dreams that leave you feeling that you know someone or have been somewhere although, in real life, it means nothing to you.

It was getting light. It was February, and sunrise was late – just before seven in the morning, I think. We never had to get up early in the winter because if there was no power it was hard to cope, so breakfast was not until nine o'clock. Everyone else in the dormitory was fast asleep.

"Look! Look!" Sophie was excited. "It's white out there! Really white!"

Well of course, you who are reading this, you know about frosts, but remember that this was taking place decades ago, and us kids had never knowingly seen frost, not first hand. I knelt up on my bed to peer out through the window. It was just light enough to see outside, but dark enough for my own reflection in the glass to distort what I was looking at.

"Are you sure it's frost?" I asked. There was condensation on the window pane. I tried to clear it with my hand but the glass was bitterly cold, and the mist was frozen to it.

"Let's go and see!" Sophie was hopping up and down with excitement on my rag rug, so that her hair seemed to go up and down round her head like a piece of cloth.

"All right!" I jumped out of bed and we headed for the spiral stairs.

I had lived in that house, which was called Xunzi House, for longer than I could remember. I think that when I first arrived there was a different caregiver, maybe two. I vaguely remember a man and woman. Back then this room, the girls' room, had not been created, but as soon as it was built by a team of freeloaders controlled by a Civic Police boss, I had moved upstairs. As a result, I was really used to those stairs, and could go up and down very quickly and without making a sound. Sophie had only arrived a couple of years ago, and she was anyhow more clumsy than me, so I had to wait at the bottom, on the boys' landing, while she tiptoed down.

We girls all slept in one large dormitory, with the smaller children at the dark end and us older girls by the dormers. This was because we went to bed in three groups, according to our ages, with the little ones first, and if they were at the back we were less likely to disturb them when we came to bed. If they woke in the night with bad dreams or feeling ill, it was our job to comfort them and sort them out. Caregivers are contractually entitled to eight hours' uninterrupted sleep at night and they stopped having night watchers as the economy started to get back on its feet and people were needed to work in factories and shops, and on public transport.

The boys' area was different, though. Originally the house must have been a home for a family. There were three large bedrooms and a bathroom on the boys' floor, and each bedroom had two beds in it. In theory, therefore, there was room in our house for thirteen kids – six boys and seven girls – but in the last few months, just before the time I am telling you about now, there had been a lot of coming and going among the boys. I cannot now remember who all the boys were. I know Noah and Elijah were both there, sharing the room that looked out over the river, and Toby slept in the room by the bathroom of course, with a whole series of smaller boys who seemed never to stay for very long. Arof the Clown had already gone, just before the time I am telling you about now. Although they did not share a room, Arof the Clown and Noah were best friends. They took classes together, fooled around a lot, and kept us all laughing when the power went off. But Arof the Clown had been selected to do some sort of IT diagnostics course, and had moved up to a room in the University of Winchester, despite being young to leave a care home, and Noah was a bit lost without him. Ethel-nushi had given them both mobile phones before Arof left, so that they could keep in touch, but it was obviously not the same. Arof was not a clown, of course, but he was good at telling jokes and at making the little ones laugh with his funny faces, if something happened to frighten them.

Anyway, Sophie and I crept down the last flight of stairs, which came out into a very large room that was both a kitchen, and the place where us kids ate, lived and studied if we were not in our bedrooms. Our house was joined on to another, and we had the downstairs part of both houses, but only the upstairs part of ours. Ethel-nushi said that the furniture and the stuff of the people who used to live next door was all stored in their upstairs rooms, but the authorities had requisitioned the downstairs because we were a dozen or more kids in a small house, and we needed the space. You could still see the ridges on the wall and the metal beam which they had put in when they knocked down the dividing wall. The only other downstairs rooms were the old front room of the house next door, which was an office where all our records and also quite a lot of junk were kept, Ethel-nushi's bedsit, (she once told me it had been a living room) which had a fireplace in it which was never used, and a downstairs cloakroom. I was not sure why it was called a cloakroom. None of us owned cloaks, which were very old-fashioned outdoor wear – as you would have known if you had ever watched those really old remakes of *Harry Potter* films – and there were not even hooks to hang cloaks on if we had owned any. There was just a loo and a hand basin with a brown stain on it where the cold tap had dripped, and one of those wooden box things that were used to deliver vegetables, which was for the little ones to stand on while they washed their hands. There was also a cloakroom in the part of the house that used to belong to someone else, but we just used it as a cleaning cupboard.

Sophie and I went out through the kitchen door, so we were at the side of the house. Sophie was ahead of me. "Confucius reigns!" she exclaimed rudely, then slapped her hand to her giggling mouth. "Daisy, it's cold!"

I was right behind her, and experiencing the same thing. We often went barefoot around the house and out into the water meadows. We paddled in the river and tried to catch fish – usually unsuccessfully, so we knew about cold feet, but this was different. The flagstones seemed almost sticky with cold, and my feet tingled, and the air around us felt brittle with the chill.

Sophie was ahead, running round to the over-grown lawn in front of the house. "Ouch! Ouch!" she was exclaiming, with glee.

The grass was stiff, like paper, and walking on it felt like a series of little electric shocks.

"Ouch! Ouch!" I imitated Sophie, and we were both laughing. "Ouch! Ouch!" It was wonderful. We hopped up and down, and squealed.

Sophie started chanting, "Frost! Ouch! Ouch! Frost!" getting louder and louder.

Then Ethel-nushi opened her bed-sit window and called out, "Girls! What are you doing? Come inside at once!"

Sophie looked almost frightened. She hated being told off, and she ran inside immediately. I did not mind Ethel-nushi calling us like that. She was a really kind caregiver, and, although we knew we must obey her and respect her, I did not find her scary. So I stayed outside, just for a minute or two longer, feeling the frost on my feet and thinking how wonderful it was.

It was then that I saw movement across the river. Two shapes were standing in among the leafless trees, shadowy and brown like the trees that surrounded them. I suppose I was surprised – shocked even. Never, in all the time that I had lived in Xunzi House, had I seen people over there. How could they have got there?

Then they were gone.

Ethel-nushi was calling, "Daisy!" in a voice which tried to sound strict, but was actually amused.

I went in.

★ ★ ★

We were not allowed to come down to breakfast in our nightwear. Ethel-nushi said that even in the worst of times, standards are standards. It was also true that the stuff we wore in bed was a strange mixture of clothes. During the summers, which had been really hot, we girls wore almost nothing, and I dare say it was also true of the boys. Our day clothes consisted of khaki shorts and random tee shirts, which arrived in brown paper packages with our food deliveries. In the winter we wore jeans and hoodies, with strange sizing in the labels because they came from colonies of China, where I supposed people were smaller.

There was quite an air of excitement at breakfast that day. Even Ethel-nushi looked happy, the way she had looked that time when she got a message from her sister saying that she was well and was about to be released. Ethel-nushi's sister had broken the old Civil Code. Ethel-nushi said she was not a freeloader, but a conscientious objector, and when we had asked her what that was, she said it was better for us and for herself if we did not talk about it any more, but that things had changed, and people like her sister were heroes now.

I think us older ones were more excited about the frost than the little ones. Sophie and I took Rebecca outside to see it for herself, and we held her hand down to the white, prickly grass, but Rebecca was more interested in the ducks on the river.

Noah said he could remember frost from the Old Days.

Ethel-nushi said, "I doubt it…"

Then Noah got upset, and grumbled, "I can! I can! Because it was after we were evicted and we were sleeping in the graveyard!"

Ethel-nushi answered gently, "Well, then you have a very good memory, Noah!" I thought, though, that she meant, "You need to forget all that."

Some of us had memories that went way back to that time following the third virus, to the Culture Wars, when people did things which about which the nation was now deeply ashamed. That is what they told us. So, although he went a bit pink, Noah stopped talking about having seen frost when he was little, and we all tucked into our bean broth and steamed buns – two of our favourite breakfast dishes, and much better than porridge, which Ethel-nushi said was traditional English food.

Looking back, I can see that by that time we kids were eating well. We were in the care of the state through no fault of our own, although it was wise not to ask why we were no longer with our parents. The state was a good caregiver in its way. We were housed outside the city, because it was the easiest way to keep us away from the viruses, and, although we attended school via the computers when the electricity worked, we generally ran free. It was only much later, after all the things I am going to tell you in this book, that I found out how tough it had been for children living in towns with their parents, endlessly in lockdown, unable to go outside, and sometimes even frightened to open their windows in case someone outside sneezed or coughed too close to them.

The kitchen/living room steamed up as we ate our breakfast. Ethel-nushi was drinking coffee, which none of us were allowed to touch and which was thought to be a slightly counter-revolutionary drink, although packets of it still arrived with our groceries every week, so it was obviously still being supplied legally. She was, as I have said before, in a good mood.

"When I was little," she began, putting the steamed buns in a basket in the middle of the table and putting one on Rebecca's plate, because otherwise she would not have been able to reach them, "we had frosts several times most winters. People used to say it was healthy. The frosts killed the bugs."

Toby asked, speaking with his mouth full and in his own special way, "Why they want to kill bugs?"

He was thinking of insects, which are precious and should be protected, because without them the whole eco-system would collapse. Also, Toby loved bugs. He used to draw pictures of them, and tell the rest of us all about them in his strange way, even if we already knew, because he was small and a bit unusual, and he was still discovering things.

"Not insects," said Elijah. "Viruses. They used to think that frosts killed viruses!"

"Fake news!" exclaimed Sophie. "If that was true all those people in Alaska wouldn't have died!"

"Well," said Ethel-nushi, "We hadn't learnt in those days how dangerous viruses could be. We really just had colds and flu…"

"Flu can kill," pointed out Sophie.

"Yes, and it did," agreed Ethel-nushi. "But it didn't worry us."

Elijah said, "It just goes to show." He did not need to say more. We had all learnt how the old Western regimes had put money, selfishness and individual freedoms before the well-being of the community, and so of course, it stood to reason, those old leaders would not care if people died of flu.

Ethel-nushi's thoughts were not on epidemics, though. She said, "We used to walk to school through the city, and sometimes the puddles would be frozen solid. We could break them by stamping on them. And we made slides by polishing the frozen ground with our feet, and us kids would skid across them. Very dangerous!" she added, with a smile of remembering.

I had finished my breakfast. My feet were still tingling from running around barefoot on the frosty grass, although by then I was wearing socks and the slippers Ethel-nushi had knitted for me for Christmas. It was a good feeling.

"Do you think we will have lots of frosts now?" I wanted to know. "Now that the climate is recovering?"

"Perhaps," replied Ethel-nushi. "Who knows? Then we will all have to learn how to deal with the cold in winter again."

"We might have snow one day," pondered Elijah.

We had watched a BBC documentary programme about skiing in the Alshan Ski Resort and all the older boys, as well as Sophie and I, hoped one day to go to China and experience it for ourselves.

Ethel-nushi laughed. "Well," she said, "There won't be any skiing here, even if we do have snow. It's not hilly enough."

"St. Giles' Hill is steep," pointed out Noah, and then he added, "We could walk there from here."

Ethel-nushi suggested, "Why don't you all go outside and look at the frost before it goes away?" Then, almost to herself, she added, "Perhaps I will need to remember how to knit gloves…"

However, by the time we got outside the sun had got quite strong, and the only patches of frost were in the dark corners of the garden where the sun could not reach. There was a mist over the river and the strange noises that waterfowl make to each other, the grunt of a swan somewhere and the tick-tick-tick and squeal of a moorhen.

★ ★ ★

**Report of Ethel T. Walker to the National Society for the Care of Abandoned and Displaced Children (NSADC)**
**Hampshire Division**
**Southern Colony**

**Date:** *24th February*
**Time:** *11.15 am*
**Care Home Identity Number:** *017954 Coed*
(Please omit details of exact location)
**Number of children at this location:** *13*
**Number of children in formal detention:** *0*

*The new child, Albert P, has settled in reasonably well. He has twice wet his bed, which is unusual for a seven-year-old, but given the child's background, is probably not surprising. He is sharing the small room with Toby F, who is younger and of course has special needs, and it seems to be a good combination because Toby is so unthreatening. Albert's reading skills and mathematical ability is about average for a child who has been home educated using BBC materials, but on encountering art materials he seems to be at a loss.*

*I am concerned about Toby, who has not coped well with the regular turnover of younger boys in this facility. He is a child who needs more than the usual amount of attention, although fortunately he has a very sweet temperament and is popular with the other children. He had become quite close to Finn S, the two boys played together, and he became very quiet when Finn was allocated new parents, and left. Toby has now become very friendly with Rebecca Mc, which is likely to become a more established relationship, given that girls are so much* harder to place in families, and Toby's condition makes him difficult to adopt too. I worry a little, though, that Rebecca will grow out of this alliance.

The older girls are doing well. Daisy W is confident and seems happy, although she can be a little cheeky at times. That could be her age, which is not known for certain but is estimated at fourteen years. She and Sophie A have become quite friendly, although I am concerned at the influence of Sophie on Daisy. Sophie's background is troubling, and I am concerned about the possible effect of any disclosures concerning her previous life on Daisy. Daisy has been rather sheltered – she is a credit to our system of care. She came to this facility as a young child, before I became the caregiver, and generally seems well adjusted and quite bright, although sadly, not in the area of mathematics, which is easily the most important subject for her future career prospects.

The only other child I need to mention in this report is Noah C. Over breakfast today he referred to the period before he was homed here, when he lived in a graveyard. I have looked at his records, and I see that this was ten years ago. I have checked the History and Local Affairs archive, and I see that following the fires on the housing estate in the west of the city during the Culture Wars a number of families did indeed live in the cemetery off Greater Beijing Street (previously known as St Cross Road). The community was broken up during the Re-establishment of Peace and Justice, and Noah was five at that time. I am not alarmed that he should have memories dating back to that period. Many children do, especially (in my experience) if family members speak to them about the events of their early lives, or if they watch or read something that is close to their own experience. My concerns for Noah therefore only revolve around the possibility that one memory may trigger off others, and that Noah may begin to worry about what happened to the rest of his family.

We had an especially happy start to the day today. Last night, as the records will show, there was a frost – the first real frost in the Southern Colony for years. It was this that triggered Noah's memory, of course. The children were very excited, particularly the older ones who know about the world's battle with climate change. I found Daisy and Sophie jumping around on the front lawn in pyjamas and bare feet, and after breakfast the whole group went back outside to look again at this unusual phenomenon. Only little Albert stayed inside, sitting at the table. It turned out that he had wet his bed again and was worried about telling me.

I have never told a child off for bed-wetting. We were taught in our preparation course that it is a natural reaction to stress. Little Albert and I went up and changed his bedding while the other children were outside, and then I gave him the last steamed bun as a little treat that only he and I would know about. It was stone cold and slightly slimy, but Albert ate it with relish and then ran outside to join the others.

The children are all at their lessons now. I can hear Noah practising his Chinese. He will soon be better than me. The older girls are reading poetry by Du Fu that has been translated into English by an Indian scholar. I am glad I do not have to mark their work; they are tackling an assignment I would find hard. Rebecca, Albert and Toby are following a reading lesson, although I am not sure Toby will ever learn to read. I will have to go and sit with them soon. All the other children will study for the regulation two and a half hours, but those little ones lose their concentration in no time.

I will see whether I can find knitting patterns for gloves or mittens online. We could take a break from making rag rugs in the evenings; the children would probably like that. It may be, though, that I am being too optimistic. What was that old saying, "One swallow does not a summer make"? Well, I suppose that one frost does not a winter make. It is a good sign, though, a really good sign.

★ ★ ★

I thought that Sophie was cleverer than me. She said she stopped doing online classes after the third pandemic, but she was definitely ahead of me in maths and computing and she spoke amazing Chinese, although she said she hated the subject and would rather learn Gaelic. She could explain all sorts of stuff about digital technology, and that morning I remember we had to read some Chinese poetry which I did not get at all, but Sophie did. We sent our work in when the homeschool slot was over. I was sure Sophie would get a better mark than me.

We did not all eat lunch together at that time. Ethel-nushi used to put it out on the big kitchen table and we took what we wanted. Some kids carried their plates up to their rooms, and some watched television downstairs. The little ones sometimes had a nap after lunch. Then we all did our household chores, and the rest of the afternoon was ours.

I think I can remember lunch being a really small meal. I vaguely remember that the people before Ethel-nushi used to put the food out on our plates, so that we could not take what we wanted, but just had to be satisfied with what we got. Sometime after Ethel-nushi arrived the amount of food increased, and instead of just taking what we were given, we were allowed to choose. Ethel-nushi used to make sandwiches and put fruit in a bowl in the middle of the table, and sometimes there were crisps. Then she would ring the hand bell and we would all come from whatever we had been doing and choose our meal. Ethel-nushi used to watch what we took, but she did not say anything unless someone helped themselves to too much, or only wanted the things that were bad for you. It was usually the new kids who took too much. Sophie said that they were used to food shortages.

So, that day (I am pretty sure it was the same day, the one with the first frost) Sophie and I took brown-bread sandwiches and bananas outside, with one of the new glass bottles of fruit juice – the sort that could be returned and reused – and went to sit on the concrete boat-launch next door, looking out over the river. I should explain to you that, on the other side from the joined-on house, our home was next to an old rowing-boat clubhouse of some sort. It was only used for storage by the time I am remembering, but it had previously belonged to some large school for freeloaders, the sons and daughters (although I am not sure about the daughters) of really rich people who used their money to buy advantages for their children. Anyhow, there was a slab of concrete sloping down to the water, and on a clear day it used to become really warm. The concrete heated up much better than the grass of our lawn, which remained cool to the touch even on the hottest summer days, at least until it turned brown.

Of course, when I talk about "the river" I am wrong, really. It was a navigation canal. The actual river was across the water meadows, and we knew several footpaths that joined the two, although first you had to cross the canal. We never called it a canal, though. Even now, the word "canal" makes me think of places I have been to in Birmingham or Leeds, cities in the Middle Colony, or of places people have fought over, such as the Suez Canal or the Panama Canal, or even of the sunken city of Venice. Our stretch of water looked just like a proper river, and it behaved like one, too. A lot of the houses alongside it used to flood most winters, and all the time I lived in Xunzi House there was a white area nearest to the river where the chalk from the floods had marked the high-water mark on the concrete of the old rowing club. The houses along from us had flooded so badly that nobody lived in them anymore. They were boarded up, and, during the storms, tiles blew off their roofs, and then teams of freeloaders would be sent to clear up, and to sort the broken tiles from the reusable ones. Our barbecue pit, which we had built a few years earlier, used some of the broken tiles from those roofs.

I had not learnt back then that after frosty nights there are often warm days, so I was surprised that it was so comfortable sitting on our jackets on the concrete. Our home faced west, more or less, so the sun came round to reach that side in the afternoon, quite low because it was really still winter.

Noah came and sat with us. He had a mountain of sandwiches on his plate, and a very green-looking apple. "Hi, girls!" he said, and he settled himself down right by the water's edge, where he was in full sunlight. He tucked into the first of his sandwiches, frowning a little because the light was in his eyes.

Sophie asked, "Can you really remember a frost, from the Old Days?" She was thinking about the conversation over breakfast. I thought she sounded worried.

"Yup!" grunted Noah, and he took another bite of his lunch. He was eating a sardine sandwich and little flakes of fish came out of the corner of his mouth.

"How come?" asked Sophie. "Did you live in the north?"

"Nope!" I thought Noah was going to leave it at that, but then he said, "I lived right here, in Winchester. I've never lived anywhere else."

"Me too," I said, although I was not sure that was true. I had lived in Xunzi House since I was very small, but who knew where I had come from before then?

Sophie requested in a rather small voice, "Tell?"

Noah finished the fish sandwich and started on another. It looked like Marmite, which was also what I was eating. "I was little," he said. "Like, maybe the age of Rebecca or Toby. We used to live in a house. I don't remember much of that – I only remember crying because I wanted to go outside and it wasn't allowed."

"It must have been during a pandemic," I suggested.

"Yeah…" Noah looked across the river to where a coot was swimming upstream, making those strange, clockwork-like movements with its head. "I think we had it – the virus, that is, because the neighbours came and banged on the door. That or we were on the wrong side during the Culture Wars. I think that was when we left."

"It can't have been the worst virus," pointed out Sophie. "You're not old enough to have seen that."

I remembered something I had read during homeschooling. "No," I said, "the third virus was the worst. The fourth hardly killed anyone, but everyone was so scared by then that they went a bit mad."

"So you lived in a graveyard?" prompted Sophie. "How could you do that?"

"I don't know…" Noah was still frowning across the river, although the coot had gone. "I only remember bits and pieces. I think a soldier took me away. I sort of remember her waking me up, and carrying me across the grass…"

"American?" I wanted to know. There had been a time when a lot of Americans had lived in England.

"Don't be daft!" said Noah. "I'm not that old. Chinese, of course!"

"And they brought you here?" I think I was intrigued. Since I had no story of my own, I always enjoyed other people's.

"Maybe," said Noah, vaguely. "I don't really remember." Then he seemed to look less dreamy, and he took his eyes off the opposite river bank. "Anyhow," he said, "I'm here now, and I *love* Marmite sandwiches!"

★ ★ ★

The thing about Sophie was that she would never talk about her life before she came to the home. She had only lived in Xunzi House for a couple of years, the year we learnt about capitalism, the fall of Chinese communism during the Winter of Disasters, and Confucianism, which is the Middle Way. That would have been when I was thirteen. We all studied according to a set curriculum, and took exams online at the end of the school year, in July. Sophie arrived in the middle of a unit about the United States of America, in which we were looking at Detroit as a case study, showing us how their society did not function well when the viruses started coming, and comparing that city to the Chinese city of Ningbo, which is where our computers were made. She seemed to know a lot about that unit already, I remember. We used to lie in bed talking, and she was full of tales about Detroit that were thrilling in their awfulness, about derelict buildings and people dying on the streets and poor people not being allowed to have water supplies and police shooting anyone they did not like. I did not believe half of what she said, but her stories were wonderful, and made shivers run up and down my spine, so that I always wanted her to tell me more.

Still, it was unsatisfactory that Sophie would not tell me where she came from or what happened to her before she came to the home. I thought it was basically going to be one of three things. Either her parents had died, or at least been crippled, in a virus, or they were criminals, or they were freeloaders. Only Sophie just would not talk about it, and I craved information about other people's lives. They always seemed so exciting.

I imagine that was why I followed Noah around that afternoon. Sophie had gone back inside. Ethel-nushi was going to make iced buns with the little ones and the Chatterers, and Sophie wanted to help. She always liked doing stuff in the kitchen.

Noah had finished his huge lunch, and I had eaten my rather smaller one, and he said, "Do you want me to take your stuff in?"

We had to put the bottles in the black bottle box, and our plates in the dishwasher, so he took mine and I stayed sitting on the concrete, watching the river flow past, with bits of weed in it. A fish jumped up to catch a fly, and a few birds were singing, and I could hear the television. The little ones were watching a cartoon called *Big Ear TuTu*, which I had also loved when I was little.

Then Noah came back out and put his jacket next to mine, so that he was sitting alongside me. "So what about you?" he asked. "I take it you never lived in a graveyard?"

"Not that I know of," I answered. "I've been here forever."

Noah laughed, it was a sort of subdued chuckle. "Forever, right!" he said. "One of these days you must tell me about the time that the Iron Age tribe lived on top of St Catherine's Hill!"

"I came here as a little kid," I explained. "I don't know anything else." I looked around, at the river and the rowing club and the derelict houses. "This is my home," I continued. "It's where I belong." And I remember that I had a strong, comfortable sense of security as I said it, because I was happy at Xunzi House, I felt different from the children who came and went. For them, this was a care home, a good place to be in times of trouble, but just a stop on the journey. For me it was home, and as long as the house was there and Ethel-nushi was in charge, all was well with me. Then I saw the funny side of it. "So that means all of you are people who have come to visit me, in my home!"

One thing about February days, even quite warm ones, is that the sun seems to lose its heat really quickly. A breeze blew across my shoulders and I shivered.

Noah said, "I think I'll go for a walk," and he stood up, and put on the jacket he had been sitting on.

"Can I come?" I wanted to know, and stood to put on my jacket. When he said, "Yup!" I followed him down stream.

There was a footpath that followed the river, right along the bank. During the time that the river was forever flooding, the time when they finally moved the people out from the houses along from ours, the path had been badly eroded and washed away by the high water. Ethel-nushi had asked the

Civic Police if they would send a group of freeloaders to build it back up, but the authorities had said that since nobody should be walking along there (there were still lots of rules about not being far from your home or your place of work) it was not a priority. I had been quite small then and there had been some kids whom I thought of as big boys and girls. They had started to rebuild the path themselves, and we little ones used to want to help, but Ethel-nushi would not let us. Then one day a man from the Civic Police came while the work was going on, and saw what they were doing, and after that they did send a bunch of freeloaders who grumbled all the time. I remember that we were forbidden to talk to them. And so the footpath was re-established. We must have been really isolated before that, because the old footbridge up-river from us had been damaged, apparently beyond repair, by the floods.

The big kids had needed that footpath, I can see that now, looking back. Behind our house, and a bit higher than us, was a lane that led more or less south and ended at a tennis club, which of course was closed. The same road in the other direction led to the city, and for reasons of self-isolating we were not supposed to go that way. So, with the footpath closed and the footbridge out of action, there was really nowhere for the kids to go to be away from their caregivers, and teenagers need their space. Once the path had been reconstructed, we could wander down through the countryside, alongside the river, and there was an old wooden plank bridge that took us across into the water meadows. Once there, on the other side of the river, a whole world opened up, of almost-vanished footpaths, little streams, strange metal contraptions that had once been part of a system of water control, and trees, birds, fallen logs to sit on, and half-rotten benches left over from the Olden Days when people walked along there, following the Itchen Way. We could go wherever we wanted. Ethel-nushi always knew approximately where we were, because of our bracelets, and we never met anyone else.

Noah was ahead of me. He picked up a stick and started swiping at the weeds that were growing alongside the path. "We ought to walk this way regularly," he said, over his shoulder. "When spring comes it will get really overgrown."

Talking to his back I wondered, "Do you suppose lots of people used to come this way?"

Noah stopped right in front of me, and turned to look across the river. "I suppose so," he said. "It's hard to imagine, isn't it? Lots of people, getting quite close to each other, talking to strangers… and not putting themselves in any sort of danger."

I thought about that. "I bet they gave each other colds and flu, and loads of other stuff."

Noah made a sort of "humph" sound and started walking again.

The rickety wooden footbridge which was built on ancient-looking brick supports was just ahead. At one time it had been closed, and a notice had been put up, saying "Unsafe". There was a place in the middle of the bridge where the wood had rotted away, and the previous summer, on a picnic in the water meadows with Ethel-nushi, we had used the notice to patch the bridge. Noah and I stopped half way across, and stared down into the water. Noah said, quoting a poem he had studied when he was my age, "And now, as I watch the green water flowing below my feet, my heart aches for the days gone by, and the days to come," Then he said it again, in Chinese, as if he were speaking to the river, and not to me.

It made me feel calm, hearing Noah quote those lines, and looking down into the slowly-flowing water. It was very clear, and we could see fish, quite small, swimming among the water weeds. The sun was getting low, and there was a bit of a breeze.

"It's beautiful, isn't it?" I commented, and I pulled my hood up to shield me from the cold.

Noah said, not answering me but seemingly talking to himself, "I only remember little bits of those days. I remember being stuck in the house, and people shouting outside, and throwing things at the windows. And I think I remember the cemetery, and Mum sitting there shivering, her face all blotchy. I suppose she was ill. And the Chinese soldier picking me up and wrapping me in a blanket."

I said, "They sent in lots of aid, during the third virus. The Chinese. And their soldiers stopped the rioting during the Culture Wars. They saved us, really."

Noah pulled his hood up too. "Yes, well, they saved me all right!" he agreed. Then he asked, "Why do you think we couldn't save ourselves? You know, we had once been a strong country. Why did we need the Chinese to come and rescue us? I mean, I'm not complaining – that soldier saved my life – but what do you think went wrong?"

I remembered all the conversations Sophie and I had shared at night in the dorm, about Detroit and police shooting people, and no water to wash your hands, and I said, "We made friends with the wrong people. We thought people were our friends who were not our friends, so of course it didn't work out. It was all a mess. The leaders in those days didn't see what was coming..."

"Yeah," agreed Noah. "That's always what they tell us. But how can we ever know?" Then he changed the subject. "Do you ever wonder about your family?" he asked. "I mean, where you came from, and all that? Who you are?"

We turned around and started walking back, so that I was in front. "I don't, really," I said, and it was true, I was a very contented child. "I dream about the future, mostly."

Noah laughed, and said, "That's a very positive way of looking at things!" Then he asked, "So what are your dreams for the future?"

That was easy. "I want to be a caregiver," I said. "Like

Ethel-nushi. I want to look after kids, and cook meals, and sit round drinking hot chocolate with them in the evenings while we watch television and make rag rugs, and not think about the rest of the world."

We walked on in silence. We could see Xunzi House ahead, set back a couple of feet from the bank and separated from the footpath by a hedge, cut low so that Ethel-nushi had a view of the river. Most of the lights were on, and the only window to have its curtains drawn was Sophie's dormer, right at the top of the house. It looked snug in the early dusk.

Noah must have been thinking about what I had said, although he had not replied until then. "Do you think they'll need caregivers, now that it's almost all over?"

"Don't be daft!" I said, as we went in through the back door. "Of course they will!" Then I thought some more. "There'll always be kids like Toby," I said.

The house smelt of newly baked cakes, and the little buns had been iced, obviously by the children, and were lined up on a mesh stand, ready for tea. The kitchen felt hot after the cold air outside.

"Holy Confucius!" I exclaimed. "I was supposed to clean the bathroom this afternoon!" And I rushed away to do my allotted chore before Ethel-nushi told me off.

★ ★ ★

Sundays were always different from the other days of the week. From Mondays to Fridays we had classes in the morning, and chores and free time in the afternoons, and on Saturdays the van came with the week's supply of food. That used to be a really exciting time when I was little, because we never knew how much of the stuff ordered by our caregivers would actually arrive, but by the time I am talking about now – from a while before that first frost – the food supplies had settled down. Occasionally we had substitutions, liked tinned mangos instead of fresh ones, but mostly we got what Ethel-nushi had ordered, even treats. The food always came in the mornings, and after lunch we were each given the sweets we had asked for. My favourite were London Haw Flakes, which came wrapped in little packages with a picture of London Bridge and Chinese writing on them. The little ones tended to like lychee candy; they collected the brightly coloured wrappings and made decorations which we older kids helped them to hang round their beds. Sophie had a real thing for green guava candy, which is unsafe for little children because they might choke on the bits, but as often as not it was substituted with something else. Some of the kids liked English sweets – Noah always wanted chocolate, and Arof the Clown once ordered jelly babies so that he could prove to the little ones that he was a cannibal, but his joke back-fired when Rebecca thought they were real babies, not yet born, and started to cry when he bit the head off one of the sweets. I did not really like the chocolate, except once when one of the big boys gave me some that was very dark and tasted of limes. I think the Chinese have better taste in candy than traditional Westerners.

We always had a big meal on Saturday evenings, with all of us sitting round the table, and, even if the electricity was on, we had candles on the table. I suppose that originally the big Saturday evening meal must have come from the fact that the food supplies always arrived that morning, but by the time I am thinking of, it was just a tradition. We used to eat later – at about seven o'clock instead of our more usual six o'clock meal, because first of all we all sat round the big screen in the living area and listened to one of our Three Leaders and the Chinese Premier. The Chinese Premier always spoke first, in Chinese with sub-titles running along the bottom of the picture. She usually congratulated us all on our hard work and our ordered living, and there was always at least one piece of good news.

Then one of the Three Leaders would speak, telling us about any new regulations, and encouraging us all to be involved in building up the country after so many disasters. The Three Leaders often changed, but whoever was speaking at that time always said which colony of England had performed the best in one thing or another, such as producing most eggs, or achieving negative pollution, or having the highest percentage of students earning As and A*s in the annual exams. The Southern Colony where we lived came first about once in every seven weeks, which was not surprising. There were seven colonies at that time.

We would all watch these programmes, which were still compulsory at that time, with the little ones sitting on the laps of us older ones, and Ethel-nushi hovering between the screen and the oven. This was the only time that we did not wear our tan-coloured tracker bracelets. It was a sort of ritual, Ethel-nushi unlocking them and us plugging them in to charge for another week, and if it was the summer, comparing the white marks on our left arms where the straps had stopped us from getting a tan. Then, when the broadcast was over, we stood to sing a few encouraging songs, like "Happy Are We", which had actions for smaller children. When they played the national anthem we would all be silent out of respect, and the television would show pictures of the royals doing important things. Afterwards there would be a general air of good humour, especially if the Southern Colony had achieved an honorary mention, and then we would have our special meal. We sometimes even had real meat, and we always had pudding.

Sundays were a family day – not just for us, but for the whole country. That meant that we had no classes and no chores, and we did fun things together. In the summer we had barbecues or picnics or we played silly sports. Arof the Clown and Noah used to organise those. It was during one of those

Sunday picnics that we had mended the footbridge using the "unsafe" notice. Sometimes we kids went off and explored the water meadows, and even came home with fish at the end of the day. In the winter we had craft or art exhibitions, or made pop-corn and all watched old movies together, where crowds of people walked around in the streets getting really close to each other and committing crimes, then solving them.

I am pretty sure that it was the Sunday after that first frost that some of us went out together in the middle of the morning. In fact, I am sure it must have been, because the evening before there had been a big fuss about the frosts which had happened three nights in a row and which had affected six out of seven of the British colonies. There were lots of congratulations made to all sorts of people, such as the power workers who worked on the solar and wind farms, the transport workers who now all used electric vehicles, and the civilians who had followed the guidelines and limited the number of fires they had lit in their grates to the regulation one a week, even if they lived in old houses with fireplaces. There were pictures of other parts of the Chinese world where other signs of climate cooling were to be seen, and talk of a worldwide holiday later in the year, to celebrate.

Ethel-nushi was at the house with the little ones. They were making snowflakes out of sheets of paper, by folding and cutting, although of course none of them had seen snowflakes in real life. Later we were all going to watch the epic about Lijuan, the heroine of the third virus, who had saved all the children in her school by bravely keeping the infected villain off the premises. We older kids had seen it before, but it was a real favourite, with adults because of the photography and the music, and with the children because all the goodies were children and all the baddies were adults!

I am fairly sure that there were five of us. Sophie was there, for sure, talking I think to Elijah and Beatrice, a quiet girl with the blonde plaits. And of course, Noah and I were there. We were behind the others, walking more slowly and talking about global cooling.

"Do you think the earth could cool down too much?" I was wondering. "I mean, we don't want another ice age, do we?"

"Huh!" Noah was scornful of that idea. "Well, we'd know how to warm it up, all right," he said. "Just burn some oil and coal, cut down a load of trees, buy some of those old trucks that use petrol or diesel, and Bob's your uncle!"

I laughed. He was right, of course. I said, "By the time we've grown up things might be back to the way they used to be! Can you imagine?"

And that was when we heard them. The sound seemed to be coming from quite a long way away across the water meadows, the sound of bells ringing.

We both stopped, surprised, and looked at each other. I asked, stupidly, "What do you think that is?"

Noah answered, "Daisy, it's church bells! I've heard them before, when I was little. Someone is ringing church bells! A group of people is ringing them – all together!"

★ ★ ★

**Report of Ethel T. Walker to the National Society for the Care of Abandoned and Displaced Children (NSADC) Hampshire Division Southern Colony**

**Date:** *1st March*
**Time:** *2.45 pm*
**Care Home Identity Number:** *017954 Coed*
(Please omit details of exact location)
**Number of children at this location:** *13*
**Number of children in formal detention:** *0*

*I have only good news to report today. Albert P has stopped wetting his bed, and has started to engage in craft work with the other younger ones. He has shown an interest in drawing, although it appears he has never used colouring pencils or paints before, and has become quite distressed several times when he has marked his clothing by mistake. Toby F and Rebecca Mc include Albert without question, and it seems that Albert has made no comment about Toby's appearance or idiosyncratic behaviour.*

*The friendship between Sophie A and Daisy W seems to have weakened a little. I put this down to the fact that Daisy and Noah C seem to be closer. This is a relief to me. I was worried that Noah, who has already suffered some attachment problems, would not cope well with the loss of his best friend. I am sure Noah and Arof A text each other, and we have had a card from Arof, which says he is doing well. You will know from his records – as I do – that he is, in fact, holding his own against students who are older than himself. I had wondered whether Noah would want to attend the same study centre as Arof, but Noah seems increasingly absorbed in his Chinese studies, and should certainly be encouraged in those. I hope he will be able to attend the Confucian school down by the old art school. He is becoming a very calm and steady boy, a real asset to this home.*

*Sophie has not, as far as I can tell, mentioned any of the things she saw or experienced before coming here. I have had the opportunity to watch her closely, because she has volunteered to help me with the smaller children several times, either baking or doing craft work. It is my opinion that she is a young lady who missed out on a real childhood, and is rediscovering it now to some extent. Her willingness to help with the younger ones will earn her merit if this continues, undoing the harm done by her previous life.*

*I am aware that the girls' dormitory becomes very cold during these unusually chilly nights. When the loft was converted to create additional space it was not well insulated, and the windows are not double glazed. While recognising that the Southern Colony needs to spend its limited income with care and discretion, I respectfully request that the Committee of Works consider taking action to reduce heat loss from this building, in line with agreed standards.*

★ ★ ★

And then the changes really started to happen, thick and fast.

It was probably a week later, although as I remember it now, looking back after so much has happened, it seems to me as if it were the next day. It was another Saturday, a day of pouring rain that made the windows on the river side of the house mist up. I do not remember what we had been doing earlier, but we all gathered together as always for the six o'clock broadcast.

Right from the start, I remember, it was different. Instead of the usual displays of national flags from every part of the Chinese world being shown when they played the introductory music, there were pictures of bells ringing and of people waving things out of apartment windows, everyone smiling, and of leaders bowing to each other respectfully, with big smiles on their faces. The Chinese Premier was wearing a garland of flowers around her neck, which looked strange over her usually severe suit, and which, we were told, the people of Honolulu had sent to show their gratitude and respect.

Then it was time for the Premier to speak. As she always did, she sat behind a desk and looked directly at the camera, with the large red flag with its gold, almost star-like symbol of Confucianism at its centre, displayed behind her. She had some papers on the desk in front of her, and as she talked to us, she referred to them, and the figures came up on our screen alongside her, with the same news written in English, in bullet points running along the bottom of the screen. It was, she said, a time for rejoicing the world over. For the first time since the Industrial Revolution the levels of pollution in Europe, Asia, Africa and Australasia had dipped below the

World Health Organization's 'acceptable' level, and the ice levels in both the Arctic and the Antarctic had grown, after years of melting. This, she said, was the result of so many people in so many countries – at great cost to themselves – living moderate and well-ordered lives and earning merit in society by their unselfish concern for others. She reminded us of some of the highlights of the last few years: Chinese soldiers rescuing people from floods, African doctors and nurses wearing protective clothing as they cared for sick patients in tiny, rural clinics, and students out in the fields picking fruit in the Eastern Colony here in England. As she spoke, pictures of these groups were shown on our screens. There were maps that showed the decline of air pollution over the years, and a graph to show how incidents of asthma had reduced.

Then the cameras moved to the Leader of the House of Cultural Continuity, one of our three houses of government, standing outside the door of Number 12 Downing Street, as microphones were held towards him, a safe distance away.

"This is a day for celebration!" he announced. "A day to take time away from our hard work, to remember all who have given up their lives so that this day would come. But it is not a day for mourning, although some of us have lost so much. It is not a day for planning what next to do, although such plans are being made. This is a day for rejoicing, a day for patting ourselves, our families and our communities on the back." Then he looked away, a sad expression on his face, as if to say, "I have reasons to mourn, and I have to plan ahead, I am serving you all at great expense to myself." He returned his gaze to the cameras, and smiled. "And I am happy to tell you that from midnight tonight we can further ease up on the safety measures we have become so used to. No longer will you be limited to travel between your work, grocery stores and home! No longer will our parks be closed and our footpaths neglected! No longer will our children look longingly at their bicycles and scooters, at their roller skates and skate boards! For, citizens of the Seven Colonies, we believe that the last pandemic has been defeated! Tomorrow, and for the foreseeable future, you can visit your families, you can attend your places of worship, and you can shop more than once a week."

Then the picture faded, and was replaced by video of the royal family. They were standing on a balcony of Buckingham Palace and waving, just as the people in the flats had been waving at the beginning of the broadcast. Then they turned to each other and embraced each other, and, without any of the usual rallying songs we sang at the end of such broadcasts, the national anthem started to play.

We all stood up. I remember that Toby had been sitting on my lap, his thumb in his mouth. I am sure the little ones did not understand how momentous that broadcast had been. Perhaps I did not, either, although I knew enough to understand that it was good news, that this was what we were all supposed to have wanted.

And right at that moment – while we were still standing, Ethel-nushi behind us with an oven glove draped over her shoulder, while the BBC was switching back to their commentator in the studio, while something boiled over onto a hotplate and made a sizzling sound – right at that moment there was a hammering on the kitchen door.

We all looked at each other, and then we all looked at Ethel-nushi. Nobody came to our door except the person delivering our groceries on Saturdays and the Civic Police occasionally. Ethel-nushi slowly walked over to the sink. She hung the oven gloves on their hook and turned the hotplate down. She seemed to me to be doing everything in slow motion. Then she walked across to the back door and opened it, while we all watched in silence.

A woman was standing there. Of course, I was useless at guessing ages in those days. Adults were either young or old. As far as I was concerned, Ethel-nushi was old, but this person – this woman standing at our back door – was nether old nor young. She was wearing patch-work trousers and a dark-blue padded winter jacket, and she had a blue headscarf on her head. She was carrying a large, shabby back-pack with red ribbons tied to it, which were drooping in the wet, and she had bright red hair.

For perhaps a second there was absolute silence, just two women looking at each other while the rain pitter-pattered behind the stranger.

Then Ethel-nushi said, "Edwina! *Eddie!*" and pulled the woman into the kitchen, giving her a huge hug.

As I remember it, us kids just stared. I think Ethel-nushi was crying. The stranger, this Edwina, was laughing, and looking around the kitchen then back at Ethel-nushi, and hugging her again.

Then Ethel-nushi turned to us. She was holding the woman Edwina's hand. She said, "Kids, this is my sister, Eddie. Edwina. My little sister!"

★ ★ ★

She laughed a lot over dinner that evening – they both did – but I think the rest of us must all have been quite quiet. The situation was so strange. I had known that Ethel-nushi had a sister somewhere, a sister who had been wrongfully arrested during the bad times and then released, but I suppose I thought we might all have family members somewhere. It did not mean we would ever see them again. Yet here was Ethel-nushi, laying an extra place at the table, serving up spaghetti with a wooden tool that stopped it all clumping together, settling Rebecca more firmly on her chair, and all the time talking to this stranger. "Do you remember eating spaghetti at home, do you remember the mushroom sauce Mum made?"

and "Are you still in touch with the Petersons? Do they still live in that big house on the cliff?" It was like turning on the television halfway through a drama.

By the time we had finished the first course and Ethel-nushi was taking the crumble out of the oven, their initial excitement at seeing each other must have eased a bit. Ethel-nushi asked, "So are you staying?" She glanced at the backpack with the droopy red ribbons on it, dumped by the kitchen door.

Edwina said, "I can have a week. They told me yesterday. I came in a van with one of our drivers and a delivery of cream! Did you see the broadcast? Is the news out?"

"The end of the lockdown," said Ethel-nushi. "We've just heard. Isn't it amazing?"

Then Edwina suggested, "I think you ought to introduce me to your family, big sister!" And it made me feel good, because I liked to imagine that we were all related.

We were a bit tongue-tied, I think. Remember, back in those days we met very few new people. Even the food-delivery people were pretty much the same every Saturday, and I think I had only seen two Civic Police officers in ten years, although I had seen one of them several times. Noah, though, was more confident. When Ethel-nushi said, "And that's Noah," Noah bowed his head a little out of courtesy, and said, "Welcome, Edwina-nushi. Have you come far?"

"Oh!" exclaimed Edwina-nushi, "It's so long since anyone addressed me like that!" And she sounded pleased. "Yes, I have come far! I came from the South Western Colony today, but before that I lived in the East, near Norwich. And I have been wanting to visit the Southern Colony forever!"

Somehow that broke the ice. Ethel-nushi started serving out the rhubarb crumble and we passed round a jug of soya cream. Then, afterwards, with the dishwasher stacked and the burnt saucepan left to soak, we all sat round the television, (although it was turned off) and Rebecca climbed onto Ethel-nushi's lap and Toby climbed onto mine, and Edwina-nushi started to tell us about the South Western Colony and how she had worked on a farm until recently, but that when she went back they were going to open a hotel, and by the summer people would be allowed to go there to stay, and have summer holidays.

"Like the Old Days," said Sophie, but she did not look very happy.

Edwina-nushi smiled. "Yes," she said. "A bit like the Old Days, but better." She stretched and yawned. "Ethel, it's so good to see you at last, but I'm shattered! Where can I bed down?"

★ ★ ★

As if to the prove that things were really, truly on the change, there was another frost that night. The rain must have stopped during the evening, and the clouds had cleared. There were patterns on my dormer window, like leaves and ferns, and I could see my own breath when I woke in the morning. As I went downstairs, each level of the house seemed to be a little warmer than the one before.

In the kitchen Edwina-nushi was sitting drinking coffee, with Ethel-nushi's private coffee pot beside her on the table. For a second I thought, *She shouldn't touch that!* but then I remembered that Edwina-nushi was Ethel-nushi's sister, and that they had probably shared things as children.

Edwina-nushi looked up at me and smiled. "Now, let's see," she said. "You're not Sophie. And you certainly cannot be Beatrice! You must be Daisy."

"Yes," I agreed, and sat at the table too. Edwina-nushi was still wearing pyjamas, and Ethel-nushi did not like us to wear our nightwear downstairs, but I did not say so.

"Coffee?" offered Edwina-nushi.

"We're not allowed," I explained.

"Right!" said Edwina-nushi. "Probably wise. Tea, then?"

I nodded, feeling shy, and watched as she made me a drink of tea, not in a pot, but using a whole teabag in a mug, and then putting the used teabag in the composting box, when it had only been used once.

When she as sitting down again, and I had put milk into my tea (we always did it the other way round – milk first, then tea, poured from a pot – but I supposed they did things differently in other colonies) Edwina-nushi asked, "So, Daisy, how old are you?"

"About fourteen," I replied.

"Oh, what a great age to be as we come out of lockdown! You have your whole life ahead of you!"

"Yes." I did not like to point out that I had my whole life ahead of me whether we were in lockdown or not, nor that I did not really know what these momentous changes, which were the cause of so much rejoicing, might mean.

Edwina-nushi must have picked up my hesitation. "Is it frightening?" she asked. "I don't suppose you can remember what it was like before?"

I said, "Yeah," meaning she was right. As far back as I could remember I had lived in Xunzi House. I had seen films and documentaries, I knew all sorts of things about living without lockdown, but I did not know what it would mean for me, right now. It was pretty frightening.

Edwina-nushi said, "I'll tell you what, Daisy. Why don't I ask Ethel-nushi if I can take some of you older ones out today? Just for an hour or so. To show you a little bit more of your world?"

★ ★ ★

In the end two groups went out. It was Sunday, so it should have been a family day anyway. Ethel-nushi took the little ones, but Sophie volunteered to stay at home with the Chatterers. This was the nickname that Arof the Clown had given to the middle group of kids, and it had stuck. Arof had been learning about collective nouns, and had discovered that a flock of starlings is called a "chatter". He thought it was really funny, and he said it suited the kids who were not teens and not little ones anymore, because they were always talking, especially after they had gone to bed and were supposed to be sleeping. Sophie had been very quiet since the broadcast the night before, almost as if she were not pleased with the news. The remaining four of us who were teenagers: Elijah, Beatrice, Noah and I, went with Edwina-nushi, but the Chatterers wanted to stick with our original plan, to have a barbecue at lunchtime. They did not particularly want to explore. Ethel-nushi said it was fine to leave the Chatterers on their own for a few hours, with Sophie in charge. She could always click on her bracelet if there was a problem.

There was a footpath that led up to the lane behind the house. I remember walking along in single file, with Edwina-nushi at the head and Beatrice at the rear, and I think I can remember the smell of very early plant growth. It was March, and still quite cool out, especially after last night's frost, but there were birds singing and I could hear the whine of a car somewhere not too far away.

We emerged out into the lane past an overgrown holly bush, which, even well into the spring, still had a few red berries on it, and through a broken wooden gate. I could only remember going left from here. A few times we had all walked down as far as the old tennis club and back when it was too muddy to walk by the river and Ethel-nushi thought we should get some exercise. But this time, following Edwina-nushi's lead, we turned right. Almost at once the tree-lined lane changed. There were houses on both sides, larger even than Xunzi House, and with pretty, well-kept gardens with daffodils growing in them. There were small Dongfeng and Chang'an electric cars parked in a lay-by, and straight ahead was a junction.

"Straight ahead or left?" asked Edwina-nushi, but I think none of us felt quite sure.

Directly ahead was a road with houses on both sides, built right up to the narrow pavements. A left turn would take us on a wider road across a bridge. I could not help thinking that the narrow road might be dangerous. Remember, I had survived four pandemics and I suppose that all my life I had lived with risk. What if someone with a disease opened her front door and stepped out right in front of us? We could all be infected. So, "Left!" I said, and that was the road we took.

Looking back, I remember most of all the feeling of strangeness. Every step we took seemed to take us a little further from safety. Many years later, I was exploring one of those abandoned villages in the Northern Colony, where everyone had died or been evacuated. It gave me the same sort of feeling as I had that morning – a feeling that maybe we were trespassing, that this was not where we really belonged, as if things had happened there that I could never understand.

We walked in silence, looking around us, first at smart-looking houses, some set back a long way from the road, then to the bridge. We peered over the parapet, but from there we could not see our part of the river, just someone's lawn with wrought-iron garden furniture arranged on three sides, so that everyone sitting there could see the water. From one of the houses we could hear music. It was different from anything I had heard before (we mostly studied Chinese music).

Edwina-nushi said, "Elgar."

We all kept walking. Some bells started ringing, not too far away, a steady "dong, dong, dong."

"Calling the faithful to worship," said Edwina-nushi.

There was an old man with a dog coming towards us on the other side of the road. The old man had a walking stick, and the dog looked just as ancient, and wobbly on his four feet.

"Morning!" said the old man.

"Morning!" answered Edwina-nushi, but we all murmured "*Zao!*" as we had been taught,

Edwina-nushi laughed, and said to us, "You might do better using the English, you know!" Then, when she must have seen the perplexed look on our faces, she explained, "Old people only know the English ways, and there is nothing wrong with them. Even the Great Premier greets English people in English."

We walked further, down a tree-lined road, until on our left it opened out into water meadows again, although not a part of them that I knew. There were cows grazing, making greenhouse gases which must have been within the permitted limits, and we could hear children playing somewhere, although we could not see them. The road seemed very empty. There were no more people and no cars.

"Are you sure it's all right to be out?" Noah was feeling as ill at ease as I was.

Edwina-nushi sounded confident. "Oh yes, I'm absolutely sure," she said, "but people are not used to so much freedom. It'll take time before it feels safe to mix socially."

The road ahead stopped at a rather grand-looking building and a pretty little cottage, but we turned right and kept walking, with meadow on our right and a high wall on our left. Ahead, set back in its own grounds, was a huge house, but we turned left again into the sort of street I found dangerous, with houses or walls close to the pavement on both sides. Perhaps I hesitated. Maybe we all did.

Edwina-nushi said, "Have we gone far enough for one day?"

We really had not gone very far at all. I doubt if we had been walking for fifteen minutes. It felt a bit cowardly to go home so soon, and the street ahead was empty of people.

I asked a little tentatively, "Do you know what's at the other end of this street?"

Edwina-nushi smiled at me. "As it happens," she said, "I do. There's an arch we can walk under and then we're nearly in the Cathedral Close. Have you seen the cathedral before?"

Three of us said, "No," but Noah said, "I think so…"

Edwina-nushi smiled. "It's worth looking at." she said. "Perhaps it's too soon to go inside, but it is part of your heritage." Then, looking at the wariness on our faces, she added, "It's perfectly safe, you know. They wouldn't have eased the restrictions if there were any risk."

Beatrice worried, "There's no one else around…"

"No." Then Edwina-nushi said, "They're probably just as scared as you. Come on!"

The cathedral was amazing. It was huge, just like the pictures we had seen on our TV screens during lessons, but, now that we were standing close to it, it looked much grander. A man was walking across the grass, wearing a long purple robe. He smiled and waved a hand in the air, the old lockdown greeting, and we waved back. There still seemed to be nobody else around.

"Not many worshippers," commented Noah.

"They will have gone in through the west doors," explained Edwina-nushi, "but I think that's enough for you for one day. And the others will have the barbecue ready soon." So we headed back, feeling – in my case anyhow – both relieved to be going home and proud to have shown so much courage. We had ventured out before most ordinary people, and it was wonderful.

★ ★ ★

Report of Ethel T. Walker to the National Society for the Care of Abandoned and Displaced Children (NSADC)
Hampshire Division
Southern Colony

**Date:** *10th March*
**Time:***10.30 pm*
**Care Home Identity Number:** *017954 Coed*
(Please omit details of exact location)
**Number of children at this location:**
**Number of children in formal detention:** *0*

*This has been a very satisfactory day. Following yesterday's announcements, and in line with recommendations sent out last week, we took some of the children out today. Kaia S and the other children in the middle group (the Chatterers) opted to stay home and prepare the barbecue and Sophie A chose to stay with them, but I took the little ones as far as the Abbey Gardens playground, and Edwina took the remaining four oldest children into the city. It was kind of the authorities to allow my sister to be with me at this time, which is a very uncertain time for the children, although a happy time for the nation and the world. I thank you.*

*Edwina took the children as far as the cathedral. She reported to me that they were very quiet and rather reserved, and three of the four children acted as if they had never walked these roads before. Noah C thought he might have seen the cathedral when he was young, and that is perfectly possible given his background.*

*They actually only met one other person. The older children used the Chinese greeting they have learnt when meeting a stranger. Edwina has suggested that I ask whether it would be better, now that we are coming out of lockdown, for the children to begin to use their native tongue around the city. They will need to learn to blend in with those who have not grown up in the care of our generous state. I will, of course, continue with official policy unless I hear otherwise.*

*I would like to take this opportunity to remind you that I have brought to your attention the need for further insulation in the girls' dormitory. While the girls all seem very well at present and warmer weather is on the way anyhow, I would not be taking my responsibilities seriously if I did not look ahead to next winter. There is no heating in the attic and already we have seen frost on the inside of the windows up there.*

★ ★ ★

I realise, having read various official documents that have been released since those days, that there was a deliberate policy of introducing children into a freer world gradually. It was not just those of us who had been in the care of the state. Children with family members were also thoroughly trained to stay away from other people not in their households, and there were high levels of anxiety among many young people as the restrictions were lifted. It was quickly understood that reopening schools was not a possibility until the world had become more relaxed, and there was some concern about how easily children might adapt to a classroom situation after years of following the National Curriculum from workstations in their homes.

To me, though, the changes seemed to come really quickly. A new course was introduced, which we each studied at our own level, called *Friendship, Fun and Freedom*. We learnt that, while close family ties were important, we would also benefit from having friends. We learnt about parties and playing sports with others, and about the importance of music, of joining choirs or orchestras, and of inviting others to come and eat with us. We were shown pictures of whole family groups – grandparents, parents and children – sitting round tables talking about all manner of things. We were taught about restaurants and theatres and places of worship. At times it seemed as if we were watching those old, pre-pandemic documentaries or dramas, but every now and again the voice-over would say things like, "If you are invited to someone's house..." or "When you go to a restaurant..." which would remind us that these things might really happen.

I remember us older ones sitting on the footbridge we had mended, dangling our feet over the edge, and discussing it all.

I think it was Beatrice who started it. She was a really quiet girl and rarely seemed to show any deep feelings, but it was she who said, out of the blue, "So, are we family or friends?"

It was not an odd question. We had always learnt that our first loyalty was to our family members, and we had always understood, since we all lived together, that we were that family. We spent Saturday broadcasts and Family Sundays together and we showed Ethel-nushi filial respect. Now, though, we were learning about friendship, about being close to people outside the family.

"I think we're family," I replied. It made me feel uncomfortable to think we might not be.

"We're friends," said Noah. "I had a family once. We're sort of special friends. We're not really related, like sharing DNA or anything."

"You don't have to share DNA!" I am sure I felt threatened. "A husband and wife don't share DNA but they are family."

Noah was not one to argue. "That's different," he answered, but not aggressively.

I knew it was, really. Only, if this was not my family, what was? Perhaps Noah realised how I was feeling. He said, "Well, in a way we are family. I mean, we will always owe Ethel-nushi our gratitude and our love, for looking after us. And we will always have shared memories of doing stuff together. Like now, sitting on this bridge. The sort of memories Ethel-nushi and Edwina-nushi share."

"Perhaps we are both, then?" I wondered.

★ ★ ★

I think it must have been late April or early May when we found our way right across the wetlands to the roads and buildings on the other side. Of course, we knew the water meadows well, the footpaths and little streams, the places that flooded in the winter and the fallen trees, the birds and the little mammals. They were our territory. They had been safe as far back as we could remember, because nobody ever went there except us. We had always known, though, to stay well away from the buildings beyond. People were there, and maybe sickness. We earned merit by keeping ourselves safe, and anyhow, who wanted to become ill?

Yet Edwina-nushi had insisted that it was safe now. Of course, there would always be illnesses, it was a fact of life, but there were also doctors and nurses, vaccines and medicines, to say nothing of our own healthy immune systems. And Ethel-nushi had taken the little ones to a park, with swings and slides that had just been mended after years of neglect, and there had been another child there, although our children had stayed well away from her. In our lessons they were teaching us that it was safe, too. The *Friendship, Fun and Freedom* classes which us older kids took suggested that neighbours might meet together to form musical groups or to practise yoga together, and suggested that when martial arts schools opened later in the year, we might like to sign up. Arof the Clown texted Noah to say that students were having classes together at the university, and that people kept interrupting each other because nobody could quite remember how it worked if you were all in one room and the teacher could not mute you. He also told Noah that he had been asked to join a music group. They were playing mostly C-pop and they were practising all together, all in one room, for hours. They were hoping to get some gigs soon.

Perhaps, though, we would not have been so daring if Noah had not been with us.

Since those first frosts, he had said several times, "The cemetery where I lived must be over there," or "I would like to see if I recognised it on the other side of the water meadows," but I do not think we set out, that morning, to go so far. Remember, we were just kids, young teenagers used to wandering free. I think it just happened.

It was one of those bright, green-and-blue days, when every plant seemed to have buds opening and there were patches of bluebells growing under trees, and a deep blue sky. It was certainly a Sunday. There were church bells ringing and we had packed lunches, so we were obviously out for the day. It was the usual four of us: Beatrice and Elijah, Noah and me. As always seemed to be the case by then, Sophie had wanted to stay with Ethel-nushi and the younger ones. They were going to make boats out of pieces of wood and old rags, to float down the river with messages of friendship for whoever might find them.

I remember it was quite soggy underfoot. I was wearing red trainers with gold stars on them, and was very proud of them. Edwina-nushi had bought them for me, but she had gone by then, back to the South Western Colony to help with the opening of the hotel, although she hoped to be back later in the year. Noah was leading the way and I was walking with Beatrice, who was younger but taller than me.

"Isn't this far enough?" Beatrice asked as we reached the fallen tree where we had once seen a woodpecker. "We're quite close to those buildings."

Noah stopped and looked at us. "I think we're nearly there. At that cemetery. Where I lived."

Elijah was behind us. He mused, "Can you really remember that? You were only a kid."

But Noah was determined. "Come on," he said. "It's perfectly safe!"

So we followed him.

There was a low brick wall between the meadows and civilization, and the road was narrow, almost a lane rather than a street. There were houses on either side, set back safely from the pavement in a way that left me feeling secure. We followed the road round, joined another road, and then, up ahead, was a bigger street, and cars going past in both directions.

Noah had a sort of gritty look on his face. He was determined to go on, apparently unaware of our hesitation. Beatrice was hanging back, so that it looked as if she was socially distancing herself from us, although actually she was just being cautious. I felt excited. I remember running to catch up with Noah as he reached the main road.

He stood there, looking left and right, a slightly confused expression on his face. Where our road met the main road there were signs telling you the names of the streets. We had just come up Kingsgate Street, and the main road was labelled Greater Beijing Street.

"I don't remember this road," said Noah, and he sounded disappointed. "It looks right, but I don't think it was called this…" Then he spotted an old, broken-down bus shelter just along from us. "Yes!" he exclaimed. "This is it! Look!"

He ran along the pavement, and just beyond the decrepit shelter he started to jump up and down to look over the messy hedge. I caught up with him. "Look, Daisy! There it is! Look!"

I started to jump up and down next to him, trying to see beyond the bindweed-covered privet. We must have looked a little mad. A car drove past and they hooted their horn at us. There were four people in it, two adults in the front and two kids behind, and the man, who was in the passenger seat, waved at us in that socially distancing sort of way, and grinned.

And it was true. Every time I jumped, I caught a glimpse of old stone crosses and overgrown mounds. It really could have been Noah's cemetery.

Beatrice and Elijah were still standing on the corner. "We've found it" Noah shouted. "Come and see!"

But they just stood there, not willing to come any further. The cemetery did not look as if there was a way in. "Where was the entrance?" I asked Noah.

Noah had stopped jumping. He said, "I have no idea!" Then he grinned. "Well, so now I know!" he said. "Huh! Greater Beijing Street! I bet it hasn't been called that for very long!" And he did a really surprising thing. He suddenly turned to face me, and gave me a big hug. "Thanks, Sis!" he said. "Thank you, my friend!"

★ ★ ★

We talked about it after dinner that evening, when the littlest ones were in bed and the Chatterers were cleaning their teeth and sorting out their laundry for Monday, wash day. Ethel-nushi always liked to know what we had been doing. Of course, she knew more or less where we had been because of the trackers on our bracelets, but she liked to know our impressions and anything interesting we had done while we were out. She was sorting socks into pairs while she listened to us, checking to see if they had holes in the heels, and putting them into separate piles if they needed mending or throwing into the recycling basket to be used for stuffing things – cushions or soft toys, or whatever.

"We went as far as Greater Beijing Street," Noah was saying. "And we found my cemetery."

Ethel-nushi looked impressed. "That was brave," she said. "Well done! And did you meet anyone?"

We all shook our heads negatively. I said, "Some people in a car hooted their horn at us."

Elijah was looking serious. "Beatrice and I thought it might be a bit dangerous," he said. "Do you think we'll have been reported?"

"No!" Ethel-nushi was very certain about it. "Of course not. Not anymore. You can go anywhere now, as long as it isn't onto private property. Keep exploring!" Then she said to Noah, "Did it feel strange, finding the cemetery?"

Noah wrinkled up his nose. "It was smaller than I remembered," he said. "And very overgrown." He looked thoughtful. "It feels good to know it's still there. Like a bit of my history. But it's just an old graveyard, when all is said and done! I don't think I want to go there again."

"Fair enough," said Ethel-nushi. She directed her next comment to Beatrice. "It must be hard to realise how free you are now. Don't be ashamed of it. Don't push yourself. It's going to take time to find your way in this new world. There's no hurry."

Sophie muttered, almost under her breath, "It isn't a new world, it's the same old one! And I hate it!"

Us four looked at each other, shocked, but Ethel-nushi put a hand on Sophie's shoulder. "Sophie," she said, really softly, "it really is a new world. But don't worry. You don't have to go out into it until you're ready!"

"I'll never be ready!" announced Sophie, suddenly sounding angry, and she stood up, shaking Ethel-nushi's hand away, and stormed upstairs.

★ ★ ★

**Report of Ethel T. Walker to the National Society for the Care of Abandoned and Displaced Children (NSADC)**
**Hampshire Division**
**Southern Colony**

**Date:** *20th April*
**Time:** *10.30 pm*
**Care Home Identity Number:** *017954 Coed*

(Please omit details of exact location)
**Number of children at this location:**
**Number of children in formal detention:** *0*

*I acknowledge with thanks the receipt of the work docket stating that the attic room serving as a girls' dormitory is to be upgraded, and confirm that it will be convenient to undertake the work any time next week. We have a full quota of girls, so we will need to use the room at night, but we can give the workers access from 9.30 am until 6.00 pm. I also confirm that we can provide a light midday meal for the workers.*

*On the subject of the adjustments being made by the children to their new freedoms, I agree with comments made by other care-givers on our online forum. Their reactions are, perhaps predictably, very mixed. Noah C and Daisy W are the most adventurous, though for rather different reasons, I suspect. Daisy has had a very stable childhood and has good self-esteem. Very little has happened in her experience to make her timid. Noah has a degree of resilience that I imagine comes from having survived early childhood traumas in the care of adults he trusted.*

*Beatrice F is a naturally quiet girl and is, at present, not comfortable about experimenting with her new freedoms, but it is my guess that this is more the result of her personality than of her life experiences. I have checked her records, and she was an only child of older parents who succumbed to the second virus.*

*My greatest concern is for Sophie A. She has not responded well to the relaxation of rules. She likes to stay close to me, and to spend her time with the smallest children, although when I took the little ones for their first experience of a playground, Sophie stayed at Xunzi House to keep an eye on the middle group. She reacted to the initial news of our new liberties with something almost like panic, and maintains that she will never be ready for life out of lockdown. I suspect that she fears falling into the hands of people like those from whom she was rescued. I echo the request of the caregiver of Care Home 017772 (Girls), that provision be made for some counselling in due course. In the meantime I am following instructions, of course, and reassuring the children that they will not be required to take any risks except those with which they feel comfortable.*

*I am grateful to the administrators for allowing the visit of my sister, and for the suggestion that she might come again fairly soon, and for a longer period. This job is more demanding now than when we lived uneventfully under lockdown, and she was extremely helpful last time she came. However, I understand that there is no merit in Edwina coming unless the South Western Colony can manage without her, and I leave the matter in your hands.*

★ ★ ★

It did not matter that we all had to get up a little earlier. The mornings were bright by then, even when it was not sunny, and the bird song was loud and cheerful, making it easier to feel as if the day had begun. Ethel-nushi said we needed to make our beds and tidy the dorm before breakfast, because of the workers, who were due to arrive at nine-thirty. It was quite exciting for us. These would not be freeloaders in a work gang, but proper builders who did this sort of thing for a living. I did not think I had met any people like that before.

Ethel-nushi was right, too. The van drew up in the lane and backed into place just by the holly bush, so that we heard its "vehicle reversing" warning before we saw the builders. There were three of them, all wearing green overalls with a logo on the pocket showing a smiley face in a triangle made by a hammer, a saw and something that looked like a ruler. There was a man with very little hair, a woman, and a boy who looked a little older than Arof the Clown. Ethel-nushi opened the kitchen door to them, and gave a little bow of her head out of courtesy, but at the same time the man held out his hand, to shake it, like they do in old movies. Then they both laughed, and the man said, "Good morning! You're expecting us, I think?"

Ethel-nushi opened the door wide and let them in, still

chuckling. We were all sitting round the table except Sophie, who had jumped up as soon as she heard the van arriving, and gone into the cloakroom.

The three workers smiled at us all.

The woman did the introductions. "So this is my husband, Robbie, and my son, Jamie, and I'm Mandy. I hope we won't cause you too much trouble!"

"I'm sure you won't!" Ethel-nushi was looking through a pile of stuff she had moved from the table in order to serve breakfast – some story books, a drawing by Toby of a dinosaur learning to fly, and a very old instruction manual for one of the computers, with the ring of a coffee cup on it. She found the docket for the builders and passed it to them.

"Great!" said the man, and tucked it into a pocket at the back of his boiler suit without looking at it. "Just let us look at the job first so that we can decide what we need, then we'll unload the van."

They were wearing heavy boots and they clumped up the stairs making a terrific racket. We heard them talking upstairs, and the floor creaking as they moved around.

Sophie peered out from the cloakroom and said, to nobody in particular, "Have they gone?"

Ethel-nushi went over to her. "I'll tell you what, Sophie," she said, "why don't you study in my room today? You have exams coming up and you need some peace and quiet." Then she ushered Sophie into her bedroom, said "You can work at my desk. Just put that stuff on the bed." Then she fetched Sophie's computer, and closed the door, so that Sophie was all alone.

"Huh!" grunted Elijah, almost under his breath. None of us could remember anyone going into Ethel-nushi's room before.

But Noah said, "Well, we've all got exams coming up, and we won't pass them if we don't get down to work!"

So we all put our breakfast dishes in the dishwasher and went to our separate workstations, and Ethel-nushi went upstairs to talk to the workers, and none of us said anything further about Sophie.

★ ★ ★

Sophie did not even come out at lunchtime, which was a pity, because it was a really interesting meal. It turned out that the builders were eating with us, which of course was a complete novelty. The only stranger I could ever remember sitting down at the table when we did was Edwina-nushi, and she was only a stranger for about five minutes!

Ethel-nushi had made extra sandwiches of course, and put out additional plates. She said cheerfully, "Help yourselves!"

We all stood back to let Robbie, Mandy and Jamie go first, the way they did in our courtesy lessons, and there was an odd moment when they seemed to be standing back for us too. Then Ethel-nushi said, "Please go ahead," and Mandy said, "This looks wonderful!" and the ice was broken.

The little ones used to sit in the corner by the television at that time. Albert and Rebecca had put together the old wooden train set to make a circuit, and their big game was to send toy engines in opposite directions, so that they crashed. Ethel-nushi said it was rather a violent game, and told them that if there were to be accidents, they would need an ambulance too, and so if she was around Toby was always the ambulance man. We kids knew, though, that if Ethel-nushi was not in the room the ambulance went out of action and the crashes became more and more dramatic, with screams of pain and a lot of groaning.

Of course, the girls could not take their lunches upstairs. Our dorm was out of bounds while the builders were there, and, although it was spring, there was quite a cool wind and so we did not want to go outside. I think we were quite interested in our visitors too.

So there we were: Ethel-nushi, Robbie, Mandy and Jamie, us older kids and several of the Chatterers, sitting round the table eating cheese and tomato sandwiches with crisps – a packet each.

Robbie said, "Nice place you have here," to Ethel-nushi.

"It is," she agreed. "We've been so lucky. It never flooded, even in the Winter of Disasters."

"You were lucky," agreed Mandy. "How long have you been here?"

"Oh…" Ethel-nushi was thinking. "Daisy, you're fourteen, aren't you?" She smiled at me. "Daisy has been here longer than anyone, she arrived soon after it opened. Before I came, even, and I've been here eleven years!"

The three builders all turned to look at me. Jamie was crunching his crisps in that very satisfactory way that I enjoyed, but which Ethel-nushi thought was bad manners. He swallowed and said, "I don't suppose you can remember anything else?"

"No," I agreed.

I noticed that his mum, Mandy, made a little sign to him across the table, as if to say "Mind your manners!"

Jamie said, "I've always lived in the same house too, but it's busier than this. I mean, we've got neighbours. And a road running past the house. This is like a secret place."

I was intrigued. "You must see lots of people," I commented.

"Yeah." There was still a pile of sandwiches in the middle of the table. He raised an eyebrow to Ethel-nushi, asking if he could have another, and she said, "Go ahead." Then Jamie went on, "For ages we used to *see* lots of people, and talk to them at a safe distance, but we could never play with them, from the time the schools closed. So me and Emily – my sister – we always played together." He looked over at the little ones.

Albert was getting his toy train ready for a really big crash. "It must be great, growing up with loads of other people," he mused, and I thought his voice sounded sad.

Noah said, "So how did you study, Jamie?" Noah was always thinking about studying.

"At home. On our computers." Jamie looked round the room. Of course he could see the workstations, and one of the Chatterers had not even turned her computer off. "Probably the same lessons as you," he added.

Ethel-nushi asked, "And how did you learn your trade?"

Robbie answered that. "From me. Well, he's still learning, of course. Apprenticeship exams at the end of next year." He winked at his son, and added, "You might even take them in a room full of other lads, at this rate!"

Mandy asked Ethel-nushi, "Have the changes affected you much?"

"A little." Ethel-nushi did not want to say too much, because of all of us listening.

I was thinking of Sophie, hiding in Ethel-nushi's room. The changes were really affecting her quite a lot, and I could not understand why.

Robbie said, "It's made a world of difference to us. We've been registered essential workers for the whole time, me and Mandy, but we only ever worked in empty properties or outdoors. You're only the fifth house we've actually been in while the family was there. It's like the Old Days."

Jamie had finished his sandwich and was looking hopefully and the bowl of apples. He said, "The biggest change so far has been opening up places of worship."

I was really surprised. Of course, we had all learnt that we should respect religious people, especially the older, wiser leaders who sat in the third house of government – the House of Cultural Continuity – and I remembered that, on that first outing with Edwina-nushi when we had walked almost to the cathedral, she had said that worshippers went in through a door we could not see, but somehow I had thought that only old people were religious. Jamie was just a few years older than me, and had studied the same classes, more or less. Did he not follow the teachings of the Master – of Confucius?

Ethel-nushi seemed to take it in her stride. "Where do you worship?" she asked.

"Quakers," answered Mandy. "In the middle of town. Do you know it?"

"Not personally," said Ethel-nushi. "That's more my sister's sort of thing. So, what do you… I mean, will you all meet together from now on? On Sundays? Is that when you have services?"

"Not really services," said Jamie. "Meetings. But yes, on Sundays. We started two weeks ago." He wrinkled up his nose. "To be honest, it seems odd. You can hear people's tummies rumbling and you're much more aware of them moving. And people have smells – shampoo and the detergent they washed their clothes in, and sometimes onion or garlic! You never know people's smells if you only ever see them on your computer screen! It's easier to concentrate when we meet online."

"You'll get used to it!" said Mandy. "Come on, now – back to work!"

They all three stood and headed for the stairs. As he walked past her, Ethel-nushi gave Jamie an apple. "Keeps the doctor away," she said, which I thought was pretty odd.

★ ★ ★

Noah said the next morning, "Let's take Jamie outside for lunch. And really talk to him."

It was a very bright, sunny day. Although it was still April, the mayflowers were out on the bush up by the lane, and the smell was powerfully sweet in the late afternoons. We were all, I think, looking forward to the builders coming again. Hearing things from them was better, I thought, than learning things from our computers, although the information came in a much less organised way.

I had tried to find out from Sophie why she did not want to meet these people. Lying in bed the night before, I had said, "Hey, Sophie, they're really nice. They won't hurt you. Come and have lunch with everyone tomorrow."

But Sophie had responded, "Honestly, Daisy, you don't know anything!" and had turned over and pretended to be asleep. She was not, though, because I could hear her sniffing.

Looking back, I think I could have been kinder. I should have gone over and sat on her bed, and said encouraging stuff about how I would be her friend even if she did not want to join in. I suppose, though, that I was excited, and a bit impatient with Sophie. I regret it now, of course, all these years later.

So lunchtime found us – Beatrice and Elijah, Noah and me – sitting with Jamie on the concrete by the river, eating bread rolls filled with watercress and slices of hard-boiled eggs, with the flap-jacks that the Chatterers had made the afternoon before.

"Where does Emily go," I wanted to know, "when you go out to work with your mum and dad?"

"She's younger than me," said Jamie. "She stays at home and does classes, like you. She wants to be a nurse."

"Wow!" That was pretty impressive. Front line workers deserved all the merit they earned, and more. "But she wants to deliver babies," he added, "not work with sick people."

Then Jamie started to ask us questions. It seemed as if our world was as strange to him, as his was to us.

"So, is it good," he asked, "All living in one house together? Your house mother seems nice."

We all answered together, "Yeah," "Pretty good," "All right," and "Great!" Then we all laughed.

I explained, "I've never really known anything else."

Elijah said, "This is the best place I've lived in. Better than the place in Portsmouth. It was all boys, and we had to wear naval uniforms."

Noah added, "And we get all this," and he waved at the river and the trees opposite. "Loads of space. And it's always been safe."

Jamie commented, "That other girl doesn't seem to think it's safe. The one who won't come out. Is there something wrong with her?"

Elijah and Noah looked at me, expecting that I would know the answer. Beatrice just looked at her knees. I answered, "We don't know," and there was an awkward silence.

Noah changed the subject. "Have you got any friends?" he wanted to know. The question of friendships was bothering us all a bit.

"No – oh…" hesitated Jamie. "Well, I think when we were little we used to play in each other's gardens. Mum says there was a time when children could play outside together but not go indoors, but I only remember little bits of that. I remember falling off a trampoline and hurting my arm, and I think I remember playing in a paddling pool in someone's garden, but you know… For ages it just wasn't sensible to play out. Even when we were allowed to Mum and Dad didn't like it. And there were all those civil disturbances."

That interested me, of course. I wanted to know all about it. "Did you see any riots? Were there people dying in the streets?"

Jamie laughed and said, "Well, not in a cul-de-sac on our housing estate, no! And if there had been bodies in the road, Mum and Dad would never have let me see them!"

Noah said, "Daisy loves gruesome stories!" and I was surprised, because I had not realised that he knew me that well.

Then Jamie surprised us all. "You could come over some time," he said, "and meet Emily. I told her about you. And it's allowed now."

\* \* \*

**Report of Ethel T. Walker to the National Society for the Care of Abandoned and Displaced Children (NSADC)**
**Hampshire Division**
**Southern Colony**

**Date:** *1ˢᵗ May*
**Time:** *11.00 pm*
**Care Home Identity Number:** *017954 Coed*
(Please omit details of exact location)
**Number of children at this location:** *13*
**Number of children in formal detention:** *0*

*I confirm that the work done on the attic room has been completed to a very high standard. The ceiling panelling which hides the insulation to the roof lightens the whole room, now that it has been painted white, and the new windows are ideal. It was kind of the workers to paint the floorboards and to put up the shelves, both jobs that were not on the docket.*

*It has been an interesting experience for the children to see ordinary workers, and for me to see how they coped with these relatively unusual social interactions. Predictably, Noah C and Daisy W seem to have reacted almost as teenagers might have done before these recent hard times. Elijah P-S and Beatrice F have been happy to follow the example of their two friends, and the young worker Jamie appeared to enjoy the beginnings of something that could become a friendship. The Chatterers (the middle group) and the little ones seemed rather shy initially but they have accepted the idea of strangers coming into the house with little wariness, and – especially in the case of the youngest children – with little interest.*

*The exception, of course, is Sophie A. Her reaction to having visitors in the house has been extreme. She is unwilling to have anything to do with them, and I have allowed her to spend these three days in my room. She is clearly very distressed. I went in yesterday to take her some lunch, and found her half hidden behind a curtain, looking out at the older children, who were talking to the young worker as they ate their lunch on the concrete by the river. The expression on her face was unnerving, a cross between confusion, anger and hate. It is not an expression I have ever seen on the face of a child before. Although, like all caregivers, I studied the unit on the troubled child, I do not feel that I am equipped to deal with Sophie in her present state.*

*The most significant development to come out of the events of this week, has been an invitation for four of the five older children (not including Sophie, who of course they do not know) to visit the Thomas household. This seems like an excellent development, but I would be grateful for official permission before sanctioning such a visit. Events are proceeding a little faster than I had anticipated when social mixing became permissible, and none of the other care workers on our forum have yet had this experience.*

★ ★ ★

It was agreed that we would walk to Jamie's house. It was quite a long way, beyond the water meadows, further even that Greater Beijing Street, which we crossed on the way. Ethelnushi told us we should take flowers for Mandy, and she gave us a box of home-made ginger biscuits for the whole family. We set out feeling quite excited, carrying daffodils that grew wild in the gardens of the abandoned houses.

It was a dull sort of day, with grey sky and no breeze, not cold, but not particularly warm either. I was still wearing jeans and my hoody, but the other three had gone into shorts, our standard summer clothing. There were more cars than the time we went to find Noah's cemetery, and a few people walking around, mostly going towards the centre of the city. Alongside Greater Beijing Street there were some large houses, and there were people in some of the gardens, pulling up weeds. We went under a bridge and then followed the road up to the houses where Jamie lived.

It was, as he had said, just a quiet cul-de-sac with red-brick houses on either side and at the end, set back a bit from the pavement. Each house (like Xunzi House) was joined on to one other. One or two of the houses were boarded up, and their little front gardens were wild, with long grass and, in one garden, a very shabby-looking sofa.

Jamie's house had a red front door, but before we reached it Jamie came out and said, "Hi!" and gave that little socially distanced wave which people did back then. Of course, we weren't social distancing, but it had become a habit. Even now, all these years later, you sometimes see old people greeting each other like that. They are forgetting how much times have changed.

We went in through the kitchen, which was tiny compared with the downstairs of Xunzi House, and into the other downstairs room which was furnished with a small table, a sofa and a couple of chairs. It looked like a very small space to me, although cheerful, and I could see that if there were only four of you, you might manage in such a house.

Jamie called up the stairs, "Emily! They're here!" Then he turned back to us. It was a Saturday, but Mandy and Robbie were not there and their van had not been parked outside. "Mum and Dad have just gone off to finish a job in Sleepers Hill," he said. "They'll buy fish and chips on the way home, if that suits you?"

I had never had fish and chips, bought from a shop and wrapped in greaseproof paper, but we all ate a lot of fish cooked in other ways, and it sounded good. We nodded or said "Yes," or "Fine," and Jamie sent his parents a quick text.

Noah was looking around the living room, and then peering out of the window. He turned to Jamie and said, quite quietly, "We used to live up here, somewhere. I think."

Jamie did not look surprised. "Until the third virus?" he asked. "Lots of people left then."

Noah looked sad. "I think so," he said. "Perhaps. I was little…"

Jamie was, I thought, about to say something, but just then Emily came downstairs.

Even on television I had never seen anyone like Emily. The first thing you saw – or at least, the first thing I remember seeing, was that long, almost-white hair and her bright blue-green eyes. The next thing I think I noticed, was her clothes. She was wearing a skirt made of something green and floaty, and a little long-sleeved top that finished at her waist, and which had sparkly bits sewn on it. She was barefoot, but she had painted her toe nails green, and she had a ring round one of her big toes. Her tracker bracelet, instead of being beige like ours, was made of some sort of silvery metal with green and red sparkling glass set into it. She looked, I thought, almost like one of those girls in the dance scenes of Indian movies, except for her exceptional whiteness. Suddenly I felt really bulky in my jeans and red trainers – big, in a lumpy sort of way.

"Hey!" greeted Emily. "Did you walk here? How long did it take?"

"Thirty-five minutes," said Noah, smiling at her as if she were just another person, not the most beautiful being in the room.

"We cut across the water meadows," I explained.

"Do you know," declared Emily, "I have never been into the water meadows. Not once! Jamie says your house is in the middle of them! Would you like some tea?"

So we sat around on the sofa and the chairs and drank tea and talked, and, although it was a bit odd at first, quite soon it felt as if Emily and Jamie were just two more people who lived in our house. Emily wanted to know how we had got on with the Chinese poetry unit – she was in the same year group as Elijah and me, and we both agreed with her that it was difficult at first, but that it got better. Actually, I seem to remember that despite my lack of enthusiasm I had earned quite a good mark for my work. That would have been thanks to Sophie. After drinking the tea, we went and looked in a wooden shed in the back garden, where the Thomases kept some of their tools, and Jamie showed us a table he was making with carved legs.

"It's for Mum's birthday," he said. "She never comes in here – it's Dad's shed!"

Then Mandy and Robbie arrived in the van, and we all ate fish and chips. I thought they would be greasy, but they weren't, just very crisp and quite salty. I remember thinking that they might be good for the odd meal, but that I would not want to live on them. Then a little while after that we walked home.

Beatrice said, as we climbed over the wall into the water meadows, "Isn't she beautiful?"

Elijah said, "Yeah" in a sort of long, drawn-out way.

Noah asked, looking surprised, "Emily? Is she?" Then, after a short pause he wanted to know, "Did you really find that poetry class hard, Daisy?" and I was reminded all over again how Noah was just interested in different things from the rest of us.

★ ★ ★

"And her toe nails were painted green!"

It was about ten at night. Sophie had come to sit on my bed, and wanted to know what had happened that day. I could not get Emily out of my mind. "And her hair was almost white. It made me feel…" I was struggling for a way to describe it. "It made me feel like a duck compared to a wren!" I tried. "Big and ugly!"

Sophie laughed, and I realised I had not heard her giggling for ages.

"You're not a duck!" she said. "You're more like... well, perhaps a robin? All inquisitive, and listening to other people with your head on one side! And I'm an owl. I just want to live in an old tree in the water meadows, and never be seen, but maybe just be heard, at a distance, now and again!"

The little ones were all fast asleep at the dark end of the dorm. I thought most of the Chatterers were too, although Kaia had still been reading on her tablet when we first came up. Beatrice was snoring gently in the way she usually did. We were the only ones awake. It was not quite dark, although the sun had set ages ago. The atmosphere was just right for telling secrets.

I wondered, "Sophie, why don't you come with us anymore? Why do you always stay with the younger ones?"

Sophie had heavy, dark hair that grew very straight. She used to let Ethel-nushi cut it, but she had been growing it longer recently and sometimes she would put her head forward and her hair would make a sort of screen, so that nobody could see her face. Now, though, she was sitting cross-legged at the foot of my bed twirling one lock of hair round and round with her fingers. I could not properly see her expression.

For a bit she was silent. Some bird, going late to its roosting, was making a "cluck, cluck, cluck" noise somewhere deep in the water meadows, and very faintly I could voices coming from downstairs – Ethel-nushi on her caregivers' forum, I supposed.

Then Sophie spoke. Her voice was very small as she said, "You know, Daisy... Some bad stuff happened... before."

They talk about "callow youths" in books, and usually mean boys, but when I look back on it now that is the phrase which best sums me up. I was a fledgling, an inexperienced and, I fear, a rather insensitive teenager, so I said, "You mean, like in Detroit?"

Sophie gave a little gasp of exasperation. "No, Daisy," she snapped. "Not like Detroit! Like England!"

I had the grace to feel ashamed. I asked, "Did bad things happen to your parents?"

Again, Sophie was quiet for a spell. Then she said, "I don't know what happened to my parents. I was taken away from them. I was outside and I shouldn't have been. We were in lockdown but I just wanted to pick some blackberries. They grew in a wild patch at the end of the road. And I was caught and taken away…"

I could hardly breathe, because at last I was hearing Sophie's story and I wanted to know what had happened next. Sophie gave a sort of shudder, I could feel it through my mattress and bed springs, but she did not say anything more.

At last I could bear it no longer. I tried to prompt her. I asked, "Was it the Civic Police, Sophie? Or soldiers? Did they punish you? Did they lock you up?"

"Oh, Daisy!" She answered, and she sounded quite angry. "The Civic Police and the soldiers are good. Honestly, you don't know anything!" Then she jumped off my bed and went back to her own.

"I'm sorry, Sophie!" I whispered, not sure what I had done wrong. "Good night."

Sophie did not answer.

★ ★ ★

**Report of Ethel T. Walker to the National Society for the Care of Abandoned and Displaced Children (NSADC)**
**Hampshire Division**
**Southern Colony**

**Date:** *23rd May*
**Time:** *11.15 pm*
**Care Home Identity Number:** *017954 Coed*
(Please omit details of exact location)
**Number of children at this location:** *13*
**Number of children in formal detention:** *0*

*Circular B11745 has caused me some concern, since I can see the wisdom of it, but I find it hard to know how to warn the children about being over-confident with strangers at the same time as dealing with their fears about going out and about in the city. As others will have reported, or are about to report, we spent some time on the forum this evening discussing how best to deal with these two conflicting but entirely necessary tasks. The only sort of "stranger danger" most of these children know about relates to fear of infection. I am not sure how to instil in them some caution about being too trusting of others, at the same time as encouraging them to begin to mix socially. A lesson or two on the excellent series "Friendship, Fun and Freedom" could be helpful, so would additional guidance from the Children's Bureau. My fellow caregivers and I assume that parents with their own children must be experiencing similar difficulties.*

*My particular concern at present is for Daisy W and Beatrice F. Both girls are old enough to be out and about without adults, but both are very naive. I am not too worried if Noah C and Elijah P-F are with them, but it is not to be expected that these four will always go around together as they are doing at present. Beatrice is, of course, not very likely to be on her own, she lacks the confidence, but Daisy is another matter.*

*I have a second concern, also associated with the end of lockdown and with "stranger danger". The authorities have made no attempt to rebuild the old, cobbled bridge across the navigation canal, but twice now I have seen people on the opposite bank. I am not quite sure how they might have found their way there, but the footpaths are now officially open and it is, I think, possible to reach the water meadows and the old*

*Itchen Way from the far end of the city limits, out by St Cross. I have found it disconcerting to see people looking across while the children make a barbecue, or play in the shallow water. It is, of course, perfectly natural to stop and watch children at play, but yesterday two men turned away as soon as they saw me looking at them. I would be grateful for an occasional police patrol, and for the locks on this property to be checked for security. I have thirteen children in my care and it is difficult to keep track of them all, despite their bracelets.*

★ ★ ★

People started to appear on the other side of the river that spring. The old gentleman with the dog, the one we had seen on our first venture out, walked that way several times a week, and if we were outside he waved to us across the water and we remembered to call back, "Morning!" or "Afternoon!" instead of "*Zao!*" Toby, who had started to be interested in dogs at that time, used to wave frantically and call "Woof! Woof!" He was more interested in the animal than in its owner. Once we saw a young couple. The woman had a small backpack and the man was carrying something on a sling tied to his front. It took me a moment or two to realise that it was a baby, snuggled up close to its daddy, safe and protected. I wondered if I had ever been carried around like that. I wondered if any of us had.

Once a group of Chinese soldiers walked along there. Noah, who liked everything Chinese, called across to them in their own language and they talked for several minutes, mostly just about the old Itchen Way, and the fact that the footbridge had been destroyed years ago. The soldiers would have to go back the way they came. I understood quite a lot of what was said, but not everything. I half wished that there was a way for them to cross over, because I would have liked to get to know more about them. They looked very young and I thought they were a long way from their own homes, and, after all, we owed them a lot. Our country had been in such a mess during the Culture Wars, until the Re-establishment of Peace and Justice. I knew, too, that it was a Chinese soldier who had rescued Noah, and Noah was, I felt, my closest friend.

Sophie had not said anything more to me about her life before Xunzi House. In fact, she did not seem to be saying much to anybody anymore. She had changed a lot from the girl who had told me all those wonderfully scary stories about riots and death in Detroit. She did not come outside very often, although we had a whole run of beautiful days, and, when she did come out, she would not sit on the concrete with the rest of us, right on the edge of the slope with our feet in the water. Instead, she sat on the grass outside Ethel-nushi's room, behind the hedge. It was as if she were hiding all the while.

Ethel-nushi suggested that we might like to invite Jamie and Emily to one of our family Sundays. Once she realised that their parents would not be coming, even Sophie seemed to think it was a good idea, so Noah texted them, and it was all set up.

The Chatterers were very keen on barbecues all that year, so it was decided that we would have veggie burgers and salad and that us older ones would look after our guests while the others cooked. Of course, Jamie had visited us before but we went up to the broken wooden gate by the lane to meet them, and they arrived dead on time. Their parents had dropped them off in the van, because they were carrying four huge bottles of ginger beer – enough for all of us – and a massive tub of ice-cream.

Sophie was sitting on the lawn making daisy chains for the little ones. Toby looked so sweet, with two necklaces of flowers round his neck and his tongue sticking out a little (as it often did) and a happy smile on his round face. It was because Sophie was there, and not on the concrete, that we all ended up sitting on the lawn. Toby went round each person and showed us his "jewellery", and we all made approving noises, then he ran off to play with Rebecca and Albert, who were hunting for snails.

Emily was wearing the same green, floaty skirt as before but it was quite warm and so she had a little blouse with puff sleeves. She looked great, although it was really old-fashioned clothing. Her almost-white hair was mostly loose, with one slim braid into which she had plaited a green thread of some sort. When she stretched her legs out, I saw that she had no hair on them at all, and I looked at my hairy legs and felt like a gorilla.

Noah introduced Sophie.

"So, we meet at last!" said Jamie in a relaxed and friendly way.

Sophie blushed. I explained, "Sophie is not keen on strangers," and I put my hand on hers to reassure her.

Emily said, "Sophie, you have such beautiful hair!"

The thing about living with people is that you get used to them. I had not noticed that Sophie's hair was anything to get excited about, but now I looked at it properly, and I saw what Emily meant. It was dark, almost black, and very straight. My hair was a bit nondescript, a mousy colour and slightly wavy, but Sophie's hair was really heavy, and swung a bit when she moved her head.

Sophie looked embarrassed and went a bit pink. She said, "Thank you," and looked at her knees.

Emily asked, "Can I braid it for you?"

For a moment I thought Sophie looked alarmed.

Emily said reassuringly, "Just one braid, on the side, like mine."

So, "All right," Sophie agreed, and I ran inside to find a comb and a rubber band, and we all sat on the grass behind the hedge chatting and watching the operation on Sophie's hair.

It was while all this was going on, and while the smoke from the barbecue drifted through the air in a tantalising fashion, and while one of the Chatterers was practising on his dizi, his little bamboo flute, and while Rebecca and Albert called out to Toby to come and see the biggest snail ever – it was while all these things were going on, that Elijah suddenly interrupted everyone, sounding indignant. "Hey! Who are they?"

We all looked at where he was pointing, to the bank on the opposite side of the river. Two people were standing there, and one of them had a pair of binoculars held up to his face. They were looking directly at us.

Noah jumped to his feet. He shouted across the river, *"What do you want?"*

Jamie stood too. He was even taller than Noah and he looked angry. *"This is private property,"* he called across to the people.

*"We're not doing any harm,"* the man shouted back. *"This is a public right of way!"*

Ethel-nushi must have heard the noise. She came outside wearing her pink apron over her Sunday clothes. "I'll deal with this," she said to the boys, but they stayed standing, and Elijah stood too.

The man was a bit more polite when he saw a proper grown-up. He said, "I'm sorry if we bothered your children. We're just out for a bit of bird watching."

Even at that distance I thought I could tell that the woman with him sniggered.

Ethel-nushi said, in an icy tone, "Well, I would be grateful if you would go and bird watch somewhere else!" Then she stood with her hands on her hips and stared at them. I thought that I would not want to deal with Ethel-nushi if she were ever to look at me like that.

For a few seconds the couple did nothing. Then the man with the binoculars said something to his companion. He shouted back across the river, "*Oh well! See you all later, I hope!*" And the two people turned and started waking south again.

Ethel-nushi watched until they had gone. She said, quite loudly, "Creeps!" I had never heard her so angry. Then she seemed to relax. She looked at our group, the three boys still standing, Beatrice, Sophie, Emily and me still sitting on the grass, and she said, "Well done, boys. And, girls, you must remember that there are some unpleasant people around. You're safe here, but be on your guard when you're out and about. Anyhow, lunch will be ready in about twenty minutes."

She seemed to notice Sophie's new braid for the first time, then, and she gave her a huge smile. "Sophie, that's really lovely!" she said, and went back round to the barbecue pit.

Sophie said, almost under her breath, "I'll never be out and about!" But I was thinking, *I could have seen those weirdos off, even if I had been entirely on my own!*

Thus, the innocence of the young!

★ ★ ★

The whole question of religious worship seemed to creep up on us. The *Friendship, Fun and Freedom* course did several lessons on "Visiting a Faith Community". Each lesson was introduced by someone from the third house of government, the House of Cultural Continuity. An imam talked about going to a mosque, the Archbishop of Canterbury, who was a very pretty Tibetan woman, described what might happen if we visited a church, and a Sikh man in a turban spoke about their temples. The CPP (Confucian People's Party) believed in freedom of worship, but we were warned to consider carefully the teachings of any group we came across, to talk to those to whom we owed filial obligations, and not to be easily taken in. Nobody said anything about the Quakers, which left us older ones wondering. Every Sunday, that spring, we would hear the cathedral bells ringing across the water meadows, reminding us that this was a Christian holy day. In a history class we learnt about the feudal systems of China and Europe, and it became clear that Christianity had been as strong an influence in the Seven Colonies and all across Europe as Confucianism had been in China.

That was the spring, too, when we heard a cuckoo for the first time. As the climate settled down, all sorts of birds were returning that had been lost to the Seven Colonies years ago. I remember lying in bed listening to the bird song in the early morning, and that distinctive "Cuckoo! Cuckoo!" I did not like it when Ethel-nushi told us that cuckoos threw birds' eggs out of nests and laid their own there instead. Their song was so attractive, and their behaviour so bad! I remember walking around in the water meadows looking for eggs or baby birds that had been ejected from their nests, but I never did find any.

At first it was Noah and Jamie who were friends, but after that Sunday barbecue Emily and I started messaging each other on our tablets. The first time it happened was over the lesson from *Friendship, Fun and Freedom* about "Sects and Cults". I thought the material was a bit frightening. It seemed that people could get sucked into groups where people were not rational, where they set aside the standards with which they were raised and all their family obligations, and often ignored the lawful government of their countries, too. I wondered how a person was supposed to know the difference between a sect and a cult. In the end I texted Emily.

"Question 4 U – r Quakers a sect or a cult?" I wanted to know.

"Neither," texted Emily, "Faith group."

That sort of helped. Faith groups seemed mainstream. There were representatives of all the main faith groups in the Third House.

Emily had obviously been following the same lesson. She texted, "We R rational!" Then she typed "And we R never supposed to ignore our families!"

I sent her a smiley face, and also an emoji of a panda scratching his head, showing that I still did not fully understand. I liked the stuff about religions and beliefs but it was turning out to be quite complicated.

Then Emily messaged me again. "Come + see 4 urself?" she suggested.

★ ★ ★

We were all really pleased when Edwina-nushi came back. It was mid-June, I think, about a week or so after the Sunday when Emily and Jamie came for lunch. This time we knew she was coming, and the Chatterers had made posters which were put up all over the living area saying "Welcome!" and with pictures of trains, because this time she was coming on public transport. There was also, I remember, quite a gruesome picture of a spider, drawn by Toby. The Chatterers did not want it put up, but Toby got upset, and claimed, "Spider for 'Wina-nushi!" and Ethel-nushi insisted it stay, in amongst all the much neater posters by the older children.

She arrived on a school day, just as we were finishing our morning classes. Sophie and I had been given a maths task, which was never my strong point, but for once I thought I knew how to do it. It was algebra, and I had just begun to understand the pure logic of the discipline, so I was feeling pleased with myself. Then I heard Toby call out "'Wina-nushi!" and he rushed past my workstation to the back door.

This time she did not knock, but just opened the door,

dumped her backpack on the floor by the cupboard with the casserole dishes in it, and said brightly, "Hello, everyone!"

I seem to remember that we all clustered round, workstations abandoned, and Toby clung to her leg with glee. Ethel-nushi came in from the store cupboard where she had been looking for lunch ingredients, and smiled happily at her sister. "It seems we are all pleased to see you!" she said.

We were. I think if it had not been for Ethel-nushi's quiet disciplining, we would all have left our computers on, our work not sent in to our teachers, books and papers scattered around on tables and window sills. As it was, "Lunch in ten minutes!" Ethel-nushi told us, and we all remembered to go and finish off properly, except for Toby, of course. Tidying up was never his strong point.

We all wanted to know about the train. Edwina-nushi showed us her cancelled ticket on her phone, and explained how it worked. Beatrice wanted to know whether she had sat next to someone she did not know, and whether everyone wore masks, and Edwina-nushi was kind, and told us all again what we had been told over and over for the last month, that there were no pandemics in the world anymore for us to worry about. She told us about the places where the train had stopped to let people on and off, and about the man who came down the aisle of the train serving tea – one cup free with your ticket; the second cup you had to pay for. She told us about walking down through the town, and that people had been painting the outside woodwork of the Baptist church. "It's so good to see these old buildings back in use!" she said.

That reminded me of Emily's text. We had all stayed round the table to eat, because of the happiness of having Edwina-nushi with us. I asked, "Do you think we could go and visit some places of worship?"

I saw Noah look at me, surprised. "Hey!" he exclaimed,

"That's just what I was wondering. I'd love to go to the place where Jamie goes."

Edwina-nushi looked slightly confused. "Jamie?" she asked.

"The Thomases," explained Ethel-nushi. She was sliding a second helping of sandwiches onto the plate in the middle of the table. Egg and cress, in brown bread. Noah reached over and took one.

"Oh, yes!" Obviously the two sisters talked about what was going on in Xunzi House. "Where do they go?"

Noah swallowed his mouthful. He said, "They're Quakers."

Edwina-nushi laughed. "This doesn't seem like a household which would be attracted by Quakers! You're all much too noisy!" Then she looked more serious. "I used to know some Quakers," she said. "I was in prison with some before… well, a long time ago." She, too, took another sandwich. She put it on her plate and looked thoughtful. "Actually," she said, "I would quite like to go to one of their meetings. The Quakers I knew before were interesting…" She looked at Ethel-nushi across the table. She said, "Do you remember, Sis, I told you about that time with the food?"

Ethel-nushi nodded. "Of course I remember!" she said. "But I think I just ought to get permission before anyone decides for sure to go…"

★ ★ ★

## Report of Ethel T. Walker to the National Society for the Care of Abandoned and Displaced Children (NSADC)
### Hampshire Division
### Southern Colony

**Date:** 1st June
**Time:** *3.45 pm*
**Care Home Identity Number:** *017954 Coed*

(Please omit details of exact location)
**Number of children at this location:** *13*
**Number of children in formal detention:** *0*

*I am sending in this report before the office closes, in the hope that I am giving you time to respond before the weekend.*

*I thank you for allowing an extended visit from my sister. She arrived at lunchtime today and has already started working with the Chatterers on their vegetable patch. It is something of a relief to me to have someone here who can observe the children first hand and with whom I can discuss them.*

*Over lunch today Daisy W and Noah C raised the possibility of visiting the local Quakers for a Sunday Service (or do they call it a meeting?). You will recall that their new friends the Thomases worship there and obviously there has been some discussion among the young people. I admit to having little religious knowledge, but I do recall that Quakers were heavily involved in the relief efforts that took place during in the Winter of Disasters, and I therefore suspect that their teachings will not contradict what the children have been taught since the Re-establishment of Peace and Justice. My sister would be happy to accompany the older children if you do not recommend that they visit the Quakers unaccompanied, although I suspect they would prefer to go alone. Either way, I would like clarity from you about the acceptability, and indeed the advisability, of such a trip.*

*On the matter of the lock for the newly mended gate leading to the path to this house, I thank you for the promptness with which this work was carried out. We continue to see more people on the footpath on the opposite bank but Xunzi House feels more secure now that it is so difficult for unauthorised people to walk here. I have to remember to unlock the gate on Thursday evenings and Saturday mornings, for the collection of rubbish and for the delivery of groceries but, so far, I have not forgotten for long enough to disrupt normal domestic services.*

*I will write a fuller report later, when the younger children are in bed.*

★ ★ ★

"Please come!" I coaxed Sophie. We were getting up on the Sunday morning, putting on our summer clothes of shorts and tee shirts, and I was looking for one of my trainers, which turned out to be under my bed. "You know Emily and Jamie. It's not as if they're strangers!"

Sophie had not started to dress. She was still sitting in her bed hugging her knees and looking doubtful. "I'm not worried about Emily or Jamie," she agreed. "I like them. But there will be other people there, too. Strangers. I would rather stay here."

I was about to argue, when I remembered what she had told me. She had been kidnapped. Sophie had never related the end of the story, never told me what happened, but perhaps being kidnapped would make a person a bit wary of strangers. So instead I said, "I'll check it out, and tell you all about it, and if we like it you can come next time."

I thought Sophie looked relieved. She said, "Stay with the others, won't you? Don't go off exploring."

I laughed. "I'll be all right!" I reassured her, and went down to breakfast.

I am not sure what I had expected. In the *Friendship, Fun and Freedom* classes all the places of worship had looked rather grand. Emily had messaged me on my work tablet that the meeting started at ten-thirty in the morning, and so Noah, Elijah, Beatrice and I set off, accompanied by Edwina-nushi, just after ten.

For most of the walk we followed the river, along the road I had found so threatening just a few weeks earlier because the houses were so close to the footpath, then along the Weirs, and up some steps to a winding road we had not yet explored. There were more houses up close to the pavement, but I seem to remember that we were already less worried by that. Then the road turned a corner and ahead of us, behind an old wall, was a tall red-brick building.

"I think that's it," said Edwina-nushi, who was following the map on her bracelet.

I felt a little nervous – or was it excitement? Beatrice stayed well behind us, but Noah and Edwina-nushi walked confidently up to the open gate.

When I look back on these things that happened decades ago, it seems that my memories are either very sharp, as if everything happened yesterday, or rather hazy, as if I had dreamt them and they did not happen at all. I mostly have impressions rather than a clear recollection of that first experience of Quakers. I know that the man at the gate held out his hand to shake ours, and I remember being deeply shocked. Ever since I could remember we had been taught never to touch someone unless we really knew them really well, and trusted them. I think Edwina-nushi must have shaken hands, and I think Noah did, but I am certain I did not. Probably I did a distance-wave, although I do not remember. Then we all filed in to a glass-sided hall that looked out onto a very pretty garden.

Perhaps I am muddling several meetings up, in my memory of that first experience. I can remember sitting with the others, in a row at the back of a circle that was three chairs deep. There was no social distancing, so it was like being in a private home, like being in Xunzi House, where we were in a safe bubble. Either on that visit or later, Jamie and Emily came and sat with us. As Edwina-nushi had warned, the meeting was very quiet, with no introductions, just people settling themselves in the wooden chairs and closing their eyes. Perhaps it was in that meeting that nobody said anything for the whole hour. I think I looked at my bracelet to see what the time was, and was surprised at how quickly the time had passed. I know that back then I understood nothing about how to listen to the Spirit – that all came later. I think I looked out of the window at the garden. Someone had hung a bird feeder on a tulip tree and there was a lot of activity around it.

I do know that afterwards, when the meeting ended, a few people started to talk, one by one. I am sure it was on that first occasion that someone quoted a poem I had never heard of, to do with bird: *I caught this morning, morning's minion.* Used as I was, as we all were, to Chinese poetry, it meant nothing at all to me. An elderly lady also recited something in old English: *The ousel cock so black of hue, With orange-tawny bill, The throstle with his note so true, The wren with little quill,* and people grinned, and someone remarked "Bottom!" which seemed like a pretty rude response, but everyone else smiled or laughed.

They were nice to us, I remember that.

We crossed the garden to a kitchen and drank tea and ate biscuits, and they talked to us in a friendly way, but they were so unlike us. It was as if they came from a different country, or were in a film set from those old movies we watched from before the Culture Wars, before the Re-establishment of Peace and Justice. I dare say if it had not been for Jamie and Emily we would never have gone back.

Emily looked a bit different that morning. She had her hair in two long braids and was wearing loose, wide-legged trousers made of something silky, with elastic round the ankles. Jamie looked just the same as always. We were all wearing our khaki shorts and tee shirts except Edwina-nushi, who was in her patchwork trousers, and probably that was the first time it occurred to me that we were wearing a kind of uniform and none of the Quakers were. Our world was so simple and reliable, and theirs was so strange. I liked ours best.

Then we walked home as clouds started to gather overhead, and were back in time for tomato soup and hot rolls, a Sunday treat.

★ ★ ★

I remember very clearly sitting on the concrete with Noah one evening, after the Chatterers had gone up to bed. Dusk was late, it must have been June, so in fact we had only been to Quakers a few times by then. I do not know where the others were. Noah had been reading a leaflet that one of the Quakers had given him, but he tucked it back in his shorts pocket when I joined him.

At first neither of us said anything, but then Noah asked, "Do you think there is a Spirit that people can listen to?"

The Quakers definitely thought there was. It seemed to be their main belief. I remembered one of the many quotations of Confucius that we had all learnt by heart years ago, and said it aloud. *"If you don't know how to live as a person, how can you serve the spirit?"* I recited. "If the Master thought there is a spirit to serve, there probably is, isn't there?"

Noah was frowning slightly. He said, "They don't really know about Confucius, you know."

"I know."

We both sat there in silence.

I said after a while, "They really just know about their own stuff, don't they? About art and music from the Seven Colonies, and about those weird old poets. They don't know anything about our lives."

Noah replied, "Well, Jamie and Emily do."

"Yes," I agreed. Then I thought a bit more. "Well, sort of," I said. "They've done the same lessons as us, but they've never lived like us, have they? They live like other Quakers, or like people who're not in care, wearing their own choice of clothes and going home to their own parents. Stuff we don't do."

Noah was almost thinking aloud. "Last week when I talked to that tall man, the one with the moustache, I felt as if we were speaking a different language. He wanted to know if they would take us on trips to the theatre now that we can go out. I mean, Daisy – who goes to the theatre? Why would we? I didn't know people even did that sort of thing nowadays!"

I said, "I'd like to hear a live concert, sometime. We did some work on Sizhu ballads last autumn and it's really lovely music. Did you do that unit?"

"Yes," agreed Noah. "And I loved it too. And I'd really like to go to a C-pop concert. Wouldn't you like to hear the Sages, if they toured in the Southern Colony? But I don't think the Quakers would be interested. They all want to listen to old European stuff all the time." He sighed. "Let's face it, Daisy. We're just different."

★ ★ ★

**Report of Ethel T. Walker to the National Society for the Care of Abandoned and Displaced Children (NSADC) Hampshire Division Southern Colony**

**Date:** *17th June*
**Time:** *11.00 pm*
**Care Home Identity Number:** *017954 Coed*
(Please omit details of exact location)
**Number of children at this location:** *13*
**Number of children in formal detention:** *0*

*I recall that, towards the end of the first pandemic, the Prime Minister (what was his name?) said that coming out of lockdown would be harder than going in to it. That certainly seems to be the case now.*

*The older children, not including Sophie, have visited their friends up on the Stanmore Estate twice, and the Thomas young people have been here once. They seem to get on well, and the friendship could certainly serve to help to ease those in my care into the wider world.*

*Their visits to the Quakers, however, are causing me some anxiety. Winchester is a city of many comparatively privileged people, and it seems these are the ones who are attracted to Quakers. Edwina tells me that there are frequent references to traditional English – perhaps I should say "British" or even "Western" – culture, and of course it is all quite alien to my charges. Edwina is concerned, since she fears it is bad for the self-esteem of the young people to feel constantly left out of, or confused by, conversations. Of course, our children are not without strong cultural awareness, but they have been exposed to very different influences, in most cases from a very early age. It seems that at the end of their worship sessions Quakers encourage some sort of sharing, and Noah C confided in me that on their first visit he wanted to share some words from a poem by Xi Wang Lei which he had learnt only recently in Chinese. The English translation is, I believe, "As the lark soars, so soars my heart. As the wind blows, so blows the spirit". The words had come into his head because of birds feeding at a feeder just outside the meeting room. Noah told me that he held back because he was not sure how easily he could translate, and that, even if he could give the people an English version, he was not sure they would appreciate it.*

*Edwina and I have discussed this cultural difference at some length. Being older, our awareness crosses over to some extent, at least as far as recognising that something might be a quotation from Shakespeare or a reference to a pre-pandemic artist. The young people have very little to help them to bridge the gap. I am sure that the Quakers and others like them would see the solution in education. If we were to introduce the children to more traditional English middle-class culture they might feel more at home. I have my doubts, though. Would this not imply that the culture in which they have been immersed is in some way lacking?*

*It does seem, though, that the older teenagers intend to keep going to Quakers. Edwina feels certain that, despite the significant cultural differences, the Quakers are a benign community. It is our intention to let our young people go unaccompanied from now on. It is, we feel, in the nature of adolescence that interests should be explored and then, perhaps, dropped or taken up more seriously, and we want our teenagers to feel no pressure of any sort from us.*

*On another matter, the whole household is becoming very excited about the planned celebrations for the summer solstice. It is, if I may add my voice to the many who have applauded this decision, inspired to choose a day that has been celebrated both in the Chinese homeland and in Europe. Here at Xunzi House the children know more about the worship of the fruitful earth and about Chinese customs, not least because of the BBC travelogue that was broadcast last summer. Noah C and Daisy W want us to make fresh noodles and to eat them cold, with salad, in the traditional manner of the ancients. The Chatterers, of course, want a barbecue, and the youngest children want sweets! Edwina and I think that all these desires can be fulfilled, and we hope in the evening to take the whole group into the city to see and to experience the celebrations. It will be the first time they have been exposed to real crowds, and we will need to prepare them all carefully.*

★ ★ ★

Sophie was behaving really strangely. It was not just that she would not visit Quakers with us, and refused to go on our second visit to the Thomases. She was keeping herself more and more to herself. We older ones had always occupied the concrete by the boatyard, it was more or less our space although Toby, of course, did not understand that and sometimes came to join us, and to sit on one lap or another. Before the lockdown was eased, Sophie used to join us there too. She was just one of the gang. But now, now that everything was changing, she would no longer join us there. Sometimes she sat on the grass behind the hedge and read a book, but she was wary even there, peering often between the privet twigs in case – it seemed to me – someone might come walking on the opposite bank.

I tried to talk to her about it, but I was a clumsy girl when it came to the feelings of others. Once, as we sat eating our lunch and throwing bits of bread to the disinterested ducks, I called across, "Come and join us, Sophie!"

Sophie did not answer, just gave a sort of "humph!" noise and stayed where she was.

Noah was kinder than me. He actually went across and squatted down next to her, and said something quiet which I could not hear. Sophie answered just as quietly, and Noah came back to join us.

"She doesn't like people watching her while she eats," he explained.

I knew that was nonsense. Sophie sat at the table every breakfast and dinner and ate as well as the rest of us.

Another odd thing about Sophie at that time was that she never drew back the curtain at her bedroom window. I think I have already mentioned that, as the oldest two girls, Sophie and I had the beds by the dormer windows. My window was on the other side of the house from the river, and looked out mostly on the trees that lined the lane. Sophie had a lovely view, across the river to the footpath and the trees on the other side. When she first came, she used to sit on her bed and look out with a dreamy expression on her face. Once she had said to me, "All that wildness, and not a person in sight!" Now she kept the curtains firmly closed, and, when she woke up in the morning and wanted to check the weather, she more or less peered round her curtains.

It was about this time that Beatrice and I had another matter on our minds, which had suddenly become very important to us both. It makes me laugh to think of it now, but at the time it was deadly serious.

In the summer we all – boys and girls – wore shorts. That meant, of course, that our legs were exposed. I suppose, since we were all in the same situation, we had thought nothing about it until that summer.

I had noticed that Emily did not have hairs on her legs. At first, I thought it was because she was blonde, so that any growth just would not show up, and then the first time we went to Meeting she was wearing those silky trousers so I did not think about it. On our second visit to their home, though,

Emily had also been wearing shorts, and I could see for myself. She really, truly, did not have hairy legs.

Then we went to Meeting on a particularly warm day, and some of the women were wearing dresses, so we could see their legs as well. And they, too, did not have any hair growing. It made me ashamed of myself, walking around looking like a monkey.

Beatrice had noticed it too. She said, "Do you think we're different? Do you think it might be something in our diet?"

"I don't know."

I had begun to notice everyone's limbs. The small children in the house, both boys and girls, were more or less hairless, but our older boys were hairy, and so was Jamie. Ethel-nushi and Edwina-nushi, of course, always wore trousers. Sophie, who had heavy, dark head-hair, also had very hairy legs. "It makes me feel as if I'm not a proper girl," I said. Then, "Perhaps there is something wrong with us," I suggested. "Perhaps that's why we're in care."

Beatrice looked doubtful. "I don't think so," she said hesitantly.

Everyone had been talking about the summer solstice celebrations. Ethel-nushi said, "When we go down into the town, we can all dress up. We ought to plan what we are going to wear."

I said at once, "I want to wear trousers!"

Beatrice agreed, "Me too!"

Sophie said, "I don't want to go to the celebrations. I'll stay here and keep an eye on everything."

Edwina-nushi was looking at Beatrice and me, although she put a kind hand on Sophie's shoulder. "We'll discuss that later," she reassured Sophie. "Don't worry." Then she said to Beatrice and me, "We could make you really nice outfits. We could buy some light cotton and make you attractive summer dresses. You don't need to wear care-clothes all the while."

I said, "Emily wore some really pretty trousers to the Quaker Meeting. They had elastic round the ankles. I could wear clothes like that."

Beatrice did not say anything but she had gone rather red. Then she sniffed and wiped her eyes.

Sophie ranted, "Who wants to go to a street party anyhow?" and ran upstairs as if she were angry.

I said, "I don't want to wear a skirt! I'd rather stay at home with Sophie!"

Edwina-nushi looked between Beatrice and me. "Girls, come in here a minute," she said, opening the door to the room that the two carers now shared, and ushering us in.

I had not often been in that room before; it was Ethel-nushi's room. Ethel-nushi had once told me that when she first arrived as a caregiver, when I was really small, I had sometimes slept in that room with her, because I used to have bad dreams. I had no memories of that, and now the room was out of bounds, but I had seen in through the open door often enough to know what it looked like. My first reaction, when Edwina-nushi closed the door, was "Goodness! This has changed!"

Instead of one bed in the middle of the room, there were two beds now, alongside opposite walls. There was a photo in a frame on Ethel-nushi's desk, showing two old-fashioned little girls standing in a garden somewhere, with a man and a woman standing behind them, smiling. *Their mum and dad*, I thought. I could tell which was Edwina-nushi's bed because there was a bright, tie-dyed spread over it. Next to that bed was a photo of a man, a man wearing the uniform of a Chinese Regular, although he looked European. There were books everywhere.

Edwina-nushi said, "So, what's up, girls?"

I do not know how Beatrice reacted, except of course that she was quiet. I think I looked at my feet. How could I explain to Edwina-nushi that we had realised that there was something wrong with us?

When neither of us answered, Edwina-nushi instructed, "Sit down!"

We both sat on the tie-dye-covered bed, Edwina-nushi facing us across the room from her sister's bed.

"Has something happened?" she asked.

I shook my head. After all, nothing had actually happened, except that we had discovered that we were not normal.

"So why this enthusiasm for wearing trousers on a hot summer's day?" she prodded.

Still we remained silent.

Edwina-nushi was quiet for a moment herself. "Is it because you've never worn skirts?" she asked.

I realised that this was true, but of course it was not that. I shook my head.

Then Beatrice started crying again, crying properly this time. I was surprised. She was a quiet sort of girl and kept herself to herself. Between sobs she said, "It's because we're odd!"

"Odd?" Edwina-nushi sounded really surprised. "Girls… How are you odd?"

I took a deep breath. She must have noticed. Probably they were ignoring the problem for as long as they could, before action became necessary. I mumbled under my breath, looking at the rug, "We're hairy, like boys." There, I had told her the worst. Now she and Ethel-nushi would have to decide what to do with us. They could not ignore the problem anymore.

Edwina-nushi gave a sort of splutter. For a moment I thought she was going to laugh, but she just made a sort of choking sound and then sounded serious. "Ah," she said. "I see!"

Beatrice was sobbing still. My mouth had gone dry. What would happen now? Were there places for people who were neither girls nor boys? Would we be sent away?

Edwina-nushi said, "Girls, I am really sorry. I think there are things we should explain to you. We should have explained them years ago."

Beatrice said, between sniffs, "Oh, we know all that stuff, about periods and hormones and wombs and babies. We had lessons. And Ethel-nushi talked to us, just after I arrived here. But I thought... I thought you were just a girl or a boy. I was sure I was a girl, especially when my period started. I didn't know..."

Edwina-nushi looked as if she was going to interrupt.

I suddenly felt angry. Did she not realise that we were going out into the world now, that we could compare ourselves to other people? Did they really think they could keep up the pretence that we were normal, when we could see for ourselves that we were not? I stuck one leg out in front of me, and said, "Look! See for yourself!"

"Oh, girls!" Edwina-nushi suddenly looked really sad. "What did they teach you?"

I was still angry. I pointed to Ethel-nushi's little computer, on the desk by the window. "See for yourself. All the lessons are on there!"

Just at that moment Ethel-nushi knocked, and put her head round the door. "Ah, there you are!" she said, as if it were entirely normal for her sister to be sitting in their bedroom talking to a couple of girls, where no child should go. "Most of the others are in bed. I thought I'd make cocoa for Sophie and me. Would you like some?"

"Give us a few minutes more," said Edwina-nushi calmly. "We'll be out when we're done."

Ethel-nushi nodded and closed the door again.

"Now, let's see..." said Edwina-nushi, scrolling down the menu of classes until she came to the Year 7 sex education icon. She clicked onto the first lesson and watched, without the sound, for just a minute or two.

"Oh, I see!" she said, and fast forwarded through the class. She clicked on the second, then the third, without taking any time to listen. After viewing several more sessions she clicked on the Year 9 refresher lessons. I remembered them clearly. The same pretty Chinese woman and a kind-faced Chinese man had delivered all the sex education. They had made it all seem so natural, as if growing up was something to look forward to. They had never mentioned the possibility that you could be a girl-boy.

Edwina-nushi turned the computer off, and smiled at us. "I see what has happened," she said, then paused for a moment. "They use the same sex education lessons right across the world," she explained, "wherever the Middle Way is followed. They are good lessons, I know. But you see… the thing is, some races of people grow less body hair than others. These lessons were first designed for Chinese home consumption. We Europeans, we have more body hair than the Chinese – or than Africans, for that matter. You are just typically European."

I would have believed her if I had not seen for myself that other European women also had smooth legs. I said, "But Emily…"

Then Edwina-nushi did laugh. "Yes," she said. "I'm sure Emily has lovely smooth legs. She probably does what I do, what most of us do!" Then she explained, and a huge wave of relief swept over me.

We left our carers' room that evening with smooth, hairless legs – and other parts of us too. We now knew about pink lady-shavers such as Ethel-nushi and Edwina-nushi kept in the cupboard above their basin, and about weekly routines of plucking eyebrows and smoothing elbows and knees with creams. We talked and giggled, and Edwina-nushi told us about when she had been a feminist and had not believed in changing her body to please men.

"Until I met Freddy," she said, "and I realised it is my body. If I want to shave my legs – or dye my hair – I can do. I no more have to follow the rules of the Sisterhood than I do the rules that men make!" She looked across at the photo by her bed and smiled. Then we went into the living room and drank cocoa with our two carers, just Beatrice and me, as if we were fully grown up.

As we crept up the spiral stairs that evening, long after all the other children were asleep, Beatrice said, "It's a relief really, isn't it?"

"Yes," I agreed. It was a relief, and somehow it made me feel quite different. We were perfectly normal, and we were getting ready to go out into the world.

★ ★ ★

We all knew about sewing, but we had never made our own clothes before because we just wore the clothes sent in brown paper parcels with the groceries, and stamped with "National Society for the Care of Abandoned and Displaced Children (NSADC). Hampshire Division. Southern Colony". Ethel-nushi had an old sewing machine in the room where our records were kept in a tall, locked filing cabinet. We brought it through and put it on the kitchen table, and at mealtimes we all had to bunch round it to eat. Edwina-nushi ordered material using the computer, letting us choose the colours and suggesting the styles, and it came the next day in more brown packages.

I had mousy, fair hair, and we made a skirt of pink and purple cotton, with a little waistcoat top for me. Beatrice was really blonde, and she had a blue dress with little white flowers on it, and blue ribbons for her braids. Ethel-nushi insisted that Sophie should have new clothes, whether or not she went to the street party, and all the other children got to choose coloured tee shirts.

On the day that the material arrived all the girls were measured up for summer shoes.

Edwina-nushi suggested, "Next time you need to buy new footwear we can go to a shoe shop!"

I could not imagine it, or see the point. Drawing round our feet on the special graph paper and scanning it into the computer seemed like a good way of buying shoes to me, and you did not have to worry about having smelly feet if it was a hot day.

Ethel-nushi said, "I never bought shoes like this until I came to work here. I always went to a shop and tried on dozens of pairs before I could decide."

I was shocked. "And did they have to disinfect every pair before the next person tried them on?" I thought it was a terrible waste of sanitiser.

Ethel-nushi laughed. "Oh, we didn't bother about that sort of thing in those days!" she said.

*No wonder*, I thought, *that there were four pandemics!*

★ ★ ★

Sophie got into a real state about the summer solstice street party. It was to be a huge fayre in the High Street, with music and stalls selling all sorts of things, and at ten o'clock, when it would be dark enough, there would be fireworks. The weather had been forecasted to be good, and we were all going to eat dinner at home, and then go there together. Even the little ones were allowed to stay up, and to come with us.

Ethel-nushi was quite strict about how we were to behave. She and Edwina-nushi would look after the younger ones and the Chatterers. We five older children could go off by ourselves. We were to stay together the whole time. We could talk to anyone we wanted, and they put money on our bracelets so that we could buy things, up to a point. But under only one circumstance were we to separate. If one of us became ill, or if we got into any sort of difficulty, two people were to stay with the one who was in trouble, and two people were to come back and find our care givers. We were not to accept help from people we did not know.

I do not think it was those instructions that frightened Sophie. She had never wanted to go to the celebrations. It did not help, though, those warnings not to accept help from others, always to stay together.

Noah, ever practical, asked "How will we know where to find you?"

Then Sophie moaned, "I don't want to go! I *really* don't want to go! I'll just stay here!"

I saw Ethel-nushi and Edwina-nushi exchange looks. I suppose they had been expecting this problem. Ethel-nushi said, "I'll show you where we'll be when we get down there. There will be things for the little ones in the wide part of the street between the Guildhall and the Statue, so we'll be there." Then she looked at Sophie and with a slight frown she added, "Sophie, you are coming with us! We will look after you, but you are not staying here alone, and it is not fair – or even possible – for one of us to stay with you."

Noah said, "We'll look after you, Sophie, won't we, Elijah?"

And Elijah followed his lead, and said, "We'll never leave your side."

"Then I said, "Nor me!" and Beatrice agreed.

★ ★ ★

Actually, I seem to remember being rather disappointed when I woke up that morning. We were promised bright, sunny weather for our celebrations, but it was cloudy, with no shadows on the ground. We were to get up into our ordinary clothes but there would be no school. This was a holiday. We would change before our evening meal and go into town afterwards.

I remember wandering outside with Beatrice after breakfast. We were never particularly close friends, but since the hairy-leg episode we had more of a connection. We had never talked to Sophie about it, because she was so uncommunicative, and I had a sneaky feeling that she would not approve of our newly sophisticated appearance although you would think that she must have noticed by then.

Edwina-nushi came out after us. "Girls," she said, "I've got something for you."

Then she held out two tiny, coloured bottles. I did not realise what they were, but Beatrice was quicker than me. "Nail varnish?" she asked.

Edwina-nushi smiled. "You need to manicure your nails first, and put the varnish on really carefully. I only do my toenails, because as quickly as I do my fingernails it starts chipping off, but it's up to you." She handed over the two little bottles. One was pink and other white. Then she left.

I looked at my hands, and thought that I, too, would be bound to break a nail or chip the varnish. You just use your hands all the while.

Beatrice said, "Emily only paints her toe nails."

"That's what I'm going to do, too," I decided.

Toby came out and joined us. "What you doing?" he wanted to know, and squatted down next to us, his tongue sticking out a little as always.

"Getting ready for the party," I explained, as I started on my first toe. "Making ourselves beautiful."

So there we were, smoothing down our toenails with emery boards and giggling together, when Sophie came out.

"What on the earth…?" she said, and glowered at us. "Are you mad?"

"We're painting our toenails," I announced, ever the insensitive one, "ready for the street party."

Sophie went bright red. I had never seen her look like that.

She was literally trembling. She said, as if it were the craziest thing imaginable, "Painting your toe nails? You'll look even more like tarts. First you shave your legs and then... Everyone will look at you! You... you are just going to make so much trouble. *Don't do it!* Men will..."

Her voice was getting louder and louder. Toby let out a big wail because Sophie was shouting. Beatrice stood up, stunned. I just sat there.

At once Edwina-nushi came out. She took one look at us all, Toby crying, Sophie bright red and shaking, Beatrice standing with her mouth wide open, and me just sitting there, and she said, in a perfectly normal voice, "I think that's enough, Sophie."

Sophie stood stock still apart from the shaking. She looked from Edwina-nushi to me, and then at Toby. Toby rushed to me and hid his head in my lap so that he could not see anyone. Sophie sort of gulped, but she still did not say anything.

Beatrice said, "Sophie, we just -"

Edwina-nushi interrupted. "It's all right, girls," she said. "Sophie and I will sort this out." Then she looked quite sternly at Sophie. "Won't we?" she asked.

"Yes," Sophie mumbled.

"Better find a biscuit or two for Toby," suggested Edwina-nushi, and then led Sophie back indoors.

We were very quiet when they had gone. I pulled Toby onto my lap and hugged him. He was getting quite big for sitting on laps, but he was a very comfortable child to cuddle, and he had stopped crying. Beatrice sat back down.

"What do you think that was about?" Beatrice asked, and stroked Toby's hair.

"I don't know," I answered, and it was true, although an idea was vaguely forming in my mind. Sophie had been kidnapped. She must have been taken somewhere. Had they mistreated her? She had started to say something: "Men will..." Men will what?

I said, "I think we'd better leave it to the caregivers to sort out. Come on Toby, let's get you a biscuit." Then I said to Beatrice, "I'm going to paint my toe nails white, I think."

"Pink for me," decided Beatrice, but I think a lot of the fun had gone out of it all.

"Pink and white for me!" announced Toby, and started to take off his trainers.

As I lifted Toby off my lap and stood, I thought I saw something across the river. It was not walkers exploring the Itchen Way and looking around them, enjoying all their new freedoms. It was more like the morning of the first frost – people were hiding in the trees, standing still, looking at us. I stared across. Yes, it was the same as on that other day. There were two people, facing in our direction, but at once they turned and went, even further back among the trees.

I would have told Ethel-nushi when I went in, except that Sophie was there, and Edwina-nushi was nowhere to be seen, so I said nothing. In fact, I probably thought very little more about it.

★ ★ ★

The clouds burnt off and the sun came out as we were eating our special celebratory lunch. All the adults and a couple of the Chatterers delved into our cold noodles and salad – it was perfect food for a hot summer's day. The Chatterers made burgers for themselves and the little ones, although Toby came round and sampled food from most people's plates. He had refused to put his trainers back on, and was proudly showing everyone the pink and white toenails that Beatrice and I had given him.

Elijah said, "It looks a bit odd, on a boy!"

Ethel-nushi replied, "He'll wear his trainers into the town. He's fine."

After lunch, the rest of the household all came out to join us teenagers on the concrete by the river. Sophie was hidden as usual, on the grass, but Rebecca took her favourite book to her and they spent some time reading and re-reading the story. Edwina-nushi had some coloured chalks, and the middle ones drew the Chinese characters for "Happy Solstice" upside down on the concrete, so that people could read them from the footpath on the other side of the river.

By the middle of the afternoon there were quite a few people following the old Itchen Way in one direction or the other. Of course, they could only get as far as the ruined bridge, then they had to turn back. Some of them waved to us and called across, making comments such as "Isn't it beautiful?" or "Happy Solstice!" Two Chinese soldiers came along, and saw our chalk signs, and gave us the thumbs-up sign, and we shouted our greetings across in Chinese, and they grinned. Then it was time for sandwiches and tea, and for washing and changing ready for the evening.

I do not know what our caregivers had said to Sophie, but when we went up to change, she did the same. She was wearing a long skirt that came right down to her calves, and a little top made of tee-shirt material but shaped like a little blouse, and although her clothes were very plain compared with ours – dark blue, in fact – she looked stunning. Even I, though, had the good sense not to say so. Then Ethel-nushi checked right round the house, from the attic to the office, making sure all the doors and windows were closed and locked, and Edwina-nushi finally convinced Toby to put on his socks and trainers, and we were ready to go.

Ever since that street party, for decades now, I have compared every public celebration I have ever been to, with that summer solstice street party. We walked along by the Weirs and so joined the festivities right down by the statue of King Alfred. It was, I suppose, about seven in the evening, and still daylight, but there were coloured lights strung around everywhere, in the trees and draping poor old King Alfred on his plinth. There were flags too – the Chinese flag, of course, but also the flag of the Seven Colonies, with its dragon in the middle breathing fire. There were jugglers and people wearing strange garments with bells on them, dancing. There was a puppet show just ending as we arrived, and a notice telling us that the next show would be at eight o'clock. A man stood at the foot of the statue playing haunting violin music, and there were chairs set out for the audience. Beyond the statue there were some enclosures. We knew there were to be farm animals with their young, although Edwina-nushi said the lambs would be past their friskiest stage by now. And everywhere there were people – people of all ages and dressed in all sorts of fashions, people from all across the Chinese world, from east to west and from north to south.

The little ones huddled close to Ethel-nushi. They had never seen so many people in all their lives. Well, as far as I knew, neither had I. My heart was beating hard with excitement and I did not know where to look. Everything was colourful, and everything was noisy, and I loved it.

Ethel-nushi said to us older ones, "We'll be round here, somewhere, if you need us – either by the Punch and Judy show (she meant the puppets) or by the Guildhall steps, or, if the children need a bit more space, we'll go into the Abbey Gardens." As she told us this, she pointed to the various places she was naming.

Edwina-nushi said, "I promised the Chatters we would look at the animals. You older ones might want to explore further up. Be back here by ten: that's when the fireworks will start."

I seem to remember that we five hesitated. The whole situation was so different from anything we had seen before. I thought there had been a lot of people walking the Itchen Way on the other side of the river, but I realised that was nothing. Everyone from Winchester must have been there, and people from beyond too.

Of course, Noah took the lead. "Right, Elijah!" he said. "You walk on one side of Sophie, and I'll walk on the other. Come on, everyone. Let's see what we can find!"

There was a covered area to the left as we walked up the street, and standing there, surrounded by lots of teenagers, was a band playing C-pop. That was the year that the song, "Now I'll Never Come Home" was really popular, and we stood and listened as they performed it. It was sad and moving, written as if a Chinese soldier had fallen in love with a boy from a country where she had been stationed, and she was going to marry him. She would stay in his country, and never see her parents again, and the song was supposed to be her letter to her family. The group sang the verses in English but the chorus in Chinese, and a lot of the teenagers in the audience joined in.

Further up the High Street the road became narrower. There were stalls selling all sorts of things: hats, brightly coloured paper birds, sweets, beautiful prints of Chinese paintings, amazing sparkling straps for tracker bracelets, brightly coloured African cloth, and even ornaments for people to put into their gardens. We could smell food. One stall was selling noodles, another hot dogs, and from somewhere came the smells of garlic and herbs. We walked together through the milling crowd. There were other groups of kids like us, some were eating chips out of paper cones, lots of them were laughing. I realised that in our specially made clothes we did not stand out at all. There were even girls in shorts, but not shorts like our care-clothes. These were colourful, patterned, even glittery. There were older people, men wearing flat caps and women with white hair, plaited in the fashion of the times, in one long braid down their backs. A man was carrying a child on his shoulders, high up above the crowd. A young couple stood in the doorway of a bakery and kissed. He was a soldier in uniform; she looked no older than me.

Elijah said, "Let's get something to eat!"

We moved towards the stalls Here there was a young woman selling pizza. There was an ice-cream stand and next to it...

"Hey! Mandy!" It was Noah who recognised her first. It was Mandy Thomas, Jamie's and Emily's mum.

She gave a big smile when she saw us. "Hi, kids!" she said. "Great to see you. Isn't this fun?"

"What are you doing here?" I thought it odd. They were builders, after all, and here she was standing behind the table of a toffee-apple stall!

"Ah, well," Mandy started to tell us cheerfully, then paused her conversation while she served two girls, clicking their bracelets against her receptor.

When her customers had gone, she said, "Emily and Jamie are around somewhere." She looked vaguely at the crowds of people. "We're raising money for the children's playground," she explained. "Up on the estate. Would you like to buy toffee apples? They're very good!"

Everything that evening seemed new and strange. "Toffee apples?" I queried, although I could see them for myself, shiny and brown, apple shapes on sticks, lined up on trays and covered with something transparent to keep off the germs.

Suddenly Emily was there. She was wearing those elegant trousers again but with a different top, and she had beads somehow draped round her forehead. "Hey!" she said, then added, "If you've never had one of Mum's toffee apples, you've never lived!"

Then Jamie arrived too, so we bought some toffee apples and sat on the steps of the Buttercross. We watched everyone walking past, and talking, and shouting across the street to their friends, and looking at the stalls, and at a woman playing sad tunes on a mouth organ. I remember it was the first time I had ever bought something for myself, with my bracelet. How grown-up I felt!

As the slow, summer dusk crept over us the strings of lights looked brighter and brighter. Mandy had been joined by another woman, and they lit a lamp and put it on the table, making blue shadows over their rather diminished stock of wares. When they had sold out Mandy was going to walk down to the statue to listen to the music. Jamie went off and bought them both coffees, then came back and joined us. Elijah and Noah stayed close to Sophie, but I thought she was looking more relaxed. She had her back to the stonework and the two boys protected her from each side. There seemed to be more people than ever.

"They'll come for the fireworks," said Emily.

She was sitting with Beatrice and me, and I had noticed the way some soldiers had looked at us as they strolled past. I remembered how Edwina-nushi had said to me, "You have the rest of your life ahead of you," and how silly I had thought her comment was then. Now I could see just what she meant, and it felt wonderful.

None of us had brought jackets, and once the sun had gone it became a little cooler. Noah said, "How about checking further up the street before we join the others?"

★ ★ ★

The top of the pedestrianised part of the High Street was barricaded off, with those plastic, removable barricades I have since seen used when there are road works or holes in the ground, and they too were draped with coloured, flashing lights. There was a pair of fire-eaters performing and of course

I had never seen such a thing in real life before. A huge crowd had gathered to watch them, and we joined them. They had an accompanist who gave a drum roll each time one or other of the fire-eaters did something particularly dramatic, and the crowd made "ooh!" and "ah!" noises and clapped loudly after each feat. I was completely engrossed, perhaps we all were, when suddenly a voice really close to us said, "Well, hello, Chen. Fancy seeing you here!"

Probably I would have assumed it was people we didn't know greeting each other, except that Sophie gave a little scream, more like a yelp. She was just to one side of me, still with Noah and Elijah on either side of her, and she had gone completely white.

Two men were standing right in front of Sophie, facing her, much too close for comfort even in that packed crowd. Both had long, wavy black hair and one had a bit of a beard. They were wearing a lot of clothes for a hot summer evening and their expressions were threatening.

I saw Noah reach for Sophie's hand and hold it. He said, sounding very polite, "I'm sorry, I don't think we know you. This is my good friend Sophie."

"Oh-ho, is it indeed?" said the slightly taller of the two. He reached across and put a hand under Sophie's chin, so that he raised her face to look at him. "She looks a lot like our Chen to me! Wouldn't you say so, Sid?"

The man called Sid grinned. "I would certainly say this is Chen," he agreed, "and I'm wondering where she has been all this time. Not very thoughtful of her to leave us like that, wouldn't you agree, after we'd put so much time and money into her education?"

Sophie had started to cry. The man was still holding up her face and peering at her, and I thought at that moment that she looked utterly hopeless, as if she had given in to something, as if she were lost.

The man who was not Sid said, still looking at Sophie, "I think it's time you came back with us, don't you? We have plans for you!"

Emily moved up close to Elijah. She did not look at all frightened, just angry. "I think you had better leave my friend alone," she threatened, "or I'll find a police officer."

Sid laughed. "In this crowd?" he asked looking around, just as the audience let out another big "Ooh!" and a round of applause. "I wonder where you will find one on an evening like this?"

The other man was looking at Emily. "I think this young lady might fit the bill, too," he said. "Why don't we take the two of them?" Looking at Emily he added, "We can definitely use a pretty girl like you!"

I am not sure where Jamie had been while we watched the fire-eaters. The crowd was shifting a little all the time as people tried to get a better view of the performers, but suddenly he was there, standing next to me and facing the men. I am not certain, with so many people around, that they even realised that Jamie was with us. One minute he had just appeared next to me, and the next minute he reached over and pushed the man who was holding Sophie's chin.

The man, taken by surprise, staggered back into his friend. Jamie yelled, "Run!"

At once we all turned tail and, elbowing our way through the crowds, ran back down past the stalls. I was on my own, but I could see Elijah and Noah almost pulling Sophie down the road and then ducking into the side street by the Buttercross. I followed them into the shadows and almost at once we were joined by Beatrice and Emily, and then by Jamie.

"We need a police officer!" declared Emily, panting a little.

"We need to hide!" countered Beatrice.

Jamie asked, "Where are Ethel-nushi and Edwina-nushi?"

Sophie was still crying. "Get me away from here!" she sobbed. "They'll find me, I know they will!"

I remembered the instructions we had been given. I said, "Two people ought to go and get the grown-ups, but the rest of us should stay here and hide somewhere."

Elijah asked, "Is your mum still at her toffee apple stand?"

We all looked across the street.

"I think she's gone down to hear the music," replied Jamie. "And we shouldn't just stay here."

"Why don't we all go and find Ethel-nushi?" I asked. "It's not that far."

"But look at the crowd!" whimpered Sophie, sounding desperate, and I saw at once what she meant. The fire-eaters must have finished their act and a surge of people was coming down the street. Somewhere in that crowd were the two men.

Emily said, "We can go to the Meeting House! They'll never look there. Come on!"

Jamie nodded, then said to Noah. "You and I had better find your caregivers and tell them. We can show them where to go."

Emily grabbed Sophie's hand. "Come on," she said, "this way!"

Then we were running along a street, going in the opposite direction to yet more crowds, racing towards the cathedral, following the line of that huge building which was lit up for the celebrations, panting along a little path and into the street where the Meeting House was. At last Emily was opening the big, wooden gate, we were through, and the gate was closed behind us.

Elijah leant with his back to it, panting. "Phew!" he said.

Emily was breathing hard too. "We were lucky," she said. "They sometimes lock that gate at night."

Sophie worried, "They still might find us!"

"No, they won't," I said, trying to reassure Sophie, although I was not convinced.

Emily had been bent over, catching her breath. She straightened up, and said, "I bet the kitchen door is open. Let's go inside."

So we followed her around the house and went into the kitchen, and Emily filled the kettle and suddenly things began to seem a little more normal.

It was getting quite dark by then. Emily turned a light on as we sat round the big pine table in the dining room.

Sophie said in a sort of straggled voice, "No!" so at once Emily flicked the light off again.

She gave us cocoa without asking if we wanted it, and hunted around somewhere and found biscuits. We sat there in the gloom and I think none of us knew what to say.

At last Emily asked, quite quietly, "What was that all about, Sophie?"

Sophie had not exactly stopped crying. That is, she was not sobbing as I did when I cried, or as I had heard her do in bed at night, but tears were still rolling down her cheeks. At first she did not answer. Then, in a very small voice, she said, "Those men kidnapped me, when I was little. They kept me in a house with other girls. And I ran away."

I said, "Did they hurt you?" A horrible idea had come into my head.

"No – o," Sophie hesitated. "They were going to sell us. When we were old enough. To men who wanted brides. Because there are too many men and not enough women in China."

"That's illegal!" I exclaimed, stupidly.

Sophie gave me that look again, the same look she had given me when I had asked ages ago whether the soldiers had hurt her. "Of course it is," she said. "But if there's money to be made…"

"My God!" said Emily, and I realised how close to danger she and Sophie had been.

101

Noah said, "Can we lock the house doors?"

"Yes," said Emily, and stood up at once to do so.

★ ★ ★

We found out later that Noah and Jamie had some difficulty finding either of our carers. The crowds down at the bottom of the town were enormous, with people looking for good places to watch the fireworks, and others trying to meet up with families or friends, and Civic Police officers with orange summer chrysanthemums in their buttonholes and (in the case of the women) in their hair, trying to keep order and answering people's questions. They finally found Edwina-nushi with the Chatterers on the steps to the Guildhall, and then Ethel-nushi arrived with the little ones, who had needed the bathroom. Noah said it was hard to explain what had happened, but that, when they caught on, our carers were quick to usher everyone away, back through the Abbey Gardens and to the Meeting House.

From my point of view, it seemed ages before they arrived. We finished our drinks and biscuits and Emily took the mugs back into the kitchen, and then we did not know what to say to each other. I, of course, wanted to know the rest of Sophie's story. How long had she been kept a captive? Why did Chinese men want brides from the Seven Colonies?

"Sophie," I tried. "Those men, did they -"

To my great surprise Beatrice glowered at me, and said, "No!" Then she looked at Elijah and added, "I don't think we should talk about it, do you?"

After that we sat in the almost-dark, in silence.

Suddenly there was hammering on the door – not the kitchen door, which we had used, but the big front door. Sophie gave that yelp again, I think we were all frightened, although of course we could not see each other's faces by then, but Emily was calm. "It's probably Jamie," she said. "Wait here."

Then there was a brief silence followed by an outburst of noise.

Toby came running into the room, somehow found me in the half light and climbed onto my lap. "Lambs!" he announced. "And dogs! I love dogs!"

I had thought the dining room was quite large until everyone crowded in. Someone turned on the light again and there we were, surrounded by all the people we really knew, our family, and Ethel-nushi was hugging Sophie and the Chatterers were all trying to show us the things they had bought, and Jamie had his hand protectively on Emily's shoulder, and it was light inside and dark beyond the windows, and I felt safe.

Ethel-nushi called the police at once, of course – not the Civic Police, but those who dealt with criminals. She spoke to them out of earshot, in a sort of office area, and once came through to check with Jamie, "Is this building locked now?"

There was a huge explosion – the first of the fireworks, and the distant sound of crowds responding.

Edwina-nushi said, "We need to occupy these children," and Jamie remembered that there was an empty room upstairs and we all trooped up to a high-ceilinged bedroom and gathered round the windows to watch the show. It was strange, because the younger children were so excited and full of fun, but we older ones were more or less shell-shocked. I am sure the fireworks were wonderful, but all I remember is my relief when we looked down and saw the police arrive.

★ ★ ★

**Report of Ethel T. Walker to the National Society for the Care of Abandoned and Displaced Children (NSADC) Hampshire Division Southern Colony**

**Date:** *22nd June*
**Time:** *2.45 am*
**Care Home Identity Number:** *017954 Coed*
(Please omit details of exact location)
**Number of children at this location:** *13*
**Number of children in formal detention:** *0*

*You will of course appreciate that this report is in addition to the report of Police Sergeant P.P. Wallace 86546 and the constable who attended with her, both of the Southern Colony Criminal Police Division, and to the statement already given to them. It is, therefore, in the nature of an informal account of the events which occurred earlier tonight.*

*The basic outline of what happened you will already know. The five older children went off by themselves in a group, and met up with their two friends from the Stanmore Estate. They talked with Mandy Thomas and spent some time sitting on the Buttercross watching the crowds. There is nothing to suggest that they did anything to attract attention to themselves. Sophie A had been reluctant to come out but had been persuaded by my sister and me following advice from Children's Services that there was no perceived danger to her.*

*At about a quarter past nine the five teenagers walked up to the junction with City Road where there was a street entertainment attracting a large crowd. It was while they watched this that Sophie was approached by two men who she recognised as among those who had kept her captive in the old premises of the Green Man at the time that the pub stood empty due to the prolonged lockdowns. You will know that these premises were raided two years ago following Sophie's escape, several people traffickers were arrested and the children kept there were put into the care of our organisation. They were physically unharmed but deeply traumatised. Sophie A spent several weeks in the Sarum Road Children's Hospital while attempts were made to locate her family, and then she came to us.*

*Initially Sophie seemed to adjust well. It appeared to me to be a good placement because the comparative isolation of Xunzi House* added to her sense of security. She became friends with Daisy W, and for a while seemed to flourish. She was one of the two girls I mentioned in an earlier report, who went outside in bare feet to experience the first frost.

Since we have come out of lockdown Sophie has become very much more timid. She is frightened of strangers and reluctant either to leave the house or to be observed by others. It was therefore something of an achievement that we were able to follow your advice and to coax her into joining the group for tonight's festivities.

Both my sister and I are proud of the actions of our teenagers and of the two Thomas young people. Their reactions were quick and sensible and quite possibly saved Sophie, and perhaps Emily Thomas too, from consequences I do not like to imagine.

We have both been impressed, too, by the Criminal Police, who were sensitive and patient. It was strange to me, sitting in on the interview with Sophie, that she started to speak Chinese as she told the officer what had happened. I understand that it is the only language they were allowed to speak when in captivity, and the shock of the evening's events had taken her back to that time in her life. I was grateful that, although the two police women exchanged glances at this development, neither of them commented, but just switched to Chinese themselves. Sophie was very shocked and frightened by her encounter with these two men, but gave good descriptions of them. Of course, she had seen them many times before, but not recently.

We have been able to keep the events of the evening quiet from the rest of the household. I suppose that they have seen so many changes in the last few months that almost nothing surprises them, and Edwina's explanation that we had discovered a better place than the Guildhall steps to watch the fireworks was entirely convincing, because we did indeed have an excellent view!

I am fairly sure that only the teenagers realised, too, how unusual it was for the police to provide transport to bring us home when the initial statements had all been made. Young Toby was, in fact, delighted, because one of the two vans provided had a police dog in the back. He *confided in me as we settled them all into their beds that he wants to be a police man with a dog when he grows up. It is sad that, of course, he will only ever be able to do the simplest of jobs.*

*I have mentioned in earlier reports that Sophie presents me with real difficulties. I have not had sufficient training to deal with a child who has undergone the sort of treatment Sophie received at the hands of the people traffickers. I therefore ask again and with greater urgency whether it might be possible to provide some qualified counselling.*

★ ★ ★

The next few days were strange. Lessons started again, because it was, after all, only June. The rest of the household did not know anything about what had happened and, apart from being tired the next day after a late night, and perhaps a little argumentative, everything went back to normal for them.

For us five older ones, though, nothing was normal at all. I remember Sophie and I working on a geometry unit together and the police arriving and taking Sophie off to our carers' bedroom to record another interview, and me having to finish the geometry unit on my own. Beatrice and Elijah were getting very close and only seemed to talk to each other about what had happened. Noah seemed thoughtful, and spent more time than usual with Sophie. He took his lunch to the grass behind the hedge to eat with her. I felt rather lonely, and full of questions that nobody seemed to want to answer. No, I was full of questions I did not even want to ask. I did not even want to think about them.

It was perhaps a week later that the counsellor started to visit. She was called Chin-Sun and she had grey hair in a fashionable braid, and a slow, kind smile. She did not take Sophie into our carers' room, as the police had done, but upstairs to the girls' dorm, and I heard both Sophie and Chin-sun laughing together up there. Somehow, I felt left out of everything. Sometimes Toby came and wanted me to do things for him, and I felt quite impatient with him, which had never happened before, and he would look puzzled. It was mean of me, because he could not understand, poor little kid.

Then it all came to a head one afternoon. Beatrice and Elijah had gone for a walk into town. They were going to look at a craft shop which had opened; by then we were beginning to get used to the idea of going into shops. Sophie and Noah had eaten their lunch together on the grass, as usual, and I had taken my sandwiches to join them. As I approached, though, they stopped talking and I knew I had interrupted something.

Just then Toby came to me, with a sandwich in each hand, each with a bite taken out of it. We were never allowed to walk about eating, and suddenly I just felt so angry.

Toby said, "Daisy, tell me a story! Tell me about little red!" He meant Little Red Riding Hood, of course.

Then, without thinking, I just suddenly exploded. I turned on Toby and shouted, *'Oh, go away! You shouldn't be out here. You shouldn't be walking around like that eating your lunch. Go back and join the babies!'*

Toby dropped one of his sandwiches. His face crumpled up and he opened his mouth and wailed. Out of the corner of my eye I could see the shocked faces of Sophie and Noah.

And I fled. I just took off, away from Xunzi House, along the narrow path beside the river, across the broken wooden bridge and into the water meadows. I ran until I was out of breath, and then I found a place where a small stream trickled past a fallen tree, and I sat in the shade where nobody would find me, and I cried. Everything had gone wrong.

★ ★ ★

Edwina-nushi found me. Of course, the location tracker on my bracelet told her more or less where I was. She arrived with two bottles of still-chilled apple juice and two of those round sugary doughnuts that we sometimes made when it was someone's birthday, although as far as I can remember it was just an ordinary day. She sat on the fallen tree next to me and passed the juice and the doughnut, without saying anything. A duck came quacking along the little stream with five tiny ducklings in her wake, all cheeping merrily and seeming to balance on top of the water rather than swimming in it. Toby would have loved them.

I ate my doughnut but I did not look at Edwina-nushi. I think I was confused. I was certainly ashamed. Edwina-nushi threw a crumb of her doughnut into the stream, but the mother duck was not interested and the ducklings just skittered around, cheeping. The doughnut crumb drifted away out of sight.

At last I broke the silence. "Is Toby all right?" I asked.

"He's fine." Edwina-nushi sounded calm and relaxed. "I wonder if these ducks nested near here?"

Again, there was silence. I could hear the wine of electric vehicles a long way away and, much closer, the sound of birds singing and the tinkling of the stream. The water meadows felt safe and unchanged, unlike the whole of the rest of my life. I said, "Everything's different nowadays."

"Yes," agreed Edwina-nushi.

We were both quiet again. I said, "Noah and Sophie used to be my best friends, but not now. I keep saying the wrong things. And Beatrice told me off, in the Meeting House… well, she didn't tell me off but she stopped me asking questions. And she was right. But I feel as if I am walking around not knowing what's going on. And nobody will tell me." Then I remembered how Toby's face had crumpled as I shouted at him, and I added, "I took it out on Toby. Poor Toby!"

Edwina-nushi did not answer at once. The duck family drifted off downstream and out of sight. Edwina-nushi picked up a stick and stirred a bit of water weed, frowning a little.

Then she spoke. "There's nothing wrong with wanting to know what's happening," she said. "To be honest, that's probably how we all feel. And I think you do know most of it, or anyhow up to a point. During all the disruption of the Culture Wars, and especially during the winter of the third pandemic when the Communist government of China finally gave way to the Confucian majority, crime rocketed all over the world. There was a feeling that those in charge were making laws for other people and not keeping them themselves, so law and order pretty much went by the board. If you protested you were arrested on any pretext… It was a hard time." She inspected the weed on her stick thoughtfully.

"And Sophie?" I prompted.

"Yes, Sophie…" Edwina-nushi put the stick down. "It's hard to explain without giving you lots of history," she said.

"I'm good at history," I prompted.

Then she laughed. "Good for you!" She turned serious again. "It's hard to believe after all the deaths because of the four pandemics, but, back before all this started, we had a population problem in the world. Too many mouths to feed, not enough resources to support everyone. So China had a single-child policy."

I remembered hearing about that. "Back then they preferred boys to girls," I suggested.

"Some did," agreed Edwina-nushi. "So things happened to baby girls… and the country ended up with an imbalance of genders."

"But that was ages ago," I said. "They changed those rules before they stopped being communists…"

"Oh, yes!" agreed Edwina-nushi. "But there was still left an ageing population of men without wives – men who wanted to marry and have children of their own…"

I saw where this was going. "But why didn't they just advertise? We saw a documentary last winter where all these men from the Faroe Islands married women from Thailand and the Philippines because they are short of girls. Their children were really sweet."

"Oh, you're right," agreed Edwina-nushi. "Lots of men did, and some men married much younger Chinese women – girls, really. But still, there was an opportunity for criminal gangs. They obtained girls, one way or another, and they trained them up to be good Chinese wives, and when they were old enough, they sold them. For good money."

"Obtained them," I repeated. It sounded like acquiring property, a bicycle maybe, or a second-hand book.

Edwina-nushi did not comment. We stayed quiet for a while. The sun had moved round and my hairless legs were in bright light, looking, I thought, quite elegant.

"During the bad times," said Edwina-nushi, "some people sold their daughters. You have to understand, it was difficult for the poor to feed their families and these girls were going to be wives – respectable women."

"But miles from home," I said. "More like slaves, really."

"Yes." Then she added, "And some, like Sophie, were stolen children."

"Kidnapped," I said.

"Yes."

Again, we were quiet. Somewhere in the city a clock struck five. "But what about after the Re-establishment of Peace and Justice?" I wanted to know. "Didn't they make all that illegal?"

"They did – well, in fact it was always illegal – but you know, Daisy, people make good money out of crime… To tell you the truth, the police had no idea we still had people traffickers in Winchester until this incident with Sophie. There have been a couple of missing girls, thought to be run-aways, and the authorities recognise that it has not been possible to re-educate all freeloaders, but I suppose we all thought things were pretty much under control."

I thought about it. Confucius taught that there are wise people – sages – and lesser people. The lesser people commit crimes. Perhaps, even in times of peace and justice there would still be lesser people. "Will they catch those men?" I wanted to know.

"They'll try," said Edwina-nushi. "Let's hope."

★ ★ ★

After dinner I talked to Ethel-nushi while Edwina-nushi oversaw the teeth-cleaning and showering of the Chatterers.

"I was mean to Toby today," I started.

"I heard," replied Ethel-nushi. She did not sound angry.

"I want to make it up to him," I said.

Ethel-nushi smiled warmly at me. "That's a good idea," she said. "What do you want to do?"

I had not got that far. "Make him a present? Or buy him something?"

Ethel-nushi pursed her lips. "I tell you what I think he would really like," she said. "He would love to do something special with you, just you and him."

I saw at once that she was right. "Like what?" I asked, beginning to feel a bit happier already.

Ethel-nushi was staring out of the window towards the river. "You could take him for a picnic after classes tomorrow," she suggested. "It's going to be quite a nice day."

"Oh yes!" It would be such fun. We could try to find those ducklings again, and Toby loved looking for all sorts of insects among the wild plants. We could take some old glass jars and maybe collect some caterpillars and bring them back, to watch them turn into chrysalises. We had been taken out to do that when I was little, probably when Ethel-nushi was a new carer.

"But don't go too far, will you?" Ethel-nushi was just checking. She did not sound worried.

"No, no," I agreed. "We'll stay in the water meadows."

★ ★ ★

She was right, the weather was lovely. For a couple of days after the Summer Solstice celebration it had been almost too hot, but a wind was blowing from the east bringing cooler temperatures from northern Europe. I went down to breakfast feeling cheerful, because of my plans.

Most of the children were sitting round the table, and several of them looked up as I came down the stairs. Usually Toby would give me his big, friendly grin, but that morning he just looked away. I had really upset him by shouting at him.

He was sitting between Albert and Rebecca and I could not suggest our expedition without inviting them too, so I just helped myself to toast and jam and took the empty chair next to Sophie. Then Noah came down and sat on the other side of me.

"Hi," he said, as if we were meeting in a classroom forum after not seeing each other for several days.

"Hi," I answered. I was glad he was being more friendly, but my mind was on Toby.

"Daisy." Noah was looking down at his bowl of muesli. "Sorry about yesterday. We didn't mean to leave you out…"

"That's all right," I said, although of course it really was not.

"Well, the thing is – I was trying to persuade Sophie to come to Quakers. She'd like it, don't you think? And now that she's been to the Meeting House…" I could hear a sort of pleading in Noah's voice. He wanted me to back him up.

I turned to Sophie. "I think you would like it," I said. I was thinking about what Edwina-nushi had told me. The people traffickers had tried to make their captives as Chinese as possible. The Quakers seemed to know very little about

Chinese culture, they were all into poems and art from the Seven Colonies and Europe. "I've never met people quite like them!" I said. Then I added, "And you know Jamie and Emily."

"That's just what I said!" approved Noah, and he smiled at me. "We'll go on Sunday, won't we, Daisy? So if you come with us…"

I thought Sophie looked a bit uncertain. *Well*, I thought, *if I were Sophie, I am not sure I would want to go anywhere.*

But, "All right," she said.

★ ★ ★

Toby was really excited about our picnic. From the time I suggested it, before classes, until lunchtime arrived, he talked of very little else. Twice he came over to my workstation and checked with me, "Picnic today?" and grinned happily when I reassured him, and I overheard him telling Rebecca that he was going for a walk with "my Daisy".

"That child really loves you," said Sophie as we hunted through some online documents for a time line of the Industrial Revolution, after Toby had been over for the second time.

"He's sweet," I said. "Don't you think so?"

"Yes," Sophie said, "he is. But he'll never really grow up like other children, will he?"

I thought about that as I scrolled down through a list of resources. "Got it!" I said, finding the time line. "He won't grow up like other children; he'll grow up like Toby!"

Sophie laughed. "You are so kind sometimes!" she said, and I knew that we were friends again, despite all my insensitive questions.

The day had started well, and everything about our expedition felt like fun. We chose our sandwiches and drinks from the pile Ethel-nushi had put in the middle of the table, and Ethel-nushi gave me two little cardboard food boxes with strawberries in them. "There's not enough for everyone," she explained, "so best not to mention them." Toby was very proud of his backpack, and placed his lunch carefully in it, and once he had been persuaded to put on his shoes – the last of the nail varnish still showed on his toes and he was proud of it – we set off.

They call children like Toby "special" and I thought then – and I still think – it is an excellent description. He had a round, smiley face and often stuck his tongue out a little, not as if he were being rude, but as if it were too big for his mouth. He seemed to enjoy things exactly as they happened, without thinking too much about the past or the future, but that was his disposition; it was not that he forgot. He had known at breakfast that I had been mean to him the day before. By the time we set out I was entirely forgiven.

We seemed to see something interesting every few steps. There was a ladybird on a reed, tiny little fish darting around in the shallows of the river, and a gull floating on the water "making friends" (so Toby thought) with the ducks. When we got to the foot bridge which we had mended the summer before, we played "Poohsticks" for ages. To be honest I was a little bored but Toby liked to do things over and over again. Then we reached the fallen tree by the stream, where Edwina-nushi had found me the day before, and we sat on the trunk of the fallen tree and ate our sandwiches, and I think I felt happier than I had done for days.

By that time there were people every day walking back and forth along the old Itchen Way, but I had never seen them in that wild area where trees had fallen and footpaths had gone into disrepair and low-lying land had flooded and formed marshy spaces. Those areas, I felt, belonged to us, the children an Xunzi House. It was a surprise, therefore, when we heard voices quite close by, a man and a woman talking, and then a little spaniel with a bright red collar came running into our clearing, wagging his tail and jumping up with his front paws on the knees of the delighted Toby.

"Oh, nice dog!" exclaimed Toby, speaking with a mouth full of sandwich.

The owners of the dog arrived then a woman with short, blonde hair that looked quite old fashioned, and a bald man with a flat cap that looked as if it belonged to his winter wardrobe, not to a warm June day.

"He won't hurt you," said the woman, which seemed an unnecessary thing to say, because it was obvious to anyone that Toby was far from frightened.

I stood automatically and gave a little bow of my head, as I had been taught. It was instinct. I knew by then that nobody in the Southern Colony did that. I pretended to brush crumbs off my shorts to cover up my mistake, and sat down again.

The couple came a little closer.

"This is a lovely area," said the man. "We've lived in Stanmore Lane for years, but we've never ventured this far until now."

"Not that it is very far," added the woman, watching Toby stroking the dog. "But during the troubles…"

"I know," I agreed. "Hardly anyone comes here."

"But you do?" It was a question, not a comment.

"Yes." I agreed. The two people looked perfectly normal. They were wearing ordinary clothes – except for the man's winter cap – and they were just taking their dog for a walk like any normal couple might, but somehow I did not want to tell them anything.

Toby, however, had no such reservations. "We live here!" he announced, sounding quite proud about it.

The woman looked around, as if looking for a house in the clearing, but I thought it was just show. She knew perfectly well that there were no houses right in the water meadows. "Here?" she asked, sounding surprised.

Toby giggled. "Not here!" he explained. "Not on this tree! Over there!" and he pointed in the direction of Xunzi House, although we could not see it from there. "With Ethel-nushi," he added, as if that explained everything, "and my Daisy."

The man replied, almost casually, "Oh, you mean the children's home! Yes, we knew there was one around here somewhere."

"Not a children's home!" Toby was indignant. "Grown-ups too! And nearly-grown-ups! Noah and B'trix (Toby never could pronounce that properly) and Elijah and Sophie, but not Jamie or Emily. And my friend 'Becca and lots of other people!"

I was really uncomfortable about Toby giving out all this information, although I was not sure why. Surely it was no secret that Xunzi House was there?

"Well," said the woman, "you are lucky children. It is beautiful around here. Come on, you crazy dog, let's be on our way!"

"Bye!" called Toby as they left. He was talking to the dog of course. Then he said to me, "I liked Crazy Dog!"

"I know you did," I laughed. "Come on, let's go home too!"

★ ★ ★

Now that we had outfits that weren't care-clothes, none of us wanted to go to Quaker meetings in our uniform shorts and tee shirts. We had all, by then, ventured into the city and, although I still felt unsafe in shops with closed doors, there were market stalls several days each week. Noah had bought a cap with the Chinese characters for "peace" on the front, Elijah had a backpack with the dragon of the Welsh Colony emblazoned on it, and Beatrice had braided ribbons into her hair, the way we had seen other teenagers do. Looking at us as we left the house that morning, I thought that nobody would be able to tell any more that we came from a care home. They would look at us and just think we were any bunch of kids. We even behaved more like other teenagers by then.

Sophie seemed happy to come with us. The woman officer who had interviewed us all on the night of the summer solstice celebrations had been round the evening before, just after the weekly TV presentations, and had told us that the men had been caught. She had announced it to everyone just as we were about to gather round the table for Saturday dinner, so of course the younger ones heard too, and they did not know what it was all about.

Trust Toby to pick up on it. "Who caught?" he had wanted to know.

"Just some bad men," I had explained.

"Did they shout at people?" Toby had asked. That was the extent of his understanding of badness – that, and not cleaning your teeth before bed.

"Even worse!" I exclaimed, in the same scary voice I used when I was pretending to be a lion. "Now, sit at the table if you want your dinner!"

Ethel-nushi had invited the officer to stay and eat with us, but she had declined. "My husband's cooking," she had said cheerfully. "He'll never forgive me if I arrive late and full!"

We left for Quakers in good time that morning. Toby wanted to come with us, but Edwina-nushi reminded him that they had planned to make cheese straws and that Toby was the chief cheese grater, so he waved us off happily enough. I remember the weather being quite dull that morning, grey skies and odd smatterings of rain, and I remember how we walked along the Weirs, Beatrice, Sophie, Noah and me, with Elijah walking backwards in front of us, facing us, telling us some funny story he had read the night before, and almost bumping into a buggy with two small children strapped in side by side, being pushed by a heavily pregnant woman. We were in good spirits. There is something about being a teenager with other teenagers – your friends – and feeling independent. It was an old-fashioned term by then, but I would say we felt "cool".

There was a place where a small part of the old Roman wall was still to be seen, and just before we reached it there were steps up to a small garden, and then on to the street that led to the Meeting House. In fact, when we went back just a few years ago for a conference at the university, we visited old sites, and very little has changed. There is a statue in the garden now, to the Chinese Premier who negotiated the Re-establishment of Peace and Justice, but back then it was just a short cut through for us, and there was a bench where people could sit and look down at the river.

And sitting on that bench were the two people Toby and I had seen in the water meadows, the people with the little spaniel.

"Well, hello!" said the man, touching his cloth cap like a character in a costume drama.

"Oh, hi!" I answered. I cannot say I was particularly pleased to see them.

The man, however, was not going to be satisfied with a simple greeting. "You're out and about nice and early," he said.

"We need to be somewhere by ten," I explained, hoping that would be it.

"Ah!" said the man. "A secret assignation! And where is your little companion?"

He's at home," I said, and added, "with our carers." I somehow felt the need to remind him that there were people looking out for us.

"Well," said he woman, "please say hello to him. And have a good time, wherever you are going."

"Come on," prompted Noah. "We don't want to be late." And we left.

Once we had got round the corner and there was no chance of them hearing us, Elijah asked, "So who were they?"

"Just some people we met in the water meadows," I said. "Me and Toby."

"I didn't like them," said Sophie.

"Me neither," agreed Noah. "They were a bit creepy. Never mind, look, there's Emily!"

★ ★ ★

I am guessing that was about our fourth visit to the Quakers. We were becoming accustomed to the way they did things, and they were getting used to us. As usual there was someone standing at the open gate to welcome people, and this time we all shook hands. It was a new ritual, something we had never done before but which we had seen in old films. It was not quite the sort of thing people like us did, but we were acclimatising. It felt a little as if we went into a different world when we went in through that gate.

The Quakers called each other "friend", and it was a good term, because I was finding that they were quite friendly, but in an odd sort of way. Jamie and Emily were our friends in the way described in our *Friendship, Fun and Freedom* classes, people whose likes and dislikes you got to know, people you might argue with and then make up with again. The Quakers were somehow more distant. They did not ask us questions about our everyday lives, but always wanted to know whether we had watched a particular documentary, or come across a certain book, or read the blog of a particular member of the House of Cultural Continuity who was concerned about the format of the baccalaureate exams. They talked about things, especially media things, and we talked about people and ideas, and all their jokes seemed to be in-jokes, to do with quotations or references we did not recognise.

Of course, apart from the night of the summer solstice, this was Sophie's first visit. I explained it to her as we walked round the outside of the house to the wood and glass meeting room in the garden.

"When you go in," I said, "you just sit down quietly. You don't say anything at all, you just sit there."

"So, what do you do?" Sophie wanted to know.

Noah came in on that, holding us back so that he could explain before we went in. "You listen to the Spirit," he said. "I think it makes you wise."

"But is there really a spirit?" Sophie wanted to know, and I had to admit the same question had occurred to me.

"Well," said Noah, "try it and see. That's what I'm doing."

Then we all went in, and sat with Emily and Jamie around the outside circle with our backs to the wooden panelled wall where we could see most people and also look out at the tulip tree, and tried to listen to a spirit which might, or might not, have been there.

At those meetings people stood, occasionally, and talked about things they were learning. Quite often they recited things, though never anything I recognised, and very occasionally they might take a book from the table in the middle and read from it. There were several copies of two books there – a purple volume called a *Book of Disciple* and two Bibles, one black (in old English) and one green (in new), and some little red booklets.

That morning, the day of Sophie's first visit, I remember that the man with the moustache read from a red booklet:

*Be aware of the spirit of God at work in the ordinary activities and experience of your daily life. Spiritual learning continues throughout life, and often in unexpected ways. There is*

> inspiration to be found all around us, in the natural world, in the sciences and arts, in our work and friendships, in our sorrows as well as in our joys. Are you open to new light, from whatever source it may come? Do you approach new ideas with discernment?[a]

I think the man went on to talk about a concert he had been to, the first concert for fifteen years, and the fact that he had been moved to tears by the slow movement. I, though, was struck by the words he had read out. So, they believed that this spirit was the Spirit of God, and that this spirit was there in their everyday lives? They believed that this spirit could work through any source of inspiration? Did that mean the things we knew, the poetry and music we had grown up with, and the friendships we made, just as much as the things the Quakers knew about? Could this spirit be there in the water meadows, just as it was there, I supposed, in the Meeting Room?

I saw that if this was true it might not matter that half the time I did not know what the Quakers were talking about, because the spirit could speak to me through the things I did know.

To be honest, it was not until I grasped that idea, that I really tried to listen to the Spirit in Meeting, or indeed anywhere else.

★ ★ ★

Sometimes after their hour of worship the Quakers had a sort of business meeting. For years all this had been done, like our lessons, via their computers, but they were thinking of holding them in the Meeting House again now that we were all free

---

[a] Advices & Queries used with permission of Britain Yearly Meeting 2013

to mix at last. There were pluses and minuses to this idea, so they had decided to have a discussion meeting to consider the pros and cons. In the meantime, Mandy explained over coffee and juice in the garden, they had other things that required decisions to be made.

"We like to explore things carefully," she explained to Sophie, Noah and me. "We want to know that we are really led to do the things we do. We don't want them just to be good ideas."

I could see the sense of that. "So, who makes the final decision?" I asked, "when you have all had your say?"

Mandy laughed. "No," she said, "that's not how it works. We don't make the decisions at all; we wait for the Spirit to guide us. The Spirit makes the decisions, and we act when we are confident that we have heard right."

Honestly, that seemed silly to me. You have to have a leader, everyone knows that. One of the reasons that we had peace in the Seven Colonies and had finally defeated the four viruses was that the first Confucian leader of China had been such a strong leader. Goodness knew what chaos we would still have been living in if libertarian ideals had triumphed.

Noah asked, "But does it work? I mean, do you all hear the Spirit saying the same thing?"

"I'll tell you what," said Mandy, "a small group of us is going to meet now, to talk about a project we are considering for the estate where we live. Would you like to come and see for yourselves?"

★ ★ ★

In the end only Sophie, Noah and I stayed. Elijah and Beatrice were planning to walk home via the new Sunday market. There was almost nothing you could not buy via your computer, then as now, but we had only just discovered the novelty of looking at real things displayed on stalls right in front of us, and of even being able to touch them.

In the actual Meeting House there were really five rooms downstairs: the kitchen, the dining room where we had sat in darkness on the night of the summer solstice, the office where Ethel-nushi had phoned the police, a library and a large, colourful room which was the children's room. It was in there that we met: Mandy and Robbie, Jamie and Emily, the man with the moustache, a woman with grey, wavy hair who turned out to be his wife, and a younger woman, Edwina-nushi's sort of age, called Ashanti. And us, of course. There were some small chairs and a couple of larger ones for adults, but also some bright, multi-coloured pouffes, and rugs on the floor in primary colours.

We sat in an irregular circle, and Mandy explained to the moustached man and his wife who we were. "They've come to see how we come to decisions," she said.

Then we settled down in silence to prepare ourselves for whatever was going to be decided.

It turned out that the issue was to do with the estate where the Thomases lived. Up on that estate there was, they said, a nice little church, and Mandy and Robbie had been working with the people from that church in the weeks since we had all come out of lockdown, doing things that would help the area to become more of a community.

"We've got the playground back in operation," said Robbie. "It's in use almost all the time, and we've applied for a grant from the House of Cultural Continuity, to establish a library in the church hall."

"Sounds good," approved Mr Moustache, and his wife nodded in agreement.

"We'd be happy enough just to go on working with those church people," said Mandy. "We knew some of them a decade or so ago, before all the trouble. But it's turning out to be a bit more complicated."

"What's the problem?" Ashanti wanted to know. "Not those old reservations, because we're Quakers and we don't have a creed?"

Mandy wrinkled up her nose, the way she did when she was thinking. "It's not quite that," she said.

Emily chipped in. "It is in a way," she said. "Me and Jamie…"

"Jamie and I," corrected their father.

"Yeah, Jamie and I have been talking to the other teenagers, the ones who worked with us cutting the grass and putting the rubbish bins in the playground, and they are sort of interested in faith groups, you know, because of the *Friendship, Fun and Freedom* unit, but they're not too keen on the church up there. They want to know more about Quakers."

Mr Moustache looked a bit worried. "What's to stop them coming here?" he asked. He looked at the three of us from Xunzi House. "It's not as if we don't have other young people."

His wife gave a little cough. "But is this the sort of place where estate children would fit in?" she asked. "I mean, don't you think they might feel more comfortable in somewhere with more… well, you know, somewhere where they sing and clap their hands?"

For a moment I did not understand. Why would estate children not feel at home with the Quakers? But even as I thought that, I realised that it was the same for us. We had to make all sorts of adjustments to fit in. Of course, there were only five of us, and several dozen Quakers – and we were very new – but all the adjustments had to be made by us, none by them. Did they even realise that?

Noah was always more articulate than me. "May I ask a question?"

"Of course!" Mandy looked pleased.

"Is there any reason why estate kids cannot hear the Spirit?" he wanted to know. "I mean, that reading this morning…"

All the adults looked uncomfortable. "Of course they can," said Robbie. "It's just that…"

"The thing is…" started Ashanti.

"We have to consider…" added Mr Moustache's wife.

"It's a question of…" muttered Mr Moustache.

I looked across the circle at Emily. She winked at me and raised her eyebrows, as if to say, "Would you believe it!"

We all sat quietly. Outside we could hear pigeons cooing and someone not too far away cutting grass. I was feeling uncomfortable. It seemed to me as if the adults did not want Jamie and Emily's friends to come to Meeting. What was it about living on an estate that they did not like? Then I wondered if they really wanted us.

Mandy said, "Of course, we could start a teenagers' group up on the estate."

I thought Mr and Mrs Moustache looked relieved. Ashanti asked, "Who would lead it?"

Jamie answered quickly, "We could – Emily and me."

I saw Mandy and Robbie exchange looks. It occurred to me then that this was the outcome they had expected all along, and that they were not too happy about it. "If it's to be an official group," said Robbie, "we have to get approval from everyone."

"Perhaps," suggested Mr Moustache, "we might keep it unofficial for now? No need to attach the word 'Quaker' to a small group of teenagers meeting in a private house…"

Ashanti said, "The Young Quakers are really only just getting themselves organised again nationally. It might be asking a lot of them to take on a group which is really a seekers' group, not Quaker at all."

Mr Moustache said, "You could see how things worked out, and report to Meeting later… in the new year, perhaps?"

I could see the disappointment on the faces of the Thomases. I did not understand it at all. Why did the other

Quakers seem so reluctant to encourage these unknown teenagers to join up with them? I thought of Noah's question, which nobody had actually answered. I thought, suddenly, that some of the Quakers might be a little afraid of "estate people".

Everyone nodded, in the case of the Thomases rather reluctantly, and, except for the closing silence, the meeting was over.

I went home confused. I thought that Quakers believed that everyone was equal. What was this issue about people living on estates? It seemed to me that they thought they believed one thing, but actually they believed something quite different. Did they really, truly, believe, as they claimed, that we were all equal? It was rather disappointing.

★ ★ ★

Edwina-nushi wanted to know, that lunchtime, what had happened at the group meeting. Beatrice and Elijah had returned home before us, and had explained that we were staying on to discuss something.

Noah said, "It was about some stuff up on the estate, about starting a group for teenagers up there."

"Except it wasn't really," I grumbled, "It was actually about how estate teenagers wouldn't fit in with the Quakers."

Sophie asked, "But don't you think they were right? I mean, what would the Quakers talk to them about?"

To my surprise, Elijah agreed. "Sophie's right," he said. "That's half the reason me and Beatrice don't stick around. It's embarrassing when they ask you questions about your school work, and try to tell you about things Quakers did years and years ago, in the Old Days."

Sophie stood up for the Quakers. "I think they're kind!" she said. "And intelligent."

I thought that Sophie liked the Quakers better than I did.

No, it was not quite that. I liked the Quakers a lot, but they seemed so different from me. Sophie seemed to accept them without any questions. I wondered then if her parents had been the sort of people who became Quakers – people who knew about music and theatre and all that stuff – not people from an estate. She just seemed to fit in.

For Noah and for me it was different. We discovered the following day that we were thinking along the same lines.

It was mid-afternoon, and obviously it was a Monday. I think I had been doing my household chores. We all had tasks that we were supposed to do, which helped the house to run smoothly. Anyway, I remember that I came downstairs into the living room, and there was Noah, sitting at the table reading something on his tablet.

"Hi, Daisy," he said, hardly looking up. "Look what I've found."

I sat next to him and he passed the device to me. It was the reading from the day before, the reading about the Spirit speaking through all sorts of things.

"When you look at it closely," said Noah, "it seems to say that the Spirit is all around."

"I know." I had been thinking the same ever since the previous morning.

"Do you hear the spirit when we are in Meeting?" Noah wanted to know.

"I don't know." The truth was that I had only really tried to listen properly for the first time the day before. "I feel sort of peaceful."

"But wouldn't you anyway?" prompted Noah. "If you just sat in silence with friendly people for an hour?"

He was right. "There must be more to it than that," I said.

"And there's something else," added Noah. "Do you think we heard the Spirit when we were discussing the estate kids yesterday?"

"Maybe not," I answered, thinking aloud. "Don't you think you have to be open to the spirit, if you're going to hear it? Can you listen if you're a little frightened of the people you're asking about?" As I said it, I thought again that maybe the Quakers did not really know about estate teenagers. Did they want to know them?

"Yeah," agreed Noah. "If you think they're alien!"

We were both quiet. I imagine that we were learning a big lesson, that everyone has their imperfections. With the idealism of youth, we probably wanted the Quakers to be perfect, but they were not.

"I suppose," said Noah after a while, "that just because they might get some things wrong, it doesn't mean they're wrong about everything? Let's try an experiment," he suggested. "Let's try to listen to the Spirit every day, and see what happens."

I think I found the idea quite exciting. "All right!" I agreed. "We can find out for ourselves."

★ ★ ★

**Report of Ethel T. Walker to the National Society for the Care of Abandoned and Displaced Children (NSADC)**
**Hampshire Division**
**Southern Colony**

**Date:** *1ˢᵗ July*
**Time:** *9.30 am*
**Care Home Identity Number:** *017954 Coed*
(Please omit details of exact location)
**Number of children at this location:** *13*
**Number of children in formal detention:** *0*

*Something interesting is going on with Noah C, Sophie A and Daisy W. All five teenagers have now visited the Quakers but their reactions* to these new experiences seem to be very different. Beatrice F and Elijah P-F do not talk much about it, but obviously enjoy their Sunday mornings, although I wonder about how much the attraction of being out and about is to do with the Quakers, and how much is to do with the Sunday street market!

Sophie has only been to the Quakers once, but her reaction was very positive. I have checked her records, and it looks to me as if her home background before the kidnapping was, we might say, modestly middle class, to use categories which are no longer really recognised any more. Information about her parents tails off during the turbulence of the third pandemic and it is likely that they both died, but in more settled times both parents were teachers. I suspect that Sophie has unwittingly found herself in a community which shares many of the values she was brought up to appreciate, although I am not sure how conscious Sophie will be of this.

Of the five, only Daisy and Noah seem to be genuinely exploring the spiritual side of this faith community. In the case of Noah this does not surprise me at all. He is a serious, thoughtful boy with a good brain in his head. Daisy's interest in the Quakers is less predictable. I have never thought of her as a "deep" child, given to reflection, but it may be that I have been mistaken.

There is nothing to alarm me about this new connection which the teenagers in my care have made. I am grateful for the prompt checks made by the Civic Police on the backgrounds of some of the community, and I have every reason to trust the Thomas family, given that they have already been cleared by the authorities to work in private homes. I am also pleased to note that all five teenagers are working well towards the examinations they will sit at the end of this month.

On a different subject, young Toby F seems to be developing well. You will recall that when he was brought here it was thought to be a temporary measure, because there were no places available in the Southern Colony in homes for "special" children. In fact, I think it is good for him to mix with children who are more able, and he is a popular little chap with the older children, as well as with his peer *group*. Toby has recently developed a fascination with dogs. He talks often about meeting an animal he calls "Crazy Dog" in the water meadows. I have wondered whether it might be appropriate to allow him to have a pet of his own. I would appreciate advice on this matter.

Following the receipt of circular SC0400 I have checked all the computers on which the children study. Three of them fall below the standards that are recommended, so I request replacements. Our internet connection remains excellent.

We have had no power cuts for four months. Do I need to continue logging interruptions to the energy supply, now that earlier difficulties seem to have been resolved?

★ ★ ★

We were all studying quite hard by July. Each year group took exams, although the really important ones were taken at sixteen and eighteen years old – except for Arof the Clown, of course, who had taken all his papers early. The ones we took at fifteen were only important as practice papers, and in case a person was ill, or something, for the main exams, in which case they looked back at the ones a student had entered the year before.

Some people hated exams. I think Elijah did, although he always did all right. "I just have a rubbish memory!" he said.

My memory was not too good either. If Sophie, Noah and I all read the same text, Sophie would know pretty much what it had said, Noah could almost recite it by heart, but I would have to write down the key points on a piece of paper and repeat them over and over to myself until the facts were firmly lodged in my brain. The only thing I could say, though, was that I was a good thinker. For instance, when we learnt about the Culture Wars, Sophie could easily name most of the politicians on the different sides, but it was me who realised that that there was a connection between freeloaders and those who favoured libertarian ideas.

When I pointed it out, Noah said, "Oh, I see what you mean! People who have always been privileged, like the freeloaders, they think people should be free to make their own decisions regardless of the effect on other people, because they are always going to be all right."

Sophie, on the other hand, re-read the text, and said, "But it doesn't say that here! It just says that the libertarians resisted the strict laws that would have helped control the pandemic, and the socialists and those who followed Confucian ideals favoured the laws. Where do you find that stuff about the freeloaders?"

We were going to take papers in seven subjects. "Papers", of course, was an old-fashioned term by then because very little paper was involved. The examinations were a mixture of written questions that we answered on our computers, interactive interviews and recorded responses that the examiners would play back later. The exams lasted a week, and during that time Ethel-nushi always let us off all our chores, and gave us treats at lunchtime.

The lead-up to the exams changed the atmosphere in Xunzi House. I remember that, when I was little, I imagined that taking exams must be like having to be interviewed by the Civic Police, because the big boys and girls looked so worried. The tension built up gradually, beginning at the point where the ordinary online classes stopped introducing new materials and started revisiting things we had learnt earlier in the year.

Those two things – the approach of the exams and the early visits to the Quakers, occurred at pretty much the same time. Noah and I had made our agreement to try to listen to the Spirit (if there was one) every day. It was a good plan, but a care home with thirteen children and two carers in it is not an easy place for sitting in silence listening, so I decided that when I could I would to go into the water meadows.

I loved that sunken area with the fallen tree and the little stream, the area where Edwina-nushi had found me, and where I had taken Toby. All these years later I have no idea how often I went there. Perhaps every day after I had done my chores? I know that I used to take my revision notes with me, and sit on the tree trunk and try to learn everything that Noah would just know after reading something through a couple of times.

More importantly, now I look back, I know that out there – where I felt separate from all the things that were happening in my new world, where the ducklings were growing bigger and a self-set hydrangea was flowering in lacy white, where everything was more or less the way it had always been – that was where I started doing my serious listening. Even now, after decades of experience, I find it hard to explain what happens if you truly listen, but I can remember exactly what happened the first time I truly heard.

I am sure it was still early July. The day was overcast but warm. I know that I was wearing my care-clothes, the shorts and tee shirt that were standard issue, and the trainers Edwina-nushi had given me. I have a clear memory of the backpack in which I had carried my notebook and some water. I had put it on the tree trunk beside me but it had fallen off and was lying in the long grass to the right of my feet. I had been sitting there with my eyes closed, trying to listen to the Spirit, but only hearing cars in the distance and wind in the trees, and the water trickling past. It was very peaceful, but I did not think I had encountered the Spirit.

For some reason I opened my eyes and looked down at my backpack lying in the grass. Then, as I watched, the grass seemed to become more vividly green, the way it might if I were adjusting the colour tone on the computer. It seemed almost to shimmer and sparkle, to absorb all my attention. I still knew the trees were there, and the stream, and a plane flying overheard, but the grass filled my mind. Then I heard some words. All they said was "Don't be afraid".

I cannot tell you how long it took me to hear those words. It was not like a person talking. I do not even know whether I heard it in my head or with my ears. Somehow everything seemed to pause: the breeze, the trickling water, even the bird song, and even now, all these years later, I can remember how intensely alive I felt. Suddenly the whole world felt right and complete, and I felt right and complete in the world.

It was an odd thing to have heard. I was not a child who often felt afraid. Yet somehow, at once, I believed those words. They were inside me, part of me, the way the stream and the green grass were part of the water meadows.

★ ★ ★

I was walking home that same afternoon, feeling curiously light, almost as if I were floating, when I thought I heard Toby's voice ahead of me. For a moment I was confused. Everything still felt, at the same time, dream-like and intensely real. Then some sort of alarm went off in my mind. What could Toby be doing out in the water meadows?

His voice was somewhere ahead of me, but close, definitely on the Itchen Way side of the river. He sounded happy, and was crooning, "Crazy Dog! Crazy Dog! You're my friend."

The little footpath I was following joined a track that led to Greater Beijing Street, and there, just a little further along it, was the man with the cloth cap and his wife. And there too was Toby, holding the lead of the little spaniel and looking delighted.

When he saw me, he gave a clumsy little jump of glee. "Look, Daisy!" he said. "Crazy Dog!"

For a moment I did not know what to say. It was all wrong, Toby with these people, a good long way from Xunzi House and going in the wrong direction. Instantly, though, I knew that I must not alarm him.

"Oh, hello, Toby!" I said, trying to sound as if it were the most natural thing in the world to see him so far from home, with a couple of strangers. "What are you doing?"

"We taking Crazy Dog for a walk!" announced Toby proudly. "I holding the lead! He likes me!"

"Of course he does!" I agreed, and squatted down so that I was looking face to face at Toby. "Everyone likes you!"

Toby grinned happily.

I stood, and said to the adults, "Thank you very much for letting Toby walk your dog, but it's time we went home for dinner now." Then I took Toby firmly by the hand.

For a moment he seemed reluctant to go with me. He looked sadly at the little dog, who was sniffing an interesting clump of grass and showing no interest in any of us.

I suggested, "Do you think we might have macaroni cheese tonight?" Toby had a fondness for cheese.

His expression brightened at once. "P'raps!" he said, and he gave that happy little jump again.

"Come on then!" I said, and Toby dropped the lead and came.

★ ★ ★

Of course, he had been missed. A long time before we got back to the house we could hear people calling, "Toby! Toby" and sounding quite panicky. Then, as we walked along the path on our side of the river, we saw Sophie and Noah in front of us. They must have seen us at exactly the same time as we saw them. They came running towards us, and Sophie bent down and gave Toby a huge hug.

Noah said, "Daisy, you should have told us you were taking Toby out! All we could tell from his tracker was that he was in the water meadows. We've been worried sick."

Toby, emerging from Sophie's hug, said, "Daisy not take me for a walk. Toby take Crazy Dog for a walk! On my own!"

Noah looked a bit confused.

Sophie, though, went suddenly very red. She sort of gulped, and said, "Did you go into the water meadows all on your own, Toby?"

"Not on my own!" Toby was proud and happy at the adventures he had had. "With Crazy Dog!"

"And with Crazy Dog's owners," I added, looking directly at Noah and Sophie, trying to explain without saying it, that I was sure they had lured Toby away.

Sophie had tears in her eyes. This was, I am sure, altogether too like what had happened to her. Noah seemed as calm as could be. He asked, "Hey, Toby, would you like a piggyback home?"

In the distance we could still hear people calling, "Toby! Toby!"

"Mac'roni cheese for dinner?" queried Toby as Noah hoisted him onto his back, completely unaware of the panic he had caused.

★ ★ ★

The same Criminal Police officer came as had been to the house only two weeks or so earlier, after the summer solstice. Toby was telling everyone who would listen about Crazy Dog, but the Chatterers had become quite bored with his enthusiasm and had clustered round the television to watch some programme that showed you how to make things out of scraps of packaging and other things that might be lying around the house. They were creating hats that afternoon, I remember, which some of the children wore to dinner.

The police officer was good at talking to Toby. He was with Rebecca and Albert in the corner where the train track had been set up. She knelt next to him, and asked, "So where have you been this afternoon?"

"Hello, lady!" said Toby. Then, proudly, "Went for a walk with Crazy Dog!"

"Did you, indeed!" said the officer, sounding very impressed. "And did Crazy Dog have any grow-ups with him?"

"Crazy Dog has two grown-ups!" Toby said, and held up two podgy fingers to illustrate the point.

"Where did you meet Crazy Dog and his grown-ups?" the officer wondered.

"Here!" said Toby. "They come here, for me to go for a walk."

The officer looked up at Ethel-nushi, who was standing just back from the group, watching and listening.

Ethel-nushi asked, "What were you doing, Toby, just before Crazy Dog came?"

Toby looked a bit confused. "Don't 'member," he said. "Playing?"

Ethel-nushi looked at Rebecca and Albert. "Were you playing with Toby when the people with the dog came along?"

Rebecca nodded seriously. "Looking for ladybirds," she said.

"I found one!" Albert added, "but it flew away!"

"Did you go into the water meadows to search?" asked Ethel-nushi.

"No!" Rebecca sounded scornful. "They came here, the people with the dog!"

The officer stood up and looked at Ethel-nushi seriously. "We need to check your security," she said. "Let's do that before I talk to the young lady who brought him home – Daisy, isn't it? They must have been on this side of the canal, and this is not a place a person could easily wander to by mistake. Then I'll take some statements…"

With my conscious mind I forgot all about my experience of listening and hearing until much later in the evening when only us older children were still up, and then I did not feel like talking about it. It was with me, all the same, the way you have an underlying feeling of happiness after getting a really good grade, even though you are actually having lunch and talking to other people about other things. When I went to bed that night and I was on my own, I could feel that sensation of being totally alive, again, and when I closed my eyes I could see the shimmering green grass.

★ ★ ★

Persuading Toby that it was not a good idea to go off with strangers was nearly impossible, because he did not seem to grasp the idea of "stranger". Edwina-nushi asked me to help her to explain, the following day, and we sat by Toby's workstation which was covered in his pictures of ladybirds, snails and caterpillars, and more recent drawings of dogs. Toby was on my lap, and Edwina-nushi had pulled up one of the kitchen chairs.

She said, "Yesterday, Toby, you went for a walk with two strangers."

"Yes," agreed Toby happily. "And Crazy Dog."

"How did you know they would not hurt you, Toby?"

Toby looked a bit confused. "They not hurt me!" he pointed out.

"No," agreed Edwina-nushi. "They didn't hurt you, but they might have done."

"Why they hurt me?" Toby wanted to know.

"Perhaps they were bad people," suggested Edwina-nushi. "Some strangers are bad people and sometimes they hurt children."

Toby thought about that. "Not strangers!" he announced. "Nice people. Take Crazy Dog for a walk!"

"Toby," Edwina-nushi was struggling. "You should never, ever go off with strangers. It's really important."

Toby bounced a little on my lap. He said, stubbornly, "Not strangers! Belong with Crazy Dog!"

I looked at Edwina-nushi and she looked back at me, and sighed.

I said, "People are strangers if you don't know their names, Toby, or if they are not friends with all of us, everyone at Xunzi House."

He might have been special, but he was quite cunning in his own way. He said, "Not know police woman's name! She hurt me?"

"No," we both said together. "The police are good," I explained.

"People in street strangers?" Toby asked.

"Yes." I thought he was getting the idea.

"They hurt me?" he asked.

"Not necessarily," Edwina-nushi tried to explain. "But they might. So you have to be careful."

Next Toby wanted to know, "Postman Pat stranger. He hurt me?"

Actually, I think Toby was just being naughty. He did not like being told that he must not go off with the owners of that little spaniel. He was special, but not stupid.

Edwina-nushi said, "Look, Toby, you mustn't go off with anyone at all unless Ethel-nushi or I tell you it's all right."

"Or my Daisy?" Toby wanted to know.

"If Daisy is looking after you, and she says it's all right, then it is all right," agreed Edwina-nushi.

I was not at all convinced that we had really got through to Toby. He seemed to turn it all into a game. All that lunchtime he would go up to people and say, "You stranger? Don't hurt me!" and then run away. In fact, by mid-afternoon all three of the little ones were playing that game, taking it in turns to be the stranger and running away from each other, shrieking.

Ethel-nushi watched it all, and said to Edwina-nushi and

me as we laid the table for dinner, "We just need to remember that he's more vulnerable than the other kids. We need to keep a really close eye on him."

"It's rather sweet that seems to have no concept of being hurt."

"Yes," agreed Ethel-nushi. "Sweet, but dangerous."

★ ★ ★

Noah was about to celebrate his birthday. Then, as now, we numbered our ages the Western way, so Noah was going to turn sixteen. Ethel-nushi had a birthday listed in the records of each one of us, although in some cases, as with Noah and me, the dates were guesswork.

All the younger ones were in bed, although we could hear two of the Chatterers living up to their name, talking still, in their bedroom over the kitchen area. We five older ones were sitting round the table with our two carers. It was almost dark, so about ten at night, and we only had the light over the oven on, so the big living room looked cosy with all the workstations in darkness and just a few lights blinking where equipment had been left on standby. I do not remember such gatherings happening until that year. I suppose that it was because we were growing up. Perhaps it had something to do with Edwina-nushi being with us too; she somehow bridged the age gap between Ethel-nushi and us.

Ethel-nushi always made a big thing of birthdays, even when she was new and I was little, and children seemed to come and go more frequently. We always made those round doughnuts with holes in the middle, the ones that are deep fried and coated in sugar. We did not have cakes with candles, the way they did in old films or some of the children's story books, because blowing out the candles was such a risk when viruses seemed to be all over the place. Instead, Ethel-nushi put the doughnuts in a basket in the middle of the table and the person whose birthday it was took one, closed their eyes, and made a wish. Then they had to hold their breath while everyone counted to ten. I have no idea where the tradition came from, but as we celebrated at least fourteen birthdays a year (Ethel-nushi had a birthday in January) it quickly became very well established.

A sixteenth birthday, however, and the first birthday after lockdown, was something special.

"What would you really like to do?" asked Ethel-nushi.

Noah was dunking biscuits in hot chocolate. He quickly rescued one that was about to disintegrate, swallowed the mushy mess, and said, "Why not do the same as usual?"

"It's your sixteenth," pointed out Edwina-nushi. "Not just an ordinary celebration." She looked across at her sister, and said, "Do you remember the disco in the barn? Was that your sixteenth?"

Ethel-nushi laughed. "Oh!" she said. "I think it was! Or was it my eighteenth? We got so wet, didn't we?"

Edwina-nushi was laughing too. She said to the rest of us, "We had been given permission to use this old barn just down the road from the church. We had a group and everything. Then it started to rain, and the barn leaked like a sieve. But we had paid for the group so we all stuck it out!"

That seemed to give Noah an idea. He said slowly, thinking aloud, "I want to do something in the daytime, with everyone here, just as we always do. But could I have friends round in the evening? I don't know enough people to have a proper party, but there's Jamie and Emily…"

"And Arof the Clown!" I said, having a sudden idea. "Didn't he tell you he was invited to join a C-pop group? They could play for us in the evening!"

Everyone turned to look at me.

"That's a brilliant idea!" said Noah. "Could we do that?"

The two sisters looked at each other. "Oh, I think so!" agreed Ethel-nushi. "I'll mention it to the Children's Bureau just to clear it, but I'm sure there won't be a problem."

★ ★ ★

## Report of Ethel T. Walker to the National Society for the Care of Abandoned and Displaced Children (NSADC) Hampshire Division Southern Colony

**Date:** *5<sup>th</sup> July*
**Time:** *11.00pm*
**Care Home Identity Number:** *017954 Coed*
(Please omit details of exact location)
**Number of children at this location:** *13*
**Number of children in formal detention:** *0*

*Thank you for the encouraging remarks following my report and that of the police. I have discussed your query with my sister and (informally) with a couple of my friends in the Carers' Forum. Our feeling is that, despite his disability, and despite my lack of training with special needs children, Toby is flourishing at Xunzi House. His social development continues. He has good relationships with the other two really young children, and is very fond of Daisy W. That affection seems to be reciprocated. His speech continues to be rather idiosyncratic and he can read very little, although he can write his name. He counts to seven and has a good understanding of those numbers, although I appreciate that we cannot expect him to keep pace with Rebecca Mc or Albert P. Toby loves to draw.*

*I am therefore happy to keep Toby here. In fact, I consider that moving him would be unnecessarily disruptive. I do, however, recognise – especially in the light of recent events – that he is very vulnerable and that special care needs to be taken. My sister would* like to take up your offer of online training to enable us better to provide all that Toby needs.

On another matter, you will recall that, following the cyber attacks, during the Winter of Disasters, when we lost so many essential records, we allocated birthdays to all those children who could not tell us theirs. Noah C was given 12$^{th}$ July, just after the cut-off point for academic year groups, and this year he will be sixteen. In light of the steps we are encouraging our charges to take out of isolation, we have suggested that Noah might like to have a small party. Of course, he has few friends beyond Xunzi House, but he is still in touch with Arof A, who was here until last September, and with the two Thomas young people. Arof A is now in a C-pop group, and Noah would like to invite all five members of the group to Xunzi House. Since this birthday falls on a Saturday, I propose that we do not hold the usual Saturday dinner, and that for once we miss the official broadcast. This seems entirely in keeping with the recommendations of your most recent circular, but if you have any concerns, obviously we will act upon them.

In the matter of Sophie A, I can report that she seems to be working well with Chin-Sun, and seems generally more relaxed around the house, although she is still very cautious. I have been concerned in case recent events with Toby might set her back, and she was indeed very distressed that afternoon while we searched for him, but it seems as if the fact that he was found again has been reassuring for her, the outcome being so different from what happened in her own life. I am, of course, not party to Chin-Sun's reports, but the counsellor has expressed optimism about the eventual well-being of Sophie.

★ ★ ★

It was a strange thing that while we were in lockdown we were all perfectly happy with very few clothes: a couple of pairs of shorts for the summer, a couple of pairs of jeans for the winter, tee shirts, hoodies and trainers. Already, by the time of Noah's birthday, the older girls had acquired our summer solstice clothes and sandals and various other bits and pieces of clothing bought on the market, and as we planned for Noah's party we felt the need for more.

Beatrice and I asked Edwina-nushi whether they could put more money on our bracelets, so that we could walk into town on the Friday afternoon.

"Why?" she wanted to know. "A present for Noah?"

I remember being a little embarrassed. I said, "I saw one of those sparkly ponchos on a stall last week. I thought it might be good for Saturday evening."

Beatrice added, "And, of course, we would like to buy Noah a present too!"

Edwina-nushi laughed. She said, "Sit down, you two!"

So we sat at the kitchen table, and she sat opposite us. "When I was your age," she said, "I would have felt just the same. I would have wanted new clothes for a party. But do you know – has nobody told you – that by the time of the first pandemic the people of the world were consuming about eighty billion new items of clothing every year?"

Well, nobody had told us. "Eighty billion!" Beatrice was as astounded as me.

"Yes, and most of it was consumed by Westerners," Edwina-nushi explained. "People like me. What a wasteful use of resources! Our only excuse was that we did not realise. But I'm telling you now, so that you do realise." She stared thoughtfully over our heads, out of the window. "Are you sure you can't manage with what you have?"

I was ashamed. "I can," I answered. "I just… sorry, Edwina-nushi."

"Me too," said Beatrice.

"Girls." Edwina-nushi was looking at us kindly. "Don't be sorry! You're just being normal teenagers. Only I'd like you to think before you spend…"

So in the end we wore our summer solstice clothes, and I was glad, because, when Emily turned up at lunchtime, she was wearing clothes I had seen before, too.

★ ★ ★

To Toby's great joy, we were having cheese fondue for dinner that Saturday, at Noah's request. It was a brilliant choice. If you have never lived in a large household you cannot imagine the fun of it. I suppose Ethel-nushi could have seated us around several sensibly sized fondue dishes, leading to well-mannered sharing. She never did do that, though. Ages ago she had rigged up a giant fondue dish using an old camping hotplate and a huge cast iron pot which, she told us, had been in the garden with flowers growing in it when she arrived at Xunzi House. This was filled with fondue, and placed on the table, not centrally, but rather towards the side where the little ones sat.

"Sat", though, was the wrong word. In order to reach with their forks into the pot, the little ones had to stand on their chairs, and because the pot was not central on the table, us older ones had to reach across. Ethel-nushi insisted that only five people could dip their bread-covered forks into the gloopy cheese at one time, so if you wanted more fondue you had to be quick. All this led to great hilarity, and to people reaching across the table and yelling, "Beat you!" or "Me! Me! Me!" and people running round to the little children's side where they could reach in more easily. There was, inevitably, a certain amount of cheating. If you had the knack of it, you could wait for someone else to obtain a large piece of bread, dripping with hot cheese, then you could flick it off their fork onto your plate. Naturally, it might fall on the table and occasionally on the floor, but that was all part of the fun. There were limits to what was allowed, of course. Toby always wanted to climb right onto the table, and several times during Noah's birthday meal one of the carers had to lift him off again.

Emily had arrived at lunch time, but Jamie was working and did not get there until late afternoon. I do not suppose either of them had celebrated a birthday in quite such a hectic manner before.

Arof the Clown and his fellow performers arrived as we were all sitting round on the sofas and easy chairs, recovering from the fondue. The gate had been left unlocked after Jamie arrived, so it was as if they just appeared, Arof first, through the kitchen door.

"Hello everyone!" said Arof. "Happy birthday, Noah!"

Toby looked up. A mischievous grin crossed his face. Arof had grown since we had last seen him, and was dressed in proper clothes, not the care-clothes we were used to seeing him in, but essentially he looked just the same. Toby went running over to him. "Arof! Arof!" he greeted him.

Arof squatted down to greet him. "Well, hello, Toby. You have grown!"

"Arof, are you a stranger?" Toby wanted to know. "Are you?"

Arof looked a little bemused. "Well, no, not really," he said.

"Yes, you are! You are!" Toby insisted. "Arof the Stranger. Help! Help! He hurt me!" and, feigning great fear, Toby hid under the table, with all the fondue spillages.

The four students behind Arof looked confused. They were older than Arof, of course, I suppose eighteen or nineteen, two girls and two boys. They were all wearing black tee shirts with "*Kuángfēng*" printed on the front in some sort of silvery fabric, and a design that looked like a willow tree blowing in the wind on the back. "*Kuángfēng*" means 'wild wind' of course, and we saw at once that it was the name of the group.

After that there was a sort of merry chaos for quite a while. Rebecca and Albert joined in their "stranger" game and became very brave about going up to members of the group who they did not know, asking "Are you a stranger?" and then running away and hiding. Several of the Chatterers wanted to look at the musical instruments, a violin, a cello and a guitar – Arof was the violinist, of course. Arof had gifts for us all – Wild Wind tee shirts. "You can be our first groupies!" he said. Ethel-nushi and the Chatterers had prepared all sorts of snacky food and lots more doughnuts, and there was hot or cold tea to drink. Edwina-nushi got into quite a serious conversation with the oldest-looking group member, the cellist, about his environmental studies course at the university, but she had to keep stopping and sorting out the little ones, whose game was getting louder and louder.

Eventually, of course, there was an accident. Nothing serious: Rebecca, who was running away from one member of the group, bumped straight into Toby, who was escaping from Jamie; they both fell and knocked over a mug of hot tea that had been set down on the floor. Both children started to cry, although the hot tea was really not very hot and neither of them was hurt, then for good measure Albert, who was hiding behind the curtain, started crying too. Ethel-nushi clapped her hands to get everyone's attention and said, "Right! Bedtime! Albert, Toby, Rebecca, you go up with Edwina-nushi. You Chatterers, change into your PJs and clean your teeth as soon as the little ones are out of the bathroom."

Then she turned to the rest of us, smiling. "Sorry about that!" she apologised. "It'll all calm down now. Give us fifteen minutes and, if you want, you can play for us? We would love to hear you."

As all the younger children started to disperse, one of Arof's friends asked, "Goodness! Was it always like this?"

Arof was looking flushed and happy. "No," he said. "Not always. Not often, in fact, although we did have a lot of fun. Come outside and look at the river. I always loved it out there."

We all trooped outside. It was one of those warm summer nights. Already the evenings had started to draw in, just a few minutes every day, and it was deep dusk when we left the house. There were bats wheeling and soaring over the water and the air smelt fresh and clean.

"Oh, wow!" said one of the Wild Wind girls. "This is amazing."

I tried to see it as she saw it, the water looking black under the trees on the other bank, the river moving almost silently past, the little mysterious plops and bubbles, the slight stirring of a breeze in the branches.

Another of the Wild Wind members, the tall boy who was taking environmental studies, asked, "Would the matron mind us playing out here, do you think?"

I giggled despite myself. "She's not a matron," I said. "She's a caregiver!"

"Oh, sorry, I just meant—"

Arof interrupted. "That's a really good idea!" he said. "I'll ask." And he went back inside.

There was not much light out there, just the lamp someone had rigged up by the barbecue at the side of the house, but Ethel-nushi found an old storm lantern that had been used when we had power cuts, and we brought out all the spare Saturday-night-dinner candles and put them on kitchen chairs to make a pool of light in front of the group. They organised themselves with their backs to the old rowing club building and we stood or sat on the concrete facing them, with the river to our left.

C-pop at that time was strong on melody and harmony and story. The songs were about loss and loneliness, about being far from home, of being separated from the ones you loved. They had a yearning to them, a sadness, and Arof's violin seemed to sing out in the night of families torn apart and of loved ones who had died young. They were, of course, songs of mourning following years of pandemics and civil strife, of soldiers stationed far from home and children growing up not knowing who their parents were. They were beautiful songs, songs that at the same time could make you smile and make you cry. Wild Wind did not use written music, and I am sure that some of the violin and cello interludes were impromptu. There were clouds in the sky, but once the moon shone briefly, brightly, on the face of the girl singer. Her eyes were closed and she had tears on her cheeks, as she sang of an eagle flying here and there over the snow-capped mountains, looking for its mate, who was floating, dead, in a lake far below.

We must have stayed there for a couple of hours. The children would have been able to hear the music, but none of them came down, and quite soon, when everyone inside was settled, our carers joined us. At some point Ethel-nushi went inside and brought out blankets and throws and we wrapped ourselves up in them. Beatrice and Elijah were cuddled together with the throw from Edwina-nushi's bed round their shoulders. Emily and Sophie were nearest to the barbecue, and the light shone on them, making strange shadows: two girls, one beautiful and pale and one beautiful and dark.

At last, in the distance, a clock chimed twelve. The tall singer said very quietly, "Let's end with a song we have only learnt recently. This is an old Scottish ballad…" Arof played a few notes on his violin, the cello and guitar came in, then the singers.

> *Speed bonnie boat like a bird on the wing*
> *Onward the sailors cry*
> *Carry the lad that's born to be king*
> *Over the sea to Skye*

When they had finished we were absolutely still. The trees rustled, the river glided by.

Then Arof said, "Happy birthday, Noah."
The party was over.

★ ★ ★

Arof and the rest of Wild Wind set off back to the university after that. Arof and one of the girls, being under eighteen, had needed to sign out and sign in again before one in the morning. The authorities were still strict in those days, and it was quite a long walk. Jamie and Emily, of course, had no such restrictions. Their mum or dad would come and pick them up when Emily texted, so they gathered round the kitchen table with us, the five older kids and our carers, to drink hot chocolate.

We were all quite quiet, in a contented sort of way. The music had been beautiful. I felt so close to everyone who was sitting round the table; they were my family and my friends. At that moment I did not want anything else in life.

Then little Albert came downstairs. He looked sleepy, and was trailing a white cloth of some sort that he had curled round his fist, a comfort blanket, I suppose.

He stood blinking on the bottom stair. "Toby's gone," he said.

"Hey, Albert!" Ethel-nushi said. "What are doing up so late? It's the middle of the night."

Albert looked at us with his big, brown eyes "Toby's gone," he insisted.

Edwina-nushi and Ethel-nushi looked at each other in sudden alarm. To my right I could feel Sophie suddenly stiffen as she sat there.

Very calmly, Ethel-nushi said, "All right, Albert. Let's go and find him, and put you back in your bed." I think we were all hoping, at that point, that Albert was dreaming, remembering the afternoon when his friend had been missing. She picked Albert up and went upstairs.

Then, urgently, she called out, "Eddie! Eddie, can you come here?"

All the peace and contentment drained out of the group. I think that, even before Edwina-nushi had reached the children's room, we all knew the worst.

Almost at once Edwina-nushi was back downstairs. She looked very white. "He's not there," she said, "and his clothes have gone!"

"His tracker!" said Noah.

Ethel-nushi was back downstairs too, still carrying Albert on her hip. We all rushed into the office, where the tracker-receptor was kept, and Ethel-nushi clicked it on.

Toby was still in the house.

Well, that was what the receptor showed.

"He's hiding!" said Edwina-nushi, sounding relieved. "Come on, everyone, let's find him!"

There was a sort of scrabble, people running up and down stairs, opening and closing cupboards, looking behind curtains and in places where even a small child could not really hide.

Then, "Oh no!" called Beatrice.

We all rushed to the room Toby and Albert shared. Beatrice was still kneeling on the floor. In her hand was Toby's tracker, with the supposedly unbreakable strap, broken.

Edwina-nushi was racing back down the stairs. "The police!" she exclaimed. She picked up the house mobile, the one that lived by the fire extinguisher, and immediately she was dialling the police.

And then started the nightmare. The police were on their way, but we could not wait even five minutes. Almost, it seemed, without any discussion, we were dividing ourselves into pairs, putting on shoes that had been carelessly kicked off, grabbing mobile phone and torches, deciding who would search where.

Edwina-nushi seized the key to the gate padlock. "I'll go up to meet the police," she said. Then she looked blankly at the keys in her hand. "Has the gate been unlocked all evening?"

I suppose it hit us all at once. Wild Wind had not needed to be let in or out. They had just arrived at the back door, so the gate must have been open, and nobody had gone off to lock it.

"Oh no!" Ethel-nushi was as white as her sister now.

Jamie said, "I had better text Mum and Dad. They need to know what's going on!"

Sophie was flushed and seemed almost breathless. "I want to go and look for him. Now!"

Emily said, "I'll go with you!" At once they were out of the door, heading for the path by the river.

Ethel-nushi said, "If the gate was open Toby might have wandered out that way. Will someone check the lane?"

"We will," said Elijah, grabbing Beatrice's hand. "Come on!"

Jamie was on his phone, talking to Mandy or Robbie. Noah turned to me. "The water meadows!" he said.

So we followed Sophie and Emily. We could hear them in the distance, already much further along the path. "Toby! Toby!"

At first I wanted to rush, to catch up with the other two, but Noah held me back, his hand on my arm. "No!" he said. "We need to go carefully and slowly. He could be hiding, playing his strangers game. If he wants to hide out here, in the dark, he will be hard to find. We might need to catch him unawares."

Of course, Noah was right. I turned off the torch I was carrying, and we slowed right down. "You look right," said Noah. "I'll look left."

We were very quiet.

From far ahead we could still hear Sophie's and Emily's voices. "Toby! Toby!"

Then, from the lane, Elijah's voice. "Hey Toby, where are you? Toby!"

My heart was beating hard, but what Noah had suggested was true. The chances were that Toby was playing his game. We just needed to find him.

It was a still night. Somewhere further upstream a duck was making that night-time call they sometimes make. Had it scented a fox? Was it warning its young? We heard a police siren. But would the police be any better than us at finding a mischievous Toby?

We kept walking, softly, quietly, not speaking, trying to stay in the narrow centre of the path where the grass was downtrodden and would not swish or rustle. We could still hear Elijah, but not the girls. The siren had stopped. The police would be talking to Ethel-nushi now. Would they have dogs? Toby would love to be discovered by a police dog.

We reached the bridge and stood still. Ahead on our side of the river was a wide-open meadow. It was not a good place to hide. Across the bridge were the untamed wetlands.

"This way!" whispered Noah, and we tiptoed across the creaking bridge.

We had to make a decision then. The Itchen Way followed the river in both directions, but there was a small footpath that led away, winding through rough land towards the main river and, eventually, Greater Beijing Street. It was the path we had taken all those weeks earlier, when we had gone to find Noah's cemetery. It was the path that led to my fallen tree.

"I wish I knew where the girls were looking," Noah said. We stood still and listened. We could not hear them at all.

"They've gone very quiet," I whispered. "Don't you think that's weird?"

I could not see Noah's face but I could hear something new, a sort of tension, as he whispered back, "Yes, I do!"

Without any further discussion, we took the little footpath. Noah was ahead, walking quietly, his head up, listening. I was right behind.

Then we heard a little yap. There was a dog, not far ahead.

We both froze. My thoughts were whirling round in my head. Had Toby just followed a dog out into the water meadows? Had that couple enticed him away again? What if the dog had nothing to do with anything?

We crept forward, towards my fallen tree. The little glade was empty, the water trickled peacefully past. Somewhere an owl hooted.

Then, briefly, the moon came out from behind a cloud, and right at my feet I could see something shining. I bent to pick it up – not one thing, but two.

"Oh, Noah!" I hissed. "Look!"

In my hand were two identity bracelets, one silver and glittery, the other a uniform beige. They were the bracelets, I knew at once, of the girls.

I felt sick.

"Oh God! Oh, blessed Confucius!" said Noah. "Come on, Daisy, we've got to tell the police!"

★ ★ ★

All the lights in the house were on when we arrived back, panting and breathless. Most of the children were gathered round on the sofas and chairs, although Rebecca was on Edwina-nushi's lap and Ethel-nushi was still carrying Albert. The police officer who had been there before was talking to some of the other children, and a new officer with a stern face was talking into his mobile phone.

"Look!" said Noah, and I held out my hand, showing them the two identity bracelets.

"Oh no!" Ethel-nushi looked almost panicky for a

moment, before she made an obvious effort to calm down. She came across and looked at the bracelets, lying on the palm of my hand. She said to the female officer who was watching us, "It's the identity bracelets of the two girls, of Sophie and, I assume, Emily. Sophie's one of mine."

Jamie must have been outside somewhere. He came in just then, and saw what I had in my hand. "Daisy!" he said. "What the… That's Emily's! Where…? What…?" He was about to reach over and pick it up.

The officer said, "Don't touch them! There might still be some DNA or even finger prints." Then, to me she said, "Right, young lady, come over here and tell me exactly where you found these, and what happened."

Over my head she said to the other officer, who was off the phone by then, "We need to check these, can you see to it?" Of Noah she asked, "Did you touch them? No? Good. Can you take someone to show us where they were found?"

After that the night was a bit of a blur. More officers arrived, and a dog. I seemed to tell my story over and over again to different people, officers in uniform, an elderly man in jeans and a pullover who everyone else called "Sir", and even Sophie's counsellor, Chin-Sun, who arrived just as it was getting light. At some point the younger children all went back to bed. Mandy and Robbie arrived, looking dreadful, and they sat on the old grey sofa with Jamie, mugs of tea in their hands which they did not drink, watching the officers come and go. At one point I saw them hold hands and close their eyes. They were holding Emily in the Light. Sophie too. When I saw what they were doing I went over and sat at their feet and did the same, then I felt a movement at my side and Noah had joined us. It was the only thing we could do.

Much later, when it was properly light, but before the children started to come down for breakfast, the Thomases left. There was a short discussion with an officer about whether they could tell the Quaker meeting what had happened – the police suggested not – so they said they would be back later. Most of the officers had gone to do whatever they needed to do, leaving only the same constable who had told us that her husband liked to cook for her. Ethel-nushi went into her cluttered office to talk to the boss of the Children's Bureau, and emerged looking as exhausted as ever, but perhaps slightly reassured.

Noah asked if it was allowed, and then texted Arof. I suppose it was about eleven in the morning when Arof arrived back. By then the children had all had breakfast and were doing the usual Sunday things, like playing games on their tablets or drawing, or kicking a football around on the lawn outside our carers' room, the lawn where Sophie had liked to sit. Arof also talked to the police, although of course he did not know much.

Edwina-nushi was very pale, but she seemed calm. She made a pot of coffee which we could smell right through the house, and offered mugs of it to any officer who came in. She made sure that us teenagers had some breakfast, although I do not remember feeling in the least bit hungry, and when Albert was clinging to Ethel-nushi in a frightened way, she lifted him out of her arms and read Albert and Rebecca stories from their store of worn-out books. By lunchtime the Thomases were back, looking no better than when they had left, although Mandy had wet hair. They must all have showered and changed.

I remember feeling sick all that morning. There was a sense of total unreality. This could not be happening, it just could not. I saw Beatrice crying and Edwina-nushi hugging her and trying to comfort her. Elijah kept staring blankly out of the window. Noah had a permanent frown on his face. At some point I dozed off, curled up in the big old armchair with the broken springs, and I dreamt muddled dreams of dogs barking and whistles blowing. When I woke up, I felt awful.

Ethel-nushi came over and sat on the arm of the chair. "How are you doing?" she asked.

I felt hot and uncomfortable from sleeping all crumpled up. "Not good," I said.

"You've been in here all day," she said. "Should you go and get some air? Or lie down properly, on your bed?"

"I don't want to lie down."

Noah heard me. "Come for a walk?" he asked, then looked at the police officer. "Can we?"

"Yes, of course," she said, "but not in the water meadows. Not yet. Not while the search is still on."

As we walked up the narrow path towards the gate – the gate that was still not locked, Noah said, "Do you think it's those guys? The ones we saw at the fire-eating?"

"It can't be," I retorted. "They were caught... I thought it was that odd couple, the ones with the dog."

"Crazy Dog," said Noah, and gave a sad little smile, no doubt thinking of Toby. Well, it was almost impossible to think about anything else.

We reached the lane. We both turned right, neither of us wanted to walk towards town, where life was, no doubt, going on as usual. Then Noah said, "What's this?" and bent to pick something up.

It was a typed envelope, sealed and wedged in the fork of the holly bush where someone was bound to see it. It was just a plain envelope, with no stamp, hand delivered.

It was addressed to Xunzi House.

Noah held it by one corner. They had not said so, but we had gathered that the police thought that I might have damaged some evidence, clutching those two bracelets as we ran home.

We raced back to the house.

"Look!" exclaimed Noah, as soon as we were inside.

Everyone looked in our direction. Noah took the envelope

to the officer. "It was wedged into the holly bush," he said. "We just found it."

The officer passed it to Ethel-nushi. "Perhaps you should open it," she suggested.

They made Ethel-nushi put on plastic gloves, then very carefully she peeled the flap away and pulled out the sheet of typed paper from inside. There was one sentence. "*It would be better if you did not try too hard to find the girls,*" it said, "*or you will not see the boy alive again.*"

★ ★ ★

In the afternoon people started to gather round the gate. Neighbours we did not know from closer to the town had seen the flashing blue lights of the police cars, and had come to investigate. The officer in jeans and a pullover, who was, it turned out, a detective inspector and who suggested we just call him Crispin, called a conference. Edwina-nushi organised the Chatterers into a competition to see who could make the best puppet using twigs and string. The woman PC went out to join them, and obviously to keep an eye on things outside, and Ethel-nushi put the two little ones down for a rest. Then Mandy, Robbie, Jamie, our two carers, Arof and the four of us, the remaining teenagers, sat round the big table, all looking weary and pale.

"Now," began Crispin. "First things first. The last thing we need right now is lots of publicity. We are moving the patrol cars and trying to give the impression that whatever the crisis was last night, the situation has been resolved. We will leave an officer at the gate and he will play things down if anyone asks. The story is that one child wandered out into the water meadows last night but is safely home now."

Ethel-nushi asked, "Is it really possible to keep this quiet?"

Crispin smiled kindly. "No, not at all," he said. "People

round here will know something happened. All we are doing is giving them a different story. It usually works!"

Mandy looked terrible. She asked, "But what is being done to find the children?"

Crispin sounded very controlled as he answered, but he looked worried. "We are interviewing the two men who approached the girls on the night of the summer solstice. You know, of course, that we arrested them within forty-eight hours of you contacting us." He coughed, and looked apologetic. "We strongly suspect that they are involved in this, but they are not being at all co-operative. Not at all."

We digested this in silence.

Then Noah said, "Do you think that weird couple with the dog have got Toby?"

"It seems likely," confirmed Crispin. "Almost certain. We are working on the assumption that they tried to take him once before, when you, Daisy, found him. If that initial plan had worked they would have threatened that if you called us something would happen to Toby. This time they will have realised that you have contacted the police already, so it was too late, by the time they had the girls safely in captivity, to prevent our involvement."

Ethel-nushi wanted to know, "Why would they send that note? Why tell us not to try too hard to find the girls, when they know you are already involved? Surely they must know that the police can't be threatened like that?"

"Oh, yes, they know!" said Crispin. "It's just a strategy, we think. They're telling us that they have Toby, because they know how much that complicates the situation. It's a tactic, we think, to slow us down. We're expecting that they will try to get the girls out of the country as soon as possible."

Jamie clenched his fists, then slowly, deliberately, unclenched them and stretched his fingers. Perhaps it was his way of controlling his anger. Emily was his sister, after all.

Crispin went on, "Of course, we have alerted every port and airport, and all the police forces of the Seven Colonies. The Children's Bureau in Beijing has been informed – they are very hot on people trafficking. And we are keeping ears to the ground."

"Ears to the ground?" queried Arof.

Crispin smiled at him. "It's Arof, isn't it? You're the one at the university?"

"Yes."

"Well then, we could do with your ears to the ground!" said Crispin. "Somehow students seem to discover all sorts of things. You are not isolating at all now, are you? So, listen to conversations in the canteen queue, after lectures, in the common room – anywhere where people chat."

"What am I listening for?" Arof wanted to know.

"Well," said Crispin, "that's hard to say. But anything odd – girls who have had unwelcome approaches made to them, odd things students might have seen when they're coming home late at night. Anything at all that just might be suspicious."

Then Crispin turned to us – Beatrice, Elijah, Noah and me. "These scum have targeted two girls at present, but you are vulnerable too. Boys, please stay close to the girls when you go out. Your presence probably saved Sophie and Emily on the night of the summer solstice. You did well then. Just keep it up for a bit longer, until this is over."

Ethel-nushi asked, "Wouldn't it be better if they all just stayed at home for now?"

Crispin looked thoughtful. Then, "We don't think so," he said. "We would quite like them to be seen around, behaving normally."

Robbie said, sounding suddenly a little angry, "You're not using these girls as bait, are you?"

Crispin looked sad. "Not bait," he said. "Not exactly. We think it might annoy the traffickers to see them out and about still, to see everything going on as usual. They need to think you are very confident that we will find the missing three children. It's more of a challenge than anything, to unsettle them. They're more likely to make a mistake if they feel under pressure."

I thought Robbie looked unconvinced, but he did not say anything further.

Crispin must have read the uncertainty on all our faces. He tried to reassure us. "We haven't had to deal with anything like this in the Southern Colony for quite a while, but in the North West they had a significant problem – which was resolved very satisfactorily – a couple of years ago. A specialist team from that colony has already arrived to help out here. There're things going on about which we cannot tell you. For the next few days you might feel as if nothing is happening. Try not to be too worried about that – appearances can be deceptive. In fact," he added, "in this case appearances are supposed to be deceptive!"

★ ★ ★

### Report of Ethel T. Walker to the National Society for the Care of Abandoned and Displaced Children (NSADC) Hampshire Division Southern Colony

**Date:** *14th July*
**Time:** *12.30 am*
**Care Home Identity Number:** *017954 Coed*
(Please omit details of exact location)
**Number of children at this location:** *10 (three missing)*
**Number of children in formal detention:** *0*

*I am grateful to you all at the Children's Bureau, and especially to the senior carer, for your support. It is kind of you to absolve me of* responsibility for the abduction of two of my charges and the young Thomas girl, although I can blame no one but myself for leaving the gate unlocked. Your remarks that these criminals are cunning and experienced, and would have found another way of kidnapping Toby, though true, do not bring me much comfort. I do not know if I deserve the confidence you continue to place in me.

You ask specifically about how well the children are coping with these stressful circumstances. The two remaining little ones (Rebecca Mc and Albert P) have become rather quiet and clingy. They obviously know that their friend is not in the house but I do not think they understand why. They are certainly aware, though, that something is badly wrong.

The group we call "the Chatterers" has become, over the last six or seven months, quite a self-contained group. There have been times when I have wondered whether this was good for the cohesion of the house as a whole, but it seems to have paid dividends over this weekend. Those five children, aged eight to eleven, have shown surprising sensitivity to the needs of others, demanding very little attention and cooperating with the adults around them. The woman officer who stayed with them while the officer we know as Crispin talked to the rest of us, has reported that the Chatterers embarked on the puppet challenge made by their carers quietly and sensibly, with the older ones helping the younger. They did not talk about the three missing children, none of whom, of course, is from their group. The atmosphere among the Chatterers reminds me forcibly of the way children reacted while we were still completely locked down, when a child was moved from this facility. It is almost as of the children want to block out events they cannot control, and focus only on whatever is immediately in front of them.

The reactions of the four remaining teens are almost opposite. Of course, they also have very little actual control, but they are involved in events very much as the adults are. I am pleased with the way Beatrice F and Elijah P-F support each other. They have become very close, and my sister and I are aware of possible romantic complications there, although indeed such liaisons are perfectly natural at their age, and it would not be the first time since I moved to Xunzi House that two young *people have formed a relationship. Noah C and Daisy W are also quite close, but from the outside, at least, theirs looks more like a friendship than any deeper form of attachment, and both were very friendly with Sophie, though in different ways. Detective Inspector Crispin Beale has asked that our teenagers continue to go out and about, and my instinct is that, if anyone is likely to come across information which might be useful, it will be Noah and Daisy. Daisy, of course, was very close to young Toby, so the emotional toll on her is likely to be considerable.*

*Your concern for my sister and me is kind. At present, supported as we are by Crispin and the Family Liaison Officer, we do not feel the need of extra staff, and as far as is feasible we would like to make things as normal as possible for the remaining children in our care.*

*We understand that the Children's Bureau is in direct contact with the Southern Colony Criminal Police Department, but that you would like, as always, regular reports from me describing how things are from my perspective.*

★ ★ ★

I thought I would not sleep on Sunday night. It was strange to see the covers of Sophie's bed opposite mine neat and tidy and flat, missing Sophie. Beatrice, who slept next to Sophie, whispered as we changed into our nightwear, "I don't think I'll be able to sleep with Sophie gone."

"I know." Everything felt all wrong. "I wonder what they're doing now," I added. "Sophie and Emily."

"I bet they can't sleep, either," whispered Beatrice.

Kaia, one of the Chatterers, turned over in her sleep, and I whispered, "We'd better not wake anyone." I think we were being much more careful than we might have been in normal times.

Beatrice nodded. Then she surprised me by coming over and sitting on my bed, and saying, "Should we hold them in the Light, like Quakers do? It's the only thing I can think of that might help."

So we sat there in silence in the dark, and I remembered those words I had almost heard out in the water meadows, about not being afraid. Then we hugged each other, and Beatrice went back to her bed, and I climbed into mine, and I think I must have gone to sleep at once, deeply, and without having any dreams.

★ ★ ★

I was woken up on Monday morning by Edwina-nushi and Rebecca, who were standing by my bed, and Rebecca was giggling. "Wake up, sleepy head!" she said.

I opened my eyes. The sun was streaming in through the light cotton curtain of my dormer, and all the other beds in the dormitory were empty, their covers straightened, their nightwear folded neatly at the foot of each bed.

"We brought you breakfast!" announced Rebecca proudly, and I saw that there was a tray on my bedside cupboard.

I sat up. "Thank you, Rebecca!" I answered. Then, to Edwina-nushi, "What time is it?"

"Nearly eleven," was the answer. "We decided to let you sleep in."

On the tray was one of my favourite breakfasts: bean broth and steamed buns, obviously freshly made. I suspect that was the first time I had ever had breakfast in bed. It was usually only allowed if someone was quite ill, with a cough or a broken arm, and I was the sort of girl who was always healthy.

Edwina-nushi pulled up a chair to sit by me while I ate, but Rebecca sat on my bed and bounced a little in her excitement, so that the broth slopped around a bit on my tray.

"Easy does it," said Edwina-nushi, sounding very normal, but, when I looked properly at her face, I saw the deep rings under her eyes.

"I've missed history," I said. "And most of Chinese literature."

"Never mind," said Edwina-nushi. "We messaged in. Take your time getting up, but don't go back to sleep again, or you won't sleep tonight. Come on, Rebecca, morning break's over. Let's see how you can get on with those takeaway sums, shall we?"

★ ★ ★

There was no street market on a Monday, so normally we would go into the water meadows after we had done our afternoon chores, but of course the water meadows were out of bounds to us while they were still searching. The authorities had closed the Itchen Way, with a notice that said *"Path Closed for Reconstruction"* and then a map of the city showing all the alternative footpaths where people might walk their children or their dogs instead. It was a warm day, with big white clouds drifting across the sky, and I think all four of us wanted to go somewhere – anywhere – away from Xunzi House.

Beatrice and Elijah had explored the city more than us. They tended to leave the Quaker meetings soon after they finished, while Noah and I, and more recently Sophie too, had tended to stay around. They wanted to take us to an old, ruined castle which was actually quite close to our house, on the way to the cathedral. "You can get in for free on Mondays," said Beatrice.

Ethel-nushi looked worried at the thought of us going out. She really wanted her sister to go with us, but Edwina-nushi reminded her, "Crispin told us to act as normally as possible." So Ethel-nushi checked that our bracelets were properly charged, and reminded us not to speak to strange people, and made the boys promise not to leave Beatrice or me alone for any reason at all, and then we set off.

It was the same route as we had walked when we had visited the cathedral, the very first time we had gone out after lockdown. It had seemed so scary then, and now it seemed almost normal. There was an ice-cream van parked on the corner, with a short queue of people, mostly parents and children, waiting for treats, and Elijah still had some money on his bracelet so he bought soft vanilla ices in cones for all of us. Then we followed the signs past a big, solid-looking building which Beatrice told us was the bishop's palace, and a man held a gate open for us to enter the ruins, and gave us a leaflet that explained what we were going to see.

I had always liked history, and I got good marks on all my history assignments, but I did not want to read the leaflet. It felt as if my head was so full of what was happening right then that I could not deal with any more past events. Noah, of course, was fascinated, and wanted to follow the ruins round in the direction indicated by the leaflet so that he could discover what everything was. Elijah and Beatrice, who had been there before, had a favourite place that they wanted to show us, and eventually, even allowing for Noah to check out this and that on the way, we reached the spot they wanted us to see.

It seemed to be a sort of courtyard area. Ahead and to one side there were arches, on the other side was a solid wall which Noah, consulting his leaflet, told us was not all original. High up, on what would have been the first floor, was the ruin of a second arch. Low on the ground a pile of fallen stones made a place where several people could sit.

There was nobody else there. Not far away in a different space two children were playing some sort of game and a mother was saying, every now and again, "Don't climb on there, Peter!" or "Philippa, don't go where I can't see you."

Beatrice and Elijah sat side by side on the rubble, looking towards the arch. Elijah said, "The first time we came here we saw a peregrine falcon up there. We watched it for ages. At first it was just riding the thermals, gliding overhead, circling round and round. And then, suddenly, it dived. Honestly, it was like a stone dropping."

"We asked the man," said Beatrice, indicating in the general direction of the entrance with a nod of her head. "He explained that it was hunting. There's a pair nesting in the cathedral tower. If you want to see them, he said, you have to look up at where they are searching, just circling round. Once they dive, they are so fast it's easy to miss them, but if you are already watching you will see them go."

We all sat and looked towards the old archway.

We heard the mother of the two children say, "Come on then, kids. We need to get home before your favourite programmes come on." Then, quite soon, they were gone, and there was only us left.

It was very quiet. Elijah and Beatrice were holding hands, but it was not embarrassing. We did not see a falcon. After a few minutes Beatrice said, "That's what they did, isn't it, the people who've got Sophie and Emily and Toby."

"What do you mean?" I asked.

"They circled around, looking for prey, and then they dived…"

I think I shuddered. "That's a horrible way of describing it."

"But true," said Elijah.

Noah was looking thoughtful. He said, slowly, as if he were thinking things through as he spoke, "And of course, that's how they'll be caught."

We all looked at Noah, confused. "What do you mean?" I asked.

Noah was beginning to look excited. "Those people, the people who've got Sophie, Emily and Toby. They circle around, looking for prey. They will never be caught in the act, actually kidnapping anyone, they will be too quick. They need to be caught just circling around, hunting."

At once we all saw it was true. "I bet that's what the police are doing," said Beatrice. "Looking for people circling around, people on the hunt."

"And we can do it too," agreed Noah. "That's how we can help."

"Look! Look! Up there!" suddenly exclaimed Beatrice, and we all followed her pointing arm. High, high above the highest arch we could see a falcon, gliding, soaring, using its wings, it seemed, just occasionally, lazily. It was beautiful.

Noah said, "Pity the chick it sees from up there, or the baby rabbit!" But I think we were all thinking of our friends.

★ ★ ★

I can still remember the strange feeling in Xunzi House that week. We all tried to follow our usual routines, logging in to our lessons in the morning, doing our chores after lunch, and helping our carers with the two remaining little ones and the Chatterers. Jamie, Mandy and Robbie came to dinner most evenings, and the woman officer called in every day except Thursday, which was her day off. On that day Crispin came instead, and spent a long time sitting on the floor by the train set, playing with Albert and Rebecca. I think he was trying to discover whether they could remember anything else about Toby's abductor, but I did not think he got anywhere.

We four older ones went into town every afternoon. I do not think we expected to achieve what the police were not able to do, to notice predators circling around, but at least we were doing something.

I think it must have been a Wednesday when Arof joined us. They were working them quite hard up at the university, but Arof was bright and could take it in his stride. There were never classes on Wednesday afternoons, though, because all the sports teams practised then. Way back when most kids went to school, the university had trained people to teach sport in schools, and they were re-establishing that tradition as the world came out of lockdown. They wanted all the students to take up some sort of exercise, but so far, Arof said, he had declined.

"I'll just keep up with my yoga," he said. "It helps me to think."

We met at the Buttercross. It was odd to remember that only a month earlier we had been sitting on the stone steps watching the crowds go past and celebrating the summer solstice. Of course, it was not anything like as crowded this time.

During the four pandemics and the Culture Wars there had really been no reason for anyone to come into the centre of the city. There were lots of photos on the internet of the way it had been before then, with crowds of people in old-fashioned clothes, bunting out for special occasions, or Christmas lights. There used to be a huge market reaching the full length of the pedestrianised area, and every shop had some sort of display in the window.

Most of the businesses had gone out of business by the third pandemic. During the Winter of Disasters some had been looted and set alight, and the black marks left by the smoke were still to be seen. There had been so much going on, on the night of the solstice, that I had not really realised that many of the High Street premises were still boarded up, but that afternoon, with fewer people around, we could see that it was so.

We sat on the steps waiting for Arof. Just down from us some people were preparing some shop premises for reopening. It had once been a book shop, or possibly a stationer's, but now it was going to sell and mend devices and "accessories". First, they had to clear out all the old stock: lots of paperback books and what looked like rolls of paper, and cardboard boxes that looked the worse for wear. An elderly man had a hand cart onto which the workers piled the stuff, and he pushed it down towards King Alfred's statue, where I supposed they loaded it onto a truck to take it away for recycling. It looked like hard work for an old man although it was downhill, but perhaps he was a freeloader, still paying off his debt to society.

Arof arrived looking, somehow, jaunty. I realise now that he was outside the stressful situation in which we were all existing, mixing with students who knew nothing about kidnapped children and people trafficking, talking about all sorts of other interesting things. He told us, too, that he had just achieved 98% for an assignment, which was a university record, and that he had received a note from the principal congratulating him.

He joined us on the steps of the Buttercross and, after he had told us of his recent academic success, he asked, "Anyhow, what's the news at your end?"

"No change," Elijah said.

"I've been keeping my ear to the ground, as Crispin told me, but I haven't heard anything." He sighed. "To be honest, I don't think I will. People keep wanting to talk to me about Wild Wind and the song we've just streamed. And I don't think students come down into town much. Nothing really happens here."

He was right. There were a few people walking around, but since most of the shops were closed there was nothing to attract anyone. The centre of the city was only lively on market days.

Noah said, "I read that if you wanted to really see a city you have to look at the first floors of buildings, and above. People are always changing the ground floors, making big windows for shops, or blocking out windows and doors which were there originally."

Of course, immediately we all looked at the higher parts of the buildings opposite. Noah was right. On the ground floor all along the street were boarded-up doors and windows, obviously once created to make interesting shop fronts, but above them the architecture was much more traditional, and actually much more attractive despite some soot marks.

Beatrice said, "Do you think people used to live above the shops?"

None of us knew.

Noah said, "Well, in old films you see families living over shops in big cities, but I don't know about places like Winchester. Perhaps they just kept stock up there."

"In European cities people live above shops," commented Arof. "I just saw a movie set in Paris."

"I would love to go to Paris," said Elijah.

I was looking at the upstairs windows opposite us. "I think people might have lived up there once," I said, "because they put things in the windows, like we do at Xunzi House."

It was true. In several places there were faded rainbow pictures, which I vaguely thought might date back to the first pandemic. A couple of the windows almost immediately opposite us were more or less blacked out by streaky soot marks so that it was impossible to see what, if anything, had been put up there. Just a little further up the street there were several pictures that looked like children's art work: something that could have been an owl, a drawing of children – or maybe it was two parents and their child, it was difficult to tell. Further down, beside an alleyway, someone had once put up a printed poster that could have been advertising something.

"So where shall we go?" asked Arof.

"Down to the Abbey Gardens?" suggested Beatrice. "They've re-planted them."

★ ★ ★

She was right. The first time we had walked there, just after the final end of lockdown, the grass had been long and the flower beds scrappy. Now the grass was short and there were bedding plants in the round beds, and a woman in a green worker's uniform was trimming the wild-looking rose bushes. The grass was dry, and we sat in a rough circle. Beatrice started picking daisies, which were very short-stemmed because the grass had so recently been mowed, and it reminded me of us all sitting on the lawn in front of Xunzi House with Emily and Sophie, and I felt sad, and rather empty.

There were excited voices coming from the nearby playground. Like everything else, it had been refurbished by then, and men and women with buggies or holding hands with small children were coming and going. Just a few metres away from us a man was throwing a stick for a dog. The dog, a small white fluffy animal, would stand at his owner's feet panting, waiting for the stick to be thrown. Then he would race after it, ears and tail flying, and retrieve it, bringing it back to the owner ready for another throw. Like everything so soon after the end of lockdown, the sight of a person playing with his dog was still a novelty to us, and we watched with amusement.

"I wonder who gets tired of it first," asked Noah. "The dog or is owner?"

Just then, hurtling out of the area of rose bushes which had not yet been pruned, a second dog appeared. It seemed to want to play too. It waited a metre or two away from the first dog, and when the man threw the stick, it too raced after it. The dogs reached the prize at exactly the same time. Then there was a sort of stand-off, both dogs crouching down slightly, growling, both wanting the stick, neither quite prepared to challenge the other by grabbing it.

Finally the first dog acted. As quick as lightning, he took the stick in his mouth and rushed back to his owner.

The second dog stood, and started barking. The first dog stood close by its owner.

"That's the end of that game," said Arof.

"I've got an idea," said Noah. He got up and walked across to the pile of branches that had been pruned from the roses. He carefully selected one, broke it in half, ran his fingers up and down it to make sure there were no thorns on it, and threw it in the direction of the barking animal.

At once the dog stopped making a noise. The stick had landed just a metre or so from where it was standing. The dog started to wag his tail, looking all the while at Noah, not sure how to deal with this new development.

The man with the first dog said, "Thanks, mate!" to Noah, attached the lead to his pet and left the gardens. Noah came back to our circle and sat down again.

Still wagging his tail, the stranger dog bent and sniffed the stick which Noah had thrown. Then, tail still wagging, he picked it up with his mouth and brought it to Noah.

It was only then, as the little spaniel put his front paws on Noah's leg, that I saw the red collar, and recognised the animal. "It's Crazy Dog!" I exclaimed. "This is Crazy Dog, the dog belonging to those people…"

★ ★ ★

There was a stunned silence. Then Noah asked, "Daisy, are you sure?" Of course, I was the only one who had really seen the dog up close.

Arof calmly reached out and started stroking the dog. I saw that he had taken hold of its collar. "Does anyone have a bit of string?" he asked.

Of course, we did not. I said, "You can use this," and took the long cotton scarf I had bought at the market from around my waist, and handed it to Arof to use as a make-shift lead.

Beatrice moved a little closer to Elijah. "Do you think those people are somewhere here, if this is their dog?" She was obviously frightened.

Elijah asked, "Should we tell the police?"

Noah was not sure. "If those people are round here somewhere, they will have seen us by now... We could text Ethel-nushi, or Crispin..."

He was already reaching into the back pocket of his shorts, for his phone.

"Wait!" said Arof, quite quietly. "If they're watching us, they will see you are making a call! They'll go. The police would never find them."

I was thinking hard. "They might not know we've recognised Crazy Dog," I pointed out. "Couldn't we just pretend to go looking for the dog's owners, as anyone might if they found a stray dog?"

"Then what?" queried Noah. "Make a citizen's arrest, when we find them?"

Again, we were all quiet, thinking about it. Crazy Dog, soothed by Arof's stroking, gave a little sigh and lay down with his chin on Noah's leg.

Then, out of the silence, came a frightened little voice. "Daisy!" called the voice. "My Daisy!"

I jumped up. It was Toby. I looked around, almost panicking. Where was he? I couldn't see him. Had the voice come from the overgrown area, where the bushes were still not pruned?

"Wait!" commanded Noah, almost sternly. "Daisy! It could be a trap!"

I stopped, one step away from our circle. At once I saw that this was true. Already they had two of our girls. Did they want Beatrice and me too? Was this their way of luring us to them?

Arof, Noah and Elijah were on their feet at once; Beatrice was just a fraction of a second behind them.

We all looked at each other.

"We'll go together," stated Noah, expressing a fact, not making a suggestion.

So with Crazy Dog on the lead made by my scarf, we headed for the wild tangle of bushes.

The sun went behind a cloud just at that moment. The green-clad worker was nowhere to be seen, although her wheelbarrow, still half full of cuttings, was still on the asphalt path. There were some trees in heavy, dark green summer leaf, and suddenly that part of the gardens seemed dark and almost threatening.

Noah reached out and held my hand. "Stay together!" he told everyone.

Crazy Dog seemed to know where he wanted us to go. The rose bed was long, crescent-moon shaped, with just one narrow footpath dissecting it half way round. That was where the dog took us.

Then, "Daisy!" came Toby's voice again, and there he was, crouching among the roses.

Without thinking, I let go of Noah's hand and rushed towards Toby. He reached out for me, but he was all tangled up in thorns and prickles, and after one step into the flower bed, so was I.

"It's all right, Toby!" I said, tearing at the thorns that were catching my shorts and scratching my legs. "We're here!" At last I reached him and picked him up. Noah was right behind me, gently disentangling Toby from the thorns.

"Help! Help!" said Toby, holding tightly onto me, "Bad people hurt me! Hide from bad people!" It was just like the game he used to play back at Xunzi House, but with none of the fun.

"It's all right," I said, as soothingly as I could. I could feel his not-so-little body trembling as I held him. "We'll find a police officer. You'll be all right now!"

Toby went almost rigid in my arms. "Not policeman!" he pleaded. "Policeman kill Crazy Dog!"

"Shh Toby," I said. "The police are nice. They won't hurt Crazy Dog."

But Toby was frantic. "Hide from strangers!" he insisted.

"Strangers hurt me." I could feel him getting more and more upset.

I stepped back onto the path, still carrying Toby. For a second or two we all looked at each other. Then, "Quick, quick! Hide!" cried Toby again. He was wriggling to get down, obviously really frightened. "Toby hide!" he insisted.

Noah said, "Yes, come on everyone, let's hide!"

I put the squirming child back on his feet. At once he started tugging my hand. "Come on, Daisy! Hide!" he said, pulling me towards an old gardener's hut, painted dark green. "Toby hide in here!" he said.

I suppose the hut had been in use before the pandemics, but it was obviously not used any longer. There was a rusty padlock preventing access by the door, but at some point someone had broken in by making a hole in the back. I vaguely wondered who had needed to hide in there before Toby, and what horrors they might have been hiding from, while pandemics raged and something close to civil war racked the country.

Toby was in the hut in no time, followed at once by Crazy Dog. "Daisy! Daisy!" Toby called, so I squeezed in after him.

Now I could only see the legs of the others. Noah whispered, "Is there room for anyone else in there?"

"Not really," I whispered back.

"Right," said Noah, obviously thinking hard. "Then I think we'll do what needs to be done." He meant they would phone the police, of course, but he did not want to upset Toby by saying so. "We won't be far away. Just stay where you are." Then, to others, "Come on, over here. We don't want to give their whereabouts away."

★ ★ ★

I thought it would only be a matter of minutes before the police arrived. I was very naive, of course, and my generation had watched a huge amount of television, made in times of peace and normality. I did not think about the threatening letter that Ethel-nushi had opened, the one delivered to the holly bush, and the care the police needed to take in order to try to rescue Sophie and Emily. I did not consider that, once they knew that Toby was safe, they would want to act very cautiously I did not consider that the boys and Beatrice might be in danger.

The hut was tall but the floor area was quite small; it was more of a cupboard than a shed. It took me a few minutes to get comfortable, with Toby cuddling up to me, and Crazy Dog cuddling up to Toby. It was not very warm, either. I had come out in shorts and a tee shirt, and Toby was no better dressed.

Toby said, "We hide from strangers. Strangers hurt us!"

"Did they hurt you, Toby?" I asked.

I could sense rather than see him nodding. "Hurt Toby!" he said. "Shut Toby in a room. Hit Toby."

How could people be so mean? I adjusted my arm a little so that I could stroke his hair. It felt sticky. I asked, "Why did they let you go, Toby?" In the back of my mind a suspicion was growing that this could still be a trap.

"Not let me go!" said Toby. "Me escape! Me and Crazy Dog."

I think I had loved Toby from the day he arrived at Xunzi House wrapped in a brown blanket, in the arms of a police officer, but I was not silly. I knew that Toby was young and could not learn like other children. I could not imagine how he could plan an escape. I asked, "That was clever, Toby. How did you do that?"

"I be very naughty!" said Toby, with some pride. "I scream and shout. They think neighbours hear me."

"That was a good thing to do," I said, trying to sound approving, although really I hated to think what his captors might have done to shut him up. "Then what?"

"Then they say they give me sweets if I be quiet."

"Right," I encouraged him.

"But I not be quiet. Scream and shout. Shout 'Help! Help! Strangers hurt me!'"

"I don't suppose they would like that," I commented.

"Not like it," Toby agreed, sounding thoughtful. "So they hit me." He held out his arm to show me, but in the dim light of the hut I could not really see.

"Oh, poor Toby!" I said.

"Then I say, 'I want Daisy' and I scream some more, but they say no Daisy. Only Sophie or Emily."

Suddenly I started to feel breathless. "Did they say that, Toby. That they had Sophie and Emily?"

Toby nodded in the dark. "Me see Sophie and Emily. Me stay one whole afternoon, if I be good afterwards. Me say goodbye to girls. They off to China now."

I felt as if I had a lump in my throat. Had Sophie and Emily already been taken out of the country? "When was this, Toby? When did you see Sophie and Emily?"

"When we drewed pictures," he said. "I made a spider. Sophie made an owl. Emily made us – two big girls and me. Put them up in the window."

Then, of course, I remembered. Pictures in upstairs windows, almost opposite the Buttercross – an owl and a picture of three people. Was that where the girls were being held? Were they still there?"

"Noah!" I hissed. "Noah!"

There was no answer. I said, "Come on Toby, let's go and find Noah."

"No!" Toby was adamant. "We hide."

Well, I thought, the police would be there any minute. I thought we could afford to wait. "So then what?" I asked Toby.

"Me naughty again," he replied, with great satisfaction. "Me scream and shout some more."

177

I felt almost sorry for those people – almost, but not quite.

"Then they say I can play in garden with Crazy Dog if I be good. Then I play and I be very good."

So, I was calculating, that must all have happened several days ago. What were the chances that the girls would still be locked above the derelict shop?

"I play and play," continued Toby, "and I be good. Then they go to have a cup of tea, and we run away. Me and Crazy Dog. And we hide. And we find you."

"Well done, Toby!" I said, but I think I was feeling quite low. We had got Toby back, but I was beginning to think we would not see Sophie or Emily again.

★ ★ ★

The police had still not arrived. I whispered, "Noah!" again, but again there was no answer. I guessed they had gone to the entrance of the park to await the officers, to show them where we were.

You have to remember that back then most of us kids in Xunzi House did not own mobile phones. Noah had been given his by Ethel-nushi when Arof moved up to the university, so that they could stay in touch, but during lockdown the rest of us had not needed or wanted them. At home we had our tablets and computers, and, as none of us had friends beyond our home, the ordinary business of texting or phoning just did not occur until we met Jamie and Emily, and then we were able to use our tablets. Toby, of course, was not wearing his bracelet anymore, but I still had mine. If Ethel-nushi was looking for me, she could easily locate me, at least to the general area of the Abbey Gardens. The trouble was, if she checked the tracker terminal and saw that I was there, she would feel no need for alarm, especially as the others could not be far away.

Just then Toby's tummy gave a very audible rumble. He giggled. "Me hungry, Daisy!" he said.

"Well," I comforted him, "We'll soon go home and Ethel-nushi will give us something nice to eat."

Toby seemed to ponder this for a while. Then he said, "Bad strangers gone now? Go home to Ethel-nushi?"

The police seemed to be taking a surprisingly long time to arrive. I could not really understand it. Perhaps there had been a big car crash out on the motorway, but even so, you would think that the recovery of a kidnapped child would take precedence. Surely they could at least spare one officer? And I had not heard any sirens.

We were hiding, really, because Toby was frightened, not because I was. What I really wanted to do was to join the others. So I said to Toby, "Shall we go and find Noah, and then go home to Ethel-nushi?"

"Take Crazy Dog?" queried Toby.

"Of course!" I reassured him.

"Go home," agreed Toby.

Climbing out through the back of the little hut was somehow more difficult than climbing in, but I went out first and looked around. I thought I might see the others in the distance, but all I could see was the bushes that were so overgrown, and the tall trees by the Guildhall. There were no other people in sight.

"Come on, then, Toby!" I encouraged him, and he squirmed out, trying not to let go of the little spaniel all the while.

"Where Noah?" Toby wanted to know. He looked so small and dishevelled, standing there, clutching my scarf that was still serving as the dog's lead. For a moment I just wanted to pick him up, but a four-year-old can be quite heavy, and Toby was not slim.

"I expect he's over by the entrance," I said.

Of course, he was not. None of them were.

There were two entrances to the Abbey Gardens on the High Street side. We were up by the old building called the Mayor's House, close to the Guildhall. There were a few people sitting around at the tables on the pavement outside the café which, I suppose, must just have reopened. It was already early evening.

Toby was becoming anxious again. He stared warily at the harmless-looking people at the tables and stood really close to me. "They strangers?" he asked. "They hurt me?"

"I don't think so," I answered, trying to sound reassuring. "Let's see if the others are down by the statue."

"Other strangers?" Toby was tired and hungry, and I suppose he was feeling confused.

"Noah and Arof," I said, "and Beatrice and Elijah."

"And Ethel-nushi?" Toby wanted to know.

"No, Ethel-nushi is at home," I explained. "Getting our dinner ready."

We walked along the pavement towards the statue, where the other entrance to the gardens passed some old, closed, public toilets. I could still not see the others.

Toby was holding my hand and walking slowly. "No Noah!" he announced. "No Arof, no B'trice, no 'Lija!"

"No," I had to agree. I was thinking that the best thing would be for me to take Toby back to Xunzi House by the quickest possible route, and to sort everything out from there, but then Toby asked, "They gone to China?"

I was us about to answer, "Of course not!" when a thought occurred to me. "Why would they go to China, Toby?"

A couple was approaching from the direction of the bridge. They looked nothing like the owners of Crazy Dog, but Toby hid half behind me, obviously frightened.

"Good evening," said the woman cheerfully as they passed.

"They strangers?" enquired Toby, once they were gone.

"Yes," I agreed. "But nice strangers."

I looked around. There was still no sign of the others. I planned to take Toby along by the Weirs it would only take about ten minutes and we would be safe. To be honest, I was feeling quite frightened myself. There was something odd about the others not being there, something strange about the police not coming. This big, new world which I had been becoming accustomed to suddenly seemed unpredictable and foreign.

Then Toby said, "Sophie and Emily go to China tonight. Nasty people say so."

"Tonight?" I asked. "Are you sure it's tonight, Toby?"

I must have sounded a bit abrupt to him. He answered, sounding almost defensive, "Toby hear while he be very good in the garden. They say they go tonight. Take the girls to China tonight." He stood still, seeming to think, while Crazy Dog investigated a dandelion plant that was growing against the fence. "China a long way away?" he wanted to know.

"Yes…" I said. "A long way away…"

The panic in me was growing. Where were the others? Had the people traffickers captured them too? If they were going to take Sophie and Emily out of the country, would they take Beatrice too? And what would happen to the boys? One part of me, the biggest part, wanted to run to Xunzi House, to drag Toby and Crazy Dog with me, to save ourselves. But I knew where Sophie and Emily were. What if the traffickers were right now picking then up from the flat above the derelict shop, loading them into a van? What if I wasted ten minutes getting to Xunzi House and another ten minutes trying to explain while everyone got excited about Toby's return and did not listen to me? I could feel myself going hot and cold, frightened to go one way, petrified to go the other.

And then, suddenly, out of nowhere, it swept over me. I think it was because Crazy Dog was still sniffing around the errant dandelion, and now Toby had squatted down to pet him, and the green of those leaves suddenly filled my mind. For an instance I was back in the water meadows, looking down at my bag which had fallen into that clump of vividly green grass. For an instance I heard that voice again: *Don't be afraid!*

Toby looked up at me. And then, for some reason which I will never understand or explain, he said to me, "Daisy? We not be afraid anymore."

A huge surge of relief swept over me. It was as if the two police officers, Crispin and the woman liaison officer, had suddenly joined us, not at all as if something supernatural had occurred. I found myself grinning at Toby. "Absolutely, Toby!" I said. "We're not afraid! We're going to go and find Sophie and Emily!"

"In China?" asked Toby, skipping alongside me as we headed away from the statue, away from the Weirs, away from safety.

"Not that far, I hope!" I said, and almost laughed out loud.

★ ★ ★

It was properly the evening by then. As we walked up the pedestrian precinct there were people walking down in twos and threes, chatting and laughing. I guessed they might be going to the pub by the bridge, which had a big outdoor yard, perfect for a warm, late-July drink or two. I thought one group was probably students, and thought for a moment of asking if they knew Arof, and if they had a mobile phone I could use, but they were engrossed in some intense conversation of their own, and I was not sure enough of myself.

Above the unused shops the windows were dark. Well, but it was not yet night-time, it did not mean that nobody was up there. We reached the Buttercross and I looked across at the window where we had seen the drawings before. They were still there.

"Look, Toby," I said, pointing up at them. "See those pictures? See the owl and the people? Did Sophie and Emily draw those?"

Toby peered in the direction in which I was pointing. Then he said, sounding indignant, "Where my spider? Toby drawed a spider!"

"They should have put your spider drawing up too!" I said, "Let's go and do that now!"

"Yup!" Toby sounded pleased.

I looked around. The building must once have been rather grand. On the ground floor it had been white, with a faded black door between mock pillars, and metal railings alongside the road, but on the first and second floors it was brick. It looked very closed, and I could not for one minute imagine walking over and knocking on that forbidding entrance. Except where small alleyways or side streets intersected the precinct, the old restaurants, banks and shops formed one continuous joined-up line of brick or stone, or wood and lath and plaster. I could not see a way to get in.

"How did you get in?" I asked Toby.

"Through door!" Toby explained. "Upstairs! Nasty people unlock, lock, unlock, lock… they give Toby sweets to stop him shouting for Sophie."

"Where is the door in, Toby?" I needed to know.

Toby looked around vaguely. "Door not here!" he told me.

That strange calm was still with me. I thought, *There must be a back entrance.* I looked up and down the street. Further up, where we had seen the fire-eaters, the pedestrian area met a road that still took traffic. Somehow I could not imagine finding a rear access that way. I took Toby's hand again and said, "Right-oh! This way!"

We walked a little way back down the precinct. The shop we had watched being cleared out earlier in the day was in darkness now, although there was a big notice on one of the front windows: "All Electrical Goods Mended Here!" and then, in smaller letters underneath, "Waste not, want not". In even smaller letters still it said, "Approved by the Ministry for Climate Stability". The shop was on a corner where one of those smaller alleyways led off to the left.

"This way!" I said to Toby.

As alleyways go, it was quite wide. The shop being refurbished took up almost all of one side, but on the other side everything was boarded up. There was no way through to the backs of the buildings.

Very quickly we reached another intersection. One of those odd green trucks they used back then for deliveries was driving almost soundlessly up the hill, its headlights already on. They used to turn off the fake engine noise, designed to prevent accidents, at night-time so as not to disturb the peace. I realised that it must be getting late. I checked my bracelet, which briefly lit up. It was eight-thirty in the evening already. Ethel-nushi would be worried by now. And where were the others?

If we wanted to get into the place where the girls were being held, we needed to go in the direction of the green truck, up the hill. We turned left and continued walking. I thought that both Toby and Crazy Dog were dragging their heels by then, if a dog could be said to do such a thing.

At first it was like the buildings in the precinct – just a steady row of joined buildings. Then at last we came to a place where there were large, grey, solid metal gates, and, even in the slow summer dusk, I could see that beyond them were the backs of buildings. Even better, I could see a light in one upstairs window, and a metal fire escape.

"Is this where you went to visit Sophie and Emily?" I asked Toby.

The poor little chap was exhausted. He said, "Toby hungry! Crazy Dog hungry!"

"Oh, Toby!" I said. I think it was only then that I realised that I might be getting him into a load of trouble, and he had been so clever at escaping. Was I about to get him recaptured?

It was probably that realisation that gave me the idea. "Do you want to stay here, if we find you somewhere to hide? You and Crazy Dog? And I'll go and get Sophie and Emily."

Toby nodded, the very image of dejection.

Now, you probably know that Winchester is very old, and the really ancient bits sometimes appear in the most unlikely places. We were in a street called St George Street, and about two-thirds of the way up, on the right-hand side, there was a small area of covered footpath. I was sure that it must have dated back to a time when the upstairs of buildings stuck out further than the downstairs. I did not know Winchester well in those days, but from where we were standing I could see that the pavement under the covered area was in deep shadow. If Toby stayed still in the darkest corner, he would probably not be seen by anyone unless they were really searching.

"Let's hide you over here!" I said, leading the weary child and the dog, who seemed almost as tired, across the street and into the darkened area "Will you sit here, you and Crazy Dog, and wait for me?"

At once Toby sat, right in the corner, and hugged the dog to him. I asked, "Toby, what will you do if someone finds you before I get back?"

I could not see his face, but I heard the question in his voice. "'Scape?" he suggested.

All in all, it seemed like a good enough answer. Then, "Do you know your way to our house?" I asked.

"Not know," Toby told me.

It was as I feared. If I was caught, if I did not come back, what would happen to Toby? Should I have taken him home? But if I had done, would I have lost the chance of freeing

Sophie and Emily? Was there really any likelihood that I could free them anyway?

But beneath these thoughts skittering around in my mind, was that reassurance. *Don't be afraid*, the voice-that-was-not-a-voice had said.

Then I had another idea. "Toby," I said, "shall we ask the Light to protect you?"

Toby answered at once. "Yes, ask Light!" he agreed.

So I squatted down next to him, and held his hand, and in silence I asked the Spirit, who is Light, to keep Toby safe. Then I said, "Right, Toby, I'm off!" and I kissed his head and sprinted across the road again, down to those huge, grey, metal doors.

★ ★ ★

**Report of Ethel T. Walker to the National Society for the Care of Abandoned and Displaced Children (NSADC) Hampshire Division Southern Colony**

**Date:** *Wednesday 24th July*
**Time:** *10.00 pm*
**Care Home Identity Number:** *017954 Coed*
(Please omit details of exact location)
**Number of children at this location:** *Theoretically 13. Currently 6 missing.*
**Number of children in formal detention:** *0*

*I know you said that there is no need to write reports until things are resolved, but these reports have become almost like a journal for me – a journal which I know you, at the Children's Bureau, always read. I cannot thank you enough for your continuing support. My sister and I have both taken on board your comments that the children in Xunzi*

House have been targeted by some serious criminals, and that nothing in our training as caregivers could have equipped us for this.

We are now missing all our teenagers and Toby F. According to their trackers, my four young people met up with Arof A at the Buttercross, as planned. They walked down to the Abbey Gardens and apparently stayed there until about five o'clock. At some point, for reasons that are not clear, Daisy W seems to have separated from the others, and stayed in the park while the remaining four walked down towards the statue. According to their trackers, they are still somewhere in that area. The police tell me that they are searching for the teenagers' bracelets. We all have it in mind that, when Sophie A and Emily T were kidnapped, their bracelets, which nobody should be able to remove without the Code, were found in the water meadows. It has been evident to the police, so the Detective Inspector told me, that these criminals have considerable technological ability.

The strangest element from both the police and our point of view, is that Daisy's tracker seems to place her somewhere in the centre of the city. The location indicator on these bracelets is not very precise, but it seems as if Daisy is not far from the Buttercross, perhaps in the parallel street, St George Street. The police suspect that Daisy is not there at all, but that somehow her tracker has become attached to one of the criminals, maybe in a pocket or a bag, and not dumped, which is what they expect has been done with the bracelets of the others. Of course, the police are watching the roads and precinct closely, but there appears to be nobody about.

As you know, I phoned the police at about six-fifteen. I had tried to call Noah, the only one with a mobile phone, at six o'clock but he had not answered. At that point I just wanted to remind the teenagers that it was time to come home for dinner. After I tried again about ten minutes later, and still did not get a reply, and in the light of the loss of Toby and Sophie, I thought it best to act at once. I am grateful to the police for their prompt response, and for the officers who have been stationed in the lane and the water meadows since about nine this evening.

The younger children are now all aware that their older friends are in trouble. Edwina and I have put Rebecca in Toby's bed, so that *the two little ones can be together. The Chatterers are chattering a great deal less. Their quietness is so out of character that it adds to the general strangeness of the atmosphere here. We will, of course, follow police advice and keep all the children at home until the authorities consider it is safe to do otherwise.*

*My sister and I plan to take it in turns to stay awake tonight, although I cannot imagine that either of us will actually sleep. Please feel free to phone at any time. We will, of course, keep you up to date too, although we are aware that you have ongoing contact with the police too.*

★ ★ ★

Looking back all these years later, I can think of all sorts of things I might have done differently without incurring all those risks, but I was a child, and not at all used to being out in the world. I should really have flagged down the next vehicle to drive up the street, although of course I was frightened that by doing so I would have handed myself straight in to the people traffickers. And, indeed, I might have done. I know now that if I had just waited in the shadows with Toby it would not have been long before a police car cruised silently and slowly up the road looking for me, just in case, against all odds, I was still wearing my own bracelet, but I did not know that then.

I remember standing in front of those big, solid metal gates. They must have been two metres high and there were no footholds. Of course, I pushed against them, to see if, by any chance, they were unlocked, but I had no luck there.

I looked around, feeling a bit helpless but, as far as I can recall, not at all fearful. That voice-that-was-not-a-voice was still with me. There was a broken old wheelie bin lying on its side in one corner, but, even standing on it, I would not be able to reach the top of the gates.

Then something made me look up at the brick wall which formed the side of the next-door building. Down at ground level the brickwork was good, but higher up it was damaged, with a few bricks and most of the pointing gone. If I could stand on the wheelie bin and reach that uneven wall, maybe I could climb over…

Well, three cheers for a childhood roaming the water meadows, climbing trees, not made fearful by anxious adults telling me always to be careful! The wheelie bin was actually pretty unsteady. True to its name, it was on wheels, and, every time I tried to climb on to it, it started to roll around. The lid was cracked too; I was not sure it would take my weight. I remember looking around to see whether I could find something to block the wheels, but the city was kept pretty clean and tidy by then, and there was nothing. I was only wearing my shorts and tee shirt. Even the scarf I had bought on the market to dress up my care-clothes I had left with Toby because it had been serving as a lead. There was nothing left except my trainers, the ones Edwina-nushi had given me at the end of the winter. I took them off, and managed to wedge the bin in place.

Climbing up onto the bin was quite a feat, even now that it was remaining still, but one way or another I managed it. When I tried to stand, though, I realised that my socks gave me no grip, so I took them off as well, and stuffed them into the side pocket of my shorts. Then came the business of trying to climb the wall.

It was a rather precarious exercise. I did not climb as if it were a climbing wall – not that I had ever seen a climbing wall back then. I leant against the metal gates and used the holes and niches in the uneven brickwork to my left to push myself up. In effect, I was sliding up the gates, propelled by my feet. I could tell because of the feeling on my back when I reached the top. Then it was very scary manoeuvring myself around until I was sitting up there, one leg on each side.

I had not thought about how I might climb down on the other side. I am pretty sure that if I had jumped I would have done myself some damage, maybe broken an ankle. However, luck or Light was on my side. Just below me, in the corner made by the gates and the next-door building, someone had put several of those green bags we still use to put out our garden waste in for collection. They were all full, smelling slightly of cut grass and other green things in the residual heat of the day. I wriggled round until I had my back to the street, and let myself drop. My landing was prickly but otherwise safe. I clambered off the bags and stood looking around me.

None of the buildings appeared at all the way they looked from the precinct. They were less grand, and several seemed to be made of a mixture of flint and brick. Two or three of them had metal fire escapes leading up their sides, but only one building had any lights in the windows. That was where I headed.

I could tell, even in the late dusk, that each property must have had its own area of yard, all accessed via the metal gates. Perhaps, in pre-pandemic times, people living in the flats above the shops might have cultivated those areas, with colourful pots full of flowers surrounding paved areas where residents could hold barbecues in the summer weather. By the time I am telling you about now, everything was in disrepair. There were ropes of ivy trailing across broken paving stones and weeds growing up in the cracks. There were broken things lying around too – barely visible pottery flower pots and an old bent spoon that I trod on with my bare foot. It was not easy making my way to those metal steps in the dark.

At one point I heard a vehicle driving slowly up St George Street. I remember stopping and listening. Those elegant electric cars were almost silent when their artificial engine noise was turned off, and I remember holding my breath so that I could hear. I was terrified that the vehicle would stop and find Toby, but the car cruised slowly on, and was gone.

I had reached the fire escape. It creaked a very little when I set foot on the lowest rung, but otherwise the night was quiet. One foot was hurting still from stepping on that spoon, but I tiptoed up, my heart beating hard.

There was a sort of platform by a large sash window set in a broken frame, and the steps led on up to the second floor. There was a dim light showing, not as if someone were in the room immediately on the other side of the dirty glass, but more as if the room led into a lighted corridor.

I tried the window. Of course, it did not move. I thought for a moment, and then tapped on the window.

Nothing. No movement at all within.

I knocked louder.

Still nothing happened. What should I do now?

I crept back down the steps and groped around until I found that spoon. Back on the platform, I tapped again. The spoon made more noise than I did using my knuckles, but still no one came.

So then I took a gamble. I was about to make a lot of noise. I pulled one sock out of my pocket, and put it on my right hand like a glove. I held the spoon by the bowl and smashed the handle into the glass.

The tinkling of breaking glass was not as loud as I had feared. I brushed the splinters and larger chunks off the metal platform to save my bare feet, then dropped the spoon. The sock did not properly protect my hand as I removed the remains of the broken window, but it was a great deal better than nothing. Then I threw my sock away, over the railings of the platform, and crawled in through the window.

I was right. I had climbed into an empty room, but the light came from a dimly lit corridor beyond, with three doors leading off. One room was an old bathroom, with a stained bath, a wash basin and a lavatory with one of those ancient cisterns fixed high on the wall, and a long chain hanging down.

It would have seemed disused, except that there was a towel on the side of the bath, and a hair brush on the sink.

I tried another door. It opened easily, but led into an empty room. There were some old mattresses in a pile in one corner, and a heap of what might have been old clothes, but no sign that anyone was living there now. Ahead, at the end of the corridor, was a sort of kitchen.

I stood still and listened. At first I could hear nothing, but then, from behind the final door, I heard a sort of scrabbling noise, and then a small cough.

I tried that door. It was locked. I listened again. Silence. Then, again, I thought I heard a movement.

It was time to take a risk. "Sophie," I whispered. "Are you there?"

At once came a reply, but it was Emily not Sophie speaking. "Daisy! Daisy, is that you? Have they got you too?"

"No." I sounded braver than I felt as I said, "I've come to rescue you."

"Are you alone?" Emily said. "Daisy, call the police. Call *now!* They are taking us out of the country tonight."

I heard Sophie's voice. It sounded flat, almost expressionless. "She doesn't have a phone."

"It's OK," I told them. "I'm going to break down the door. Don't get too near it!"

If you watch lots of films, as we had done during all those years of lockdown, you would think that breaking down doors is an easy enough business. You just charge at the door with your shoulder leading and – crash! – the door is open. Nothing at all like that happened for me. After a couple of attempts I stood in the corridor nursing a bruised shoulder, wondering what to do.

Emily whispered through the door. "Have you got your ID card with you? This is a Yale lock. You might be able to open it if you slide the card up…"

"We don't have ID cards," I explained. "We just use our bracelets." Then I had an idea. "Hold on a minute."

I ran to the kitchen at the end of the corridor. I clicked the light switch and one of those old, fluorescent lights flickered on. I vaguely thought how we should not be using such lighting anymore; it was not at all energy efficient. I looked frantically around and then I found what I wanted. Sitting on the stained work surface was a knife.

I grabbed it and rushed back to the locked door. It seemed too good to believe, that a person could unlock a door using just a card or a knife. People must have been forever breaking into other people's homes back in the Old Days! But it worked, the lock made a sort of slithering noise, and the door opened. And there were Sophie and Emily, looking tired, still wearing the clothes they had worn for Noah's birthday party.

★ ★ ★

Like me, they were both bare foot, although I suppose it was for different reasons.

"Come on, quickly!" I exclaimed. They were both just standing there looking at me, as if they were stunned, and I wanted us to go, go now, before something went badly wrong.

Sophie had an odd look on her face. It was as if she did not quite believe I was really there. Emily said, quite gently to her, "Come on, Sophie, let's put our shoes on."

It was then that I realised that Sophie was in a really bad way.

Emily was quick, slipping one foot and then the other into those pretty sandals, but Sophie was still doing nothing. "Come on, Sophie!" I begged, but the urgency in my voice must have frightened her even more. She backed into the far corner of the room and hugged herself, as if she were very cold.

And then I heard it. Not the van. The van must have had the fake engine noise turned off, but there was a sort of squealing, the sound of metal scraping on concrete. I ran back to the broken window and saw the van drive in. Someone had unlocked and opened the gates. He came in after the van and closed them behind him, a dark shape with a red glow on his trousers from the brake lights as the van stopped.

Emily had joined me. "Oh no!" she cried. "It's them!" Then, "Quick, Daisy, hide, or they'll take you too!"

I looked wildly around. "Where?" I asked helplessly.

Emily dragged me into the empty room. "Under the mattresses!" she said. "Go!"

The next minute she was back in her room, and I heard the lock click as she closed the door. It was a good thing I had not broken the door down. Nobody would be able to explain away something as obvious as that.

I scrambled under the top mattress and wriggled towards the wall, so that I could just see out from a slight gap between the dusty fabric on top of me and the foul-smelling cloth below. I could hear people on the metal steps.

"This way, ladies and gentlemen!" a voice was saying, not at all kindly. I could hear footsteps and shuffling on the fire escape. And then, "What the hell?" The owner of the voice must have reached the broken window. "Hey, Duff, someone's been here!"

There was the sound of another person running up the stairs, and a voice demanded, "Move out of the way, you kids! Move!"

"We've had a break-in," said the second voice. "Check the girls!"

Heavy footsteps passed the door to the room where I was hiding. A key turned in a lock. Then the voice called back, "They're still here!"

"Huh!" The owner of the first voice came from the window area. "Stick these kids in the other room," he said. "Lock the door. I want to talk to the girls!"

The next minute there was more shuffling and the voice commanded, "In you go!"

I heard Arof's voice, very close to me. "All right, mate, no need to push us! And take your hands off that girl!" Then someone landed heavily on the mattress that was on top of me, and I just managed to stop myself from making a noise.

The door closed and I heard a key turning in the lock.

I muttered, "Would you mind not sitting on me?"

"What?" Arof and Elijah were pulling the mattress off me. "What on the earth… Daisy! How did you get here? "

I stood up a bit shakily. There was no electric light in the room, but a street light was shining in, a dull orange, environmentally friendly glow. I could see Noah, Arof, Elijah and Beatrice. Their hands were tied together and there was a rope attached to their feet too. No wonder there had been a shuffling sound on the stairs!

For a moment we all just looked at each other. Then Arof asked, "Can you untie us?"

It was not easy. The knots were tight and it was hard to see, but, once I had freed Beatrice, she was able to help me with the boys. While we worked, we whispered our conversations.

"We hoped you'd got away," said Beatrice, and then added, "Where's Toby?"

"Not here," I answered. "Outside, hiding – I hope."

"Poor little Toby," said Arof. "So did they get you too?"

"No, I was trying to rescue Sophie and Emily."

"Are they here? In this place?" It was Beatrice again, rubbing her wrists where the rope had chaffed her.

At the same time Elijah asked, "How did you know where to find them?"

The thought of telling them about the pictures in the window seemed just too much. It felt to me as if explanations could wait for another day. "They're taking them out of the country tonight," I said. "Sophie and Emily."

"And me, too," added Beatrice. "We heard them discussing what to do with us."

For a few seconds we were all quiet. Next door we could hear the sound of Emily's voice, speaking calmly, and the sound of sobbing – Sophie, I knew. I wondered what story Emily was telling them.

"What about you boys?" I asked. I thought the people traffickers wanted girls, to be brides for sad old men.

"Labourers," said Arof. "Unpaid."

"Slaves," said Elijah.

Noah had not spoken at all until then. "They were following for us," he said at last. "All the way from Xunzi House. But they were keeping their distance. They didn't see us finding Toby. They didn't see you and Toby hiding. They picked us up at the statue."

"We should have been more careful," grumbled Arof.

"We thought we were safe," said Elijah. "The police were happy to let us be out and about."

Noah continued his story. "I was just on the phone to the police. I had dialled 999 and the woman was asking me which service I required, and then suddenly there was someone behind me snatching my phone away."

"It all happened really quickly," confirmed Arof. "This van drew up right by us and we were bundled in. One minute we were standing on the pavement, feeling pleased because we had at least found Toby, and the next minute we were in a heap on the floor of a moving vehicle, being driven who knows where."

I was trying to imagine it. I said, "But that was hours ago!"

"Yes," Arof agreed.

Beatrice went on with the story. "They drove us out of town somewhere. We stopped off in a sort of parking area, and they searched us and tied us up. They took Arof's phone and they had the key code to our identity bracelets. She held out her left arm, and I could almost see the white mark where her bracelet had always been.

"My phone won't do them much good," scoffed Arof. "I tried it in the van. It must have triggered the automatic lock when I landed on it, when they threw us into the van. I couldn't make it work."

"Then what?" I wanted to know.

"They kept driving us around. They brought us back into the city almost at once."

Beatrice added, "They were dumping our bracelets."

"And biding their time." It was Noah who said this last thing. "We heard them talking. They didn't want to head south until the roads were clearer. They're planning on going to Southampton."

"To leave the country," I concluded.

"Yes. We need to get out of here," Beatrice said. "Or we'll all be taken abroad."

"No!" Suddenly Noah sounded excited. "They don't know you're here, do they?"

"That's right!" Arof had seen the point at once. "You've got to hide again, Daisy. When we've gone, you've got to get out of here and call the police. Tell them we're going to Southampton."

"But how?" It was almost the same problem I had faced earlier. None of us had a working phone. There was no police station in the centre of Winchester; there had not been for years. There was very little night life, we were still too soon out of lockdown, so I could not have gone to a restaurant or pub and asked to use their phone, and if I were to stop a vehicle, who knew what sort of reception I might get?

"You'll have to go back to Xunzi House," answered Noah.

"It'll take fifteen minutes, at least," I said.

"How long does it take to drive to Southampton?" Noah was talking to Arof. He had been down there for a socially distanced demonstration of some sort before the end of lockdown.

"About twenty minutes," said Arof. "But that was when nobody much was travelling. With more vehicles on the road, it could take longer. And they've got to go to the docks. I think that's further than to the university."

"You'll have to run," prompted Noah.

"And pray!" suggested Beatrice.

Elijah had thought of something else. "You'd better tie us up again, too."

★ ★ ★

We barely made it before we heard movement from next door, where the girls were. The men came back into the corridor. "Just some kid breaking into empty properties," said Voice One.

"We shouldn't use this place again, anyhow," said Voice Two.

"No," agreed Voice One. "Anyway, we'll need to lie low as far as Winchester is concerned, for a while. Come on girls, we're off. Come on, you kids," and our door was unlocked. "On your feet! You've got a long journey ahead of you!"

I felt almost like a traitor, hiding under the smelly mattresses listening to my friends being taken away. I also had a deep urge to sneeze, so that I had to hold my nose and think hard about something else. I knew when Emily and Sophie passed the door to my room, because I could hear Sophie crying and Emily coaxing her along. "It's all right, Sophie," she was saying. "I'm here. I'll stay with you."

"For now!" said one of the men, unkindly. "Not forever!"

I think perhaps Noah and Arof were deliberately making a lot of noise climbing out of the window onto the fire escape. They were hoping someone would hear them and come to the rescue. Instead, all that happened was a soft-spoken but vicious voice said, "Keep the noise down!" and then I heard the sound of a thump and Noah said, "Ouch!" very loudly. They meant business.

The fire escape stairs creaked a bit as everyone descended. I stayed still under my mattress and listened. There was the sound of van doors opening – the sliding doors at the front, the other sort at the back, and the almost inaudible sound of an electric motor being turned on. I wriggled out from under the mattress and ran to the window. One man was opening the metal gates and the van was backing out. *Please don't lock up after yourselves!* I silently implored.

Sure enough there was the sound, almost immediately, of a van door closing and I could see the glow of their headlights as they drove up the street.

I was out of that window at once, and running, almost tumbling down the metal stairs. I needed to get back to Xunzi House at once, quickly, before my friends reached the docks and I lost them for ever.

It was properly night-time by then, of course, and very dark. Environmentally friendly street lights are, no doubt, a good thing, but they tended to make pools of orange on the pavement and road, with long, dark shadows between. There was no traffic. I ran across to the road to the place where I had left Toby.

At first I thought he was not there. Then something made a slight movement, and I realised it was Crazy Dog, wagging his tail to greet me.

Toby was fast asleep. He had my scarf wrapped round his arm, and his thumb was in his mouth.

I shook him gently. "Toby! Toby! Time to wake up. Let's go and find Ethel-nushi, shall we?"

Toby sort of grunted, but he did not open his eyes. I needed him to wake up quickly; we ought to have been on our way.

"Toby!" I shook him more firmly. "Toby, wake up. We've got to go. Now!"

Crazy Dog growled. I suppose he was warning me not to hurt Toby. "Good dog!" I said, to calm him down. "Toby, please wake up!"

At last Toby opened his eyes. It was impossible to see his expression in the dark, but he said, "Hello, Daisy. Me sleep now."

"No, Toby," I said. "Not now. We have to go and find Ethel-nushi. Right now."

Toby answered, "Daisy, it night-time! Find Ethel-nushi in the morning."

"No," I said. I could feel a sort of panic rising up inside me. We must have lost five minutes already. "Please, Toby!" Then I had an idea. "We have to go to Ethel-nushi; we have to run away from bad strangers who hurt us!"

At last Toby was wide awake. He sounded frightened. "Where bad strangers?" he wanted to know.

I said, "The bad strangers can't get us if we find Ethel-nushi. Come on!"

Toby stood at last. "Take Crazy Dog?" he asked.

"Of course!" I said. "Come on!"

The streets seemed strange at night. We walked back the way we had come, into the pedestrian precinct. Once we saw a car approaching slowly up St George Street. It was quiet, with the engine noise switched off and the headlights dimmed. I thought it might be someone looking for Toby. They did not know about me, but the people traffickers obviously knew that Toby was still missing.

"Quick!" I said to Toby, and pulled him into a deep shadow as the vehicle passed. Afterwards I thought perhaps it might have been a police car, but I could not be sure.

Once in the precinct the going was easier. Of course, I was still in bare feet, and the stone flagging was cool and clean, easy for running on. Crazy Dog was willing to run too, but moving fast was really not Toby's thing. He had been created clumsy, and, although he was still only a little boy, I would say he lumbered rather than ran.

We had not even got to the bottom of the precinct, to the place where cars can drive, before Toby stopped and sat down, right there in the middle of the path. "Toby tired," he announced. "Not run anymore."

The clock in the Guildhall struck, lots of chimes but I did not count them. Was it eleven or midnight? How far would the van have got now? I could imagine it driving between huge containers, like something I had seen on a detective series.

I insisted, "Toby, we have to find Ethel-nushi!"

But Toby could be obstinate. He looked around, as if searching for something or someone. "It's night-time," he told me. "No strangers! We stay here."

"No, Toby!" I felt desperate.

Then an idea struck me. I sat down beside Toby, as if I were not in a hurry at all. I said, "Toby, I bet Crazy Dog is hungry."

Toby stroked the little spaniel. "Crazy Dog and Toby hungry," he agreed.

"I think we ought to find some food for Crazy Dog, don't you?" Then I said, "No, it's all right. He's only a dog. He can wait until morning!"

At that Toby stood, indignant with me. "Daisy!" he said, imitating Ethel-nushi when she was disappointed in me. "Crazy Dog not just a dog. Crazy Dog hungry! We find food for Crazy Dog, now!"

I said, "But, Toby, we're both tired!"

"We find food now!" insisted Toby, and started leading the little dog down the street.

I jumped up. "Oh, all right!" I said as I joined him. "What shall we get him?"

Things were easier now that Toby had a reason for being on the move, a reason he understood. We passed the Guildhall and the turning to the Abbey Gardens, and the pub on the bridge which was closed for the night, and at last we were walking along beside the river. Crazy Dog seemed to be enjoying the expedition. He sniffed around at everything and tugged at the makeshift lead.

I must have become lazy. There seemed to be nobody around. We were talking in quite normal voices, discussing what Crazy Dog might like to eat when we reached Ethel-nushi. Toby thought he would like cake and hot chocolate. I suggested that maybe dogs like biscuits and water. Toby was telling me, "Bad strangers give Crazy Dog biscuits and water. We nicer. We give him cake. Crazy Dog wants cake!"

We were making good progress. Up ahead was the mill that was turned into flats, then it was just a little way to the lane, and the gate to Xunzi House. I was feeling less panicky, although I thought we had taken a long time, much longer than if I had been running on my own.

Then, "Ah, there you are!" Out of the shadows, standing right in front of us, was the man with the cap, Crazy Dog's real owner.

We both stopped dead, Toby and me. I could feel him sidle up to me, holding the hem of my shorts, looking for reassurance. Neither of us said anything.

The man was looking at Toby. "We missed you," he said, in a falsely friendly voice. "I've been looking for you all evening! But here I am, to take you home."

I was surprised at Toby's reaction. I could tell that he was frightened. The little hand holding on to my shorts was shaking, but he answered the man, "Toby not like strangers. Strangers hurt him. Toby going home to Ethel-nushi!"

"Oh, I don't think so," said the man. He looked at me. "In fact, you're both coming with me now!"

I took my lead from Toby. "No, we're not!" I said, sounding much more confident than I felt.

For a moment I thought the man looked quite disconcerted, although it was hard to be sure.

I suggested, "In fact, if I were you, with the police looking for you, I would get away quickly!"

"The police?" The man sounded confused.

"Oh, didn't you know?" I lied. "They've got your friends. Arrested them about half an hour ago, in that place you were using off the High Street!"

It was, of course, a ridiculous story. None of the ends tied up. If I had really witnessed such an arrest, why would Toby and I have been wandering around Winchester in the middle of the night, making our own way home? But I suppose we had taken the man by surprise, and he obviously knew that there had been a place where girls were locked up in St George Street.

For a few seconds we were all silent. It was then that I thought I heard voices, somewhere beyond the Weirs. But in that moment, that brief pause, the man must have pulled himself together. He sprang at me, knocking me to the ground, and then he was kneeling on me, holding me down.

"We can make good money out of you!" he panted, and he started reaching for my arms. I was sure he was going to tie my wrists and I thrashed around, fighting as hard as I could, even though it might be hopeless.

"*Run, Toby!*" I shouted. "*Now! Run!*"

But Toby did not run. He started crying and then he started shouting. I did not know until that minute how loud he could shout. It was just like his game, but desperately real. "Help! Help! Strangers catch me! Strangers hurt me! Strangers hurt my Daisy!"

And then Crazy Dog start to bark, to bark and to howl into the darkness.

I heard Toby say, "Crazy Dog, bite stranger!" and I heard the man exclaim, "Ouch!"

Then, suddenly, there were bright lights shining on us all, from both directions.

A wonderfully familiar voice was saying, "Well done, Toby!" – the voice of Ethel-nushi.

Almost at the same time I heard the police officer we called Crispin say to someone else, "Handcuff him, will you, and take him to the wagon? Let's get these kids home."

★ ★ ★

## Report of Ethel T. Walker to the National Society for the Care of Abandoned and Displaced Children (NSADC) Hampshire Division Southern Colony

**Date:** *Thursday, 25th July*
**Time:** *1.15 am*
**Care Home Identity Number:** *017954 Coed*
(Please omit details of exact location)
**Number of children at this location:** *9. 4 children missing*
**Number of children in formal detention:** *0*

*I have wondered whether there was any need for the children to wear trackers anymore. They were initially used, as you will know, to alert us as to whether the children had been anywhere near anyone carrying the virus during the second pandemic. For years we have all worn them, and gradually extended their use, so that we could make purchases and use them as ID cards. However, their global positioning is weak, and I have considered whether it might not be better to issue the children with mobile phones.*

*Tonight, though, I have every reason to be thankful for Daisy's tracker. The tracker-receptor in my office is old and the portable one* brought by the police to the house was not much better. We saw that Noah's, Beatrice's and Elijah's trackers seemed to leave the city briefly but then return to the bottom end of town, by the statue. They were found in the compostable rubbish put out by a resident in Eastgate Street, at about nine o'clock. The receptor seemed to indicate that Daisy's bracelet was somewhere else, never leaving the centre of the city.

As you know, the police suspected that Daisy, too, had been kidnapped, and perhaps that her tracker was in a vehicle or on one of the kidnappers, that it was a simple mistake on the part of the criminals not to dump it with the others. Nevertheless, the police have been patrolling the city on the look-out for Daisy all evening.

It was only when the tracker seemed to indicate that whoever had it about their person was walking along the Weirs that we all realised that someone might be approaching Xunzi House. It was my sister's idea, supported by the police, that we go to meet the person. The police hoped to make an arrest, but they invited me to go along with them, with the unlikely possibility in mind that it might actually be Daisy.

As I write this, the police will be surrounding Southampton docks. They believe that they will be in time. Daisy and Toby are in the middle of a crowd of excited Chatterers, my sister, the police liaison officer and Robbie Thomas, and are eating cake and drinking hot chocolate. Crazy Dog has also wolfed down a plate of cake, to Toby's great delight, and has drunk a good bowl of water.

★ ★ ★

It was mid-August. The little ones were on the grass by the hedge, playing with Crazy Dog. He was Toby's pet, but Albert loved him too and Rebecca had overcome her fear of dogs enough to play happily with the boys.

We were sitting on the concrete right down by the river, in a row. The results of our end-of-year exams had just been published. Arof had completed his first year at the university with flying colours, of course. Noah and Emily were both celebrating being in the top ten per cent, and I was celebrating the fact that I had reasonable passes, with a distinction in history. Sophie had not taken her exams. She had been very traumatised when they were brought back to Xunzi House in the early hours of the morning, and spent an hour a day with Chin-Sun, her counsellor, for a couple of weeks. She would go on having counselling for years after that, once a week and then once a month, dealing with all that hurt and insecurity.

We knew, by then, that we had one more year of studying the full curriculum before we started to choose subjects to study in greater depth. It was already certain that Noah would specialise in Chinese language and literature. Emily was still keen on nursing, and Sophie was interested in going in the same direction. Elijah and Beatrice were impressed by what Edwina-nushi had told us all about opening up the hospitality sector, now that all the pandemics were over. I did not know for sure what I wanted to do, but Ethel-nushi reassured me that it really did not matter yet.

So, there we sat, our feet in the river, chatting and watching the water weed floating down stream. It was midweek, and, although the Itchen Way was open again and there was talk of rebuilding the old stone bridge, there were, in fact, no people around. The clouds were building up, ready for a thunderstorm. Ethel-nushi told us that this was typical English weather, now that the immediate risk of global warming was over. She laughed, and said that when they were children there was still an old saying around, that an English summer consisted of three hot days and a thunderstorm.

We had all struggled a bit in the month that had passed. It was hard to believe that at the beginning of the year we had not seen a frost, we had not come out of lockdown, we had not even dreamt of street parties or friends who lived in other parts of the city. We had not imagined kidnappers or people traffickers, or police officers, of adventures in the middle of the night. We had not been to a place of worship, or sat and tried to listen to a Spirit that could give us courage and strength. There we sat, with the sound of a blackbird whistling up the storm, and of ducks just beginning to work themselves up to their autumn call, which made it sound as if they were laughing. We were friends, and I think that we knew then that we would be friends for life. As Edwina-nushi had told me, our whole lives were ahead of us.

There was a world waiting for us, beyond the water meadows.

# Why write *Beyond the Water Meadows*?

**Introduction**

A group of us from my local Quaker Meeting was studying the Gospel of Luke together, via Zoom because of Covid 19. We had just reached Luke 5: 29 – 32, where Levi, newly recruited as one of Jesus' disciples, gives a banquet in His honour. Verse 30 refers to "tax collectors and sinners." We had all done some preparation, consulting different commentaries, and one Friend read out what one commentary had to say. The tax collectors and sinners were referred to as "the lower classes". (1)

There were several things that struck me about this. First came the assumption that wrongdoers would necessarily be from a lower class. Why should anyone suspect that? The text did not indicate that this was so. The second thing that bothered me was that in our small group I seemed to be the only one who noticed the commentator's bias. The third worrying thing was that, when I pointed it out, the initial reaction of the group was laughter, although to be fair, more thought was afterwards given to the issue.

This small incident more or less sums up why I have written this novel, *Beyond the Water Meadows*. I am taking a long time following the Quaker Woodbrooke course "Equipping for Ministry", and my personal project, inspired partly by a friend who has recently become a member of our Meeting, has been on the general issue of Quakers and the working class. I should probably add that while my friend has been a regular source of stimulation and good conversation on the topic, I have drawn upon my own experiences too. While definitely middle class now, my background was rural working class, and to this day I suffer from imposter syndrome, the underlying lurking sense that I do not really belong here, and that sooner or later my social and cultural inadequacies will be discovered. I suspect that I am far from alone in this, and that my experience is not unique to Quakers.

**Social Class Is Not a Hot Topic**

Quakers are currently very exercised about being a fully and honestly inclusive community, but being accepting of others requires at least some understanding of where our friends are coming from. Social class is not a hot topic at present, and perhaps partly for that reason Quakers, no doubt reflecting society in general, are not always clear about the meaning of the term "working class". Indeed, I heard it claimed, during a question and answer session at Woodbrooke, that we are virtually all working class, in that we have all had to work to make a living! More years ago than I care to admit, while I was studying to become a teacher, social class and some of its implications in the classroom were part of my training. Years later I found that I had teachers in a team I then led who had studied no sociology themselves during their teacher training. A political elite which believes that there is no such thing as society had removed the study of sociology from initial teacher training. Having come from traditional middle-class backgrounds themselves, some of my team had no awareness of the significant cultural differences of the working-class children in their classrooms.

Knowing of my interest in these matters, I was asked by the clerk of my area meeting to talk at an area meeting gathering. The reactions of Friends was interesting. Some seemed to find what I had to say about the middle-class ethos of Quakerism difficult to accept. There were those who did not seem to believe that in the twenty-first century there still exist class distinctions, and others who apparently thought that, if we are pleasant to all comers, nothing further by way of understanding is needed. This is in direct contradiction to the work of Betsy Leondar-Wright in *Missing Class*, a book to which I will refer frequently in this paper: *"Lack of class awareness prevents activists from noticing how class dynamics play out and so keeps them from effectively bridging class differences."* (2) There were also those present who seemed fully engaged in what I had to say, and who afterwards told me stories that illustrated the point that I was trying to make: that the "Quaker establishment" as it now exists, is generally only accessible to middle-class people.

In the pages that follow I intend to explain a little of what I have learnt about social class. I will look first at the question of whether class is a matter of income, and then at the relationship between class and education, especially higher education. Finally, I will look in a little more detail at social class as primarily a matter of culture, and at the implications of this to British Quakerism.

*Income and Social Class*

One big mistake in the understanding of some of us seems to lie in the conflating of social class with income. These two things probably never went together entirely. The NRS (National Readership Survey, 1956) based social class upon the occupation of the head of the household, as follows: (3)

| Grade | Occupation |
|---|---|
| A | Higher managerial, administrative |
| B | Intermediate managerial, administrative or professional |
| C1 | Supervisory or clerical and junior managerial, administrative or professional |
| C2 | Skilled manual workers |
| D | Semi and unskilled manual workers |
| E | Casual or lowest grade workers, pensioners and others who depend on the state for their income |

Anyone looking at these categories will recognise that at times in the twentieth century, and still in the twenty-first, it has been entirely possible that some skilled manual workers (C2) would earn more than some supervisory, clerical, junior managerial, administrative or professional workers (C1). Indeed, I remember a discussion in the staff room during my first year of teaching, when an ex-pupil had gone to work in a local business as a canteen worker, and was reportedly earning more than a teacher in her probationary year. As I write this, and as a result of a huge number of redundancies brought about by the current pandemic, there will be many people on painfully low incomes who are, in terms of qualifications and cultural capital, thoroughly middle-class. Income and social class are not the same thing.

*Education and Social Class*

In the 1950s, 3.4% of young British people attended university, although there were many others involved in higher education: for example, teachers in colleges of education, nurses and librarians, who all studied for up to three years post eighteen, but were not awarded degrees. In 2017, 32.6% of eighteen-year-olds were awarded places at university. (4). Since higher education is frequently regarded as a doorway into professional life, these statistics might suggest that more people nowadays are middle class. "University", however, can describe a variety of different experiences, and not all places of study are likely to open the doors that the most elite establishments open. In *The Educated Underclass*, (5) Gary Roth notes that there seems to be an implied promise to those who achieve higher education, that they will have more prosperous and fulfilling work lives, but that, in reality, this is not the case. Those who graduate from "good" universities do indeed often achieve much, but students who study in lesser institutions regularly fail to break into genuine middle-class occupations or lifestyles. Indeed, as more people have more qualifications, there has been a sort of qualification inflation, so that workers are now required to have qualifications which a generation ago would not have been needed. Leondar-Wright (6) refers to those for whom a degree has not provided entry into the middle-class as "blocked aspirants". In Leondar-Wright's terms this means college graduates who are now unable to make the step into the professional middle class. James Bloodworth in *Hired* (7) notes that a 2015 report by the Chartered Institute of Personnel and Development found that 58.8% of graduates were in jobs that did not actually require a degree.

When I trained to teach, *Education and the Working Class*, (8) was a staple text. From it one could see that a grammar school education followed by further or higher education could serve to enable a child from a working-class background to achieve middle-class status. However, in the twenty-first century, good A levels from a comprehensive school and a degree from a non-elite university is unlikely to have the same results. Sadly, for those of us who have dedicated our professional lives to education, and who still value it greatly, higher education does not necessarily correlate with social class or with upward mobility.

*Culture and Social Class*

If social class is not determined by either income or education, how can it be understood? My suggestion is that it can only be recognised by a person's culture, although whether the culture defines the class or the class gives rise to the culture is a question for a different discussion.

The French sociologist Bourdieu observed that there is something he called cultural capital, which is extremely important in the identity of social class groups. Leondar-Wright (9) explained it like this:

> *People feel most comfortable with those who share their tastes in food, humour, media, and clothing. Like congregates with like. Those who make the decisions in any field (whether educational, occupational, intellectual, or artistic) resonate with and reward those whose cultural capital is similar to their own.*

From her detailed work with campaigning groups in the USA, however, Leondar-Wright discovered that the differences in culture went much further than the afore-mentioned tastes in food, humour, media or clothing, and some of the differences she uncovered could prove to be very enlightening to Quakers who have a genuine concern to be inclusive. It is my contention that these other factors, which are sometimes very subtle differences in culture, are likely to be the most alienating factors for working-class people encountering Quakers. It is perhaps worth noting here that Leondar-Wright found that "straddlers" – those who had changed their social class – tended to retain many of the characteristics of their original social class.

There are several key areas where differences between working- and middle-class culture might impact on Quakers. Before exploring them, however, it is perhaps important that readers consider their own attitudes towards cultures other than their own. We are learning to be accepting of the ways people from different ethnic backgrounds see the world, but are we as accommodating when it comes to white, working-class Brits? In *Chavs. The Demonization of the Working Class* (10) Jones points out that, while the traditional aspiration of the working class has been to raise the quality of life of workers, the accepted aspiration nowadays is to raise oneself above one's class. In other words, there seems to be a general understanding that it is not a good thing to be working class. If we carry that perception into what follows, we are unlikely to learn much.

**Language**

Back in the 1960s and 1970s, when social class was widely discussed in education and political circles, awareness of differences in linguistic cultures was generally acknowledged. This is not just a question of vocabulary, although that is undoubtedly part of it. Children brought up in a middle-class environment tend to share conversation with adults in ways that are less typical in working-class situations. They are questioned more about what they have done in school, they are encouraged to voice opinions, and, as a consequence, they grow up confident in putting forward arguments or points of view. By contrast, those who grow up in a working-class environment tend to be "quizzed" less often, and as adults may feel intimidated if asked to give an opinion, especially in a formal setting. (11) Quaker Meeting for Worship is therefore an occasion when middle-class Friends are likely to be much more confident than their working-class brethren – and to feel more at home.

It will be no surprise that styles of humour are different in different social groups. Middle-class groups tend to elicit laughter through wordplay and cultural allusions, while working-class groups elicit laughter by teasing and fake bad behaviour. (12) I have become especially aware of frequent references to high culture such as Shakespeare quotations, references to Renaissance artists and so on, in my local Quaker meeting. Of course, this is in no way wrong. Indeed, it can be enlightening and enriching. However, I cannot help wondering how a working-class visitor might feel when, for example, Gerard Manley Hopkins is quoted, when to the visitor Hopkins' poetry is as alien as Chinese literature?

In addition, middle-class speech tends to use general organisational words and quite a lot of abstract speech, while working-class people tend to refer to concrete political issues and operational details. (13) As I mentioned earlier, I was born working-class and I am now, in most respects, middle-class, but this is a linguistic difference I have become particularly aware of since I resumed studying more than two years ago. In 2019 I found myself in a small discussion group at the Quaker study centre, Woodbrooke. I cannot now recall what we were discussing, but I clearly remember introducing specific examples to explain why I did not agree with a purely theoretical point put forward by another member of the group. Afterwards, in the summing-up, I was thanked for introducing down-to-earth illustrations. Reflecting on that very stimulating group experience, I now recognise that I was bringing my working-class approach to conversation into a middle-class discussion. Despite majoring in philosophy when studying for my master's degree, I still anchor my thinking in the actual and the concrete. What is more, in my heart of hearts I still believe that is the best and most realistic approach to confronting issues.

**Decision Making and Leadership**

The Quaker business method is something many of us hold in very high esteem. We believe that we are listening to the Spirit and looking for divine guidance. I trust that none of us believe that the Spirit is class bound! However, on the matter of decision making, and in the associated question of leadership, there tend to be very different norms in working- and middle-class cultures.

It is obvious that middle-class people tend to work in situations where they have some control over their own professional lives and the lives of other people. They may be teachers, health care workers, human services providers or consultants. They may work in the arts or the media, or in a host of different managerial positions. By contrast, working-class people tend to work in jobs where they are instructed what to do, and live lives where they have decisions made for them. This was brought home to me very recently as a close friend and I discussed our childhoods. He was sent to an independent school where he received an excellent education. I passed the eleven-plus examination and went to a grammar school, and I too received a good education. The difference was that my friend's parents chose his school, and I went where I was sent. My parents were allowed to express a preference, but they did not choose my school. My friend came from a family that could make choices; I came from a family where choices were made for us.

In *Blessed Are the Poor?* by Laurie Green the author relates part of a conversation between a parishioner in a poor, working-class neighbourhood and the parish priest. *"It doesn't help much that Jesus said do to others what you want them to do to you, father,"* says the parishioner, *"because all we get is people doing things to us. When did we last get a chance to do anything to them?"* (14)

How might that early working-class experience of comparative powerlessness impact on a Friend approaching Meeting for Worship for Business? How alien might the process seem, of making important and occasionally very expensive decisions – to a person who comes from a family which depends upon the local authority to decide on even such basic questions as where they may live?

The way in which meetings are held can also reflect different class practices. Leondar-Wright notes that middle-class groups tend to prefer very stylised group processes, while working-class groups are much more comfortable with "natural" conversational patterns. (15) What could be more stylised than the Quaker practices of standing to indicate the desire to speak, or responding to a suggestion with the phrase "I hope so"?

Further, Leondar-Wright observed that members of the middle-class tended to speak less frequently but to use more words when making a point. Working-class contributors speak more often but more briefly. (16) Again, the Quaker tradition of only speaking once to an issue favours middle-class culture.

Finally, Leondar-Wright discovered that, in the groups she studied, the concept of "leadership" was very different in working-and middle-class cultures. In middle-class groups, the concept tends to be of the leader as manager, *"designing and running processes that require everyone to speak..."* (17) This is very much the role of the clerk and assistant clerk in a Quaker Business Meeting. By contrast, in working-class culture a respected leader is one who exercises strong control and who nurtures warm and helpful personal relationships – much closer to the leadership role that might be expected of a traditional priest or pastor.

## Outreach

While Quakers are not, strictly speaking, an evangelical group, nevertheless at various times in our history we have felt it to be our responsibility to reach out to others, either to share our spiritual insights or to promote social justice issues. Once again, though, it seems that the forms of outreach which feel comfortable to those of different social classes can be quite different.

Leondar-Wright finds in her research that, as one might have guessed from what has gone before, middle-class people were most comfortable promoting their concerns through an emphasis on ideology, while working-class outreach tends to be on the basis of relationships. (18) Consider then the much-loved "Quaker Quest", a popular form of organised Quaker outreach in the UK. While individual contributors may well refer to concrete experiences of their own, the usual titles of the sessions tend to be abstract and theoretical: simplicity, worship, peace, Jesus, God and equality. What is more, the format of each session involves several Quakers expressing different points of view on the topic under consideration. The appeal is clearly to those whose life experiences equip them to decide issues for themselves, to select and reject ideas. By comparison, a not insignificant aspect of outreach in some other churches is the giving of accounts of dramatic change along the lines of *I once was lost but now I'm found, was blind but now I see*. The former appeals to those whose thought patterns are at home in the abstract (the middle-class), the latter to those who anchor their understanding in the concrete (the working-class).

In the same way, there seems to be a difference in the way different class cultures approach social issues such as the problem of inequality and linked issues such a hunger or homelessness. Middle-class people, according to Leondar-

Wright, tend to use what she calls "a wide angle lens" when confronted with such problems. They might look for political or structural solutions, and be willing to take action which is unlikely to bear immediate fruit, while working-class people are more inclined to consider practical measures that could impact victims more quickly. (19) Looked at in this light, peace vigils and demonstrations against nuclear weapons would seem to be the stuff of middle-class activism, while involvement in trade union activity and local efforts to support food banks fall more naturally into the working-class sphere. If Quakers are really only involved in the former, then working-class attenders are unlikely to feel at home with us.

**Personal Relationships**

During the course of my reading I came across cultural differences which initially surprised me. For example, Leondar-Wright (20) noted that, when people disagreed, working-class people were much more inclined to believe that the disagreement was personal, and therefore to be hurt or upset, while middle-class people saw such disagreements as merely differences of opinion. The implications of this observation could be, and I suggest often are, very significant in the everyday life and work of a local Quaker Meeting, with Friends being hurt by the responses of others, and those others being completely unaware of it.

Another discovery that surprised me was noted by Edwards. (21) He quotes a working-class man who had recently joined a local church. The man is discussing the different culture he found in the church, compared with that of his family and friends: *"For example, it took me a good three or four months of attending church to feel comfortable shaking hands with people."* The reason is, according to Edwards, that in working-class culture men do not touch other men, except to give them a friendly punch or to act a little camp, as a joke. Quakers, it seems to me, are forever shaking hands – especially with people arriving at meetings and at the end of meetings. In my local Quaker Meeting we all hold hands in a circle at the end of activities in some smaller groups. How alienating someone from Edwards' background might find that!

**Conclusion**

It has been my intention to show that British Quakerism as most of us know it is culturally extremely middle-class. The aspects of our community life which might alienate people from working-class backgrounds are not primarily to do with either income or education, but with the more subtle, and perhaps much more deep-seated aspects of the class-specific cultures from which we come. My suggestion is not that one class culture is better than another, although I fear that such is the belief of many middle-class people. My intention is merely that we should recognise these differences and be sensitive to them. Unless we can achieve that much, it seems to me, there will be little chance of becoming a truly inclusive community.

# References

1. Despite serious attempts to locate this quotation, the Friend who shared it at our study group cannot now locate where he found it. Perhaps it is just as well!
2. Leondar-Wright, B. *Missing Class* p.2
3. http://www.nrs.co.uk/nrs-print/lifestyle-and-classification-data/social-grad
4. https://www.ucas.com/corporate/news-and-key-documents/news/largest-ever-proportion-uks-18-year-olds-entered-higher-education-2017-ucas-data-reveals
5. Roth, G. *The Educated Underclass*
6. Leondar-Wright, B. *Missing Class* p.51
7. Bloodworth, J. *Hired* p.153
8. Jackson, B & Marsden, D. *Education and the Working Class*
9. Leondar-Wright, B. *Missing Class* p.31
10. Jones, O. *Chavs. The Demonization of the Working Class* p.80
11. Leondar-Wright, B. *Missing Class* p.139
12. Ibid. p.91
13. Ibid. p.152-153
14. Green, L. *Blessed Are the Poor?* p.149
15. Leondar-Wright, B. *Missing Class* p.138
16. Ibid. p.184
17. Ibid. p.124
18. Ibid. p.102 – 103
19. Ibid. p.97
20. Ibid. p.209
21. Edwards, D. *Chav Christianity* p.55

# Questions for Discussion

1. Instead of writing about a clash between middle- and working-class cultures, the author has substituted a clash between middle-class and Chinese-influenced mores. How effective do you think this substitution is, and why?

2. Although all five of the teenagers in *Beyond the Water Meadows* are living in Xunzi House during the period covered by the novel, there is evidence that originally they came from very different backgrounds. In particular, what do you discover about Sophie's and Noah's early childhoods?

3. To which of the five teenagers do you relate most closely, and why?

4. The five teenagers respond rather differently to their exposure to Quakers. Can you suggest why they react differently? Do the reactions of any of them chime with your initial responses to Quakers, or to any faith community with which you have had contact?

5. Reflecting on their experience of Quakers, Noah and Daisy decide that the Quakers "really just know about their own stuff... About art and music from the Seven Colonies [the UK], and about those weird old poets. They don't know anything about our lives." To what extent might this be true of your local Quaker Meeting or faith community?

6. When Daisy considers the corporate decision making process of Quakers she says:

   "You have to have a leader; everyone knows that. One of the reasons that we had peace in the Seven Colonies and had finally defeated the four viruses was that the first Confucian leader of China had been such a strong leader."

   Do you agree with Daisy about the importance of strong leadership? In your opinion is leadership within Quaker communities or in your faith community effective? Would your community benefit from change, and, if so, how?

7. Of the five teenagers, Noah and Daisy seem best to grasp the true nature of Quakerism when they begin to understand that at the heart of the message is the belief that the Spirit is everywhere, and accessible to everyone. Do you agree that this is at the heart of the Quaker message? Is that what visitors might hear if they attended your Quaker Meeting for the first time? If you belong to a different faith group, what do you think is the true nature of your faith? Would visitors to be likely to grasp that in their first few visits?

8. In their *Friendship, Fun and Freedom* lessons the teenagers learn about places of worship and faith communities. At one point Emily makes the distinction between a faith group and a cult, saying that faith groups are rational and cults are not. Do you agree with that? If you have a faith, to what extent do you believe that your faith is rational?

9. At one point Daisy describes herself as being like a duck – big and ugly. Sophie says that she is like an owl, preferring

not be seen. If you were to liken yourself to a bird, what would it be, and why?

10. There are several references to birds throughout this novel. Why do you think the author chose to make these references? In your opinion, do these references add anything to the novel?

# Bibliography

Advices & Queries used with permission of Britain Yearly Meeting 2013
Armstrong, S. *The New Poverty*. Verso. 2017
Bell, Dan A. *China's New Confucianism: Politics and Everyday Life in a Changing Society: Politics and Everyday Life in a Changing Society.* Princeton University Press. 2010
Bloodworth, J. *Hired. Six Months Undercover in Low-Wage Britain.* Atlantic Books Ltd. 2018
Carraway, C. *Skint Estate.* Ebury Press. 2019
Charlesworth, M. & Williams, N. *The Myth of the Undeserving Poor.* Grosvenor House Publishing Ltd. 2014
Chester, T. *Unreached. Growing Churches in Working Class and Deprived Areas.* InterVarsity Press. 2012
Chinn, C. MBE. *They Worked All Their Lives.* Carnegie Publishing Ltd. 2006
Chinn, C. MBE. *Poverty Amidst Prosperity.* Carnegie Publishing Ltd. 2006.
Davie, G. *Religion in Britain. A Persistent Paradox.* (second edition) Wiley Blackwell. 2015
Davie, G. *The Sociology of Religion.* Sage. 2013
Day, A. *Believing in Belonging.* Oxford University Press. 2011
Edwards, D. *Chav Christianity.* New Generation Publishing. 2013
Fussell, P. *Class. A Guide Through the American Status System.* Touchstone. 1983
Garthwaite, K. *Hunger Pains. Life Inside Foodbank Britain.* Policy Press. 2016

Green, L. *Blessed Are the Poor? Urban Poverty and the Church.* SCM Press. 2015

Hanley, L. *Respectable. Crossing the Class Divide.* Penguin Books. 2016

Jackson, B. & Marsden, D. *Education and the Working Class.* Penguin Books. 1966

Jones, O. *Chavs. The Demonization of the Working Class.* Verso. 2016

Leondar-Wright, B. *Missing Class. Strengthening Social Movement Groups by Seeing Class Cultures.* Cornell University Press. 2014

Roth, G. *The Educated Underclass.* Pluto Press. 2019

Savage, M. *Social Class in the 21$^{st}$ Century.* Pelican. 2015.

Sherman, J. *Those Who Work, Those Who Don't. Poverty, Morality, and Family in Rural America.* University of Minneapolis Press. 2009

Simmons, M. *Landscapes of Poverty.* Lemos and Crane. 1997

Sugrue, T.J. *The Origins of the Urban Crisis.* Princetown University Press. 2005.

Vance, J.D. *Hillbilly Elegy. A Memoir of a Family and Culture in Crisis.* William Collins. 2016

**Websites**

(National Readership Survey) http://www.nrs.co.uk/nrs-print/lifestyle-and-classification-data/social-grad

UCAS survey https://www.ucas.com/corporate/news-and-key-documents/news/largest-ever-proportion-uks-18-year-olds-entered-higher-education-2017-ucas-data-reveals